BLACK OPS WARRIOR

Amelia Autin

HARLEQUIN® ROMANTIC SUSPENSE

Recycling programs
for this product may
not exist in your area.

ISBN-13: 978-0-373-40240-3

Black Ops Warrior

Copyright © 2017 by Amelia Autin Lam

Printed in U.S.A.

"A challenge?" Niall murmured. "I love a challenge."

He would. Savannah didn't know how she knew that about him, but she did. He wasn't talking about carrying on a conversation with her, of course. She wasn't *that* naive. He was talking sex, plain and simple. She caught her breath, then shook her head. "I won't be much of a challenge," she said before she could think about how unwise it was to admit it.

He didn't move closer, but somehow it felt as if he had. And instead of that choked-up feeling that always overcame her whenever she feared she couldn't escape, this time her shortness of breath had nothing to do with fear and everything to do with excitement.

"You're no pushover," he told her, that tantalizing smile in his eyes matching the one on his lips. "Damned if I know *what* you are, but I know that much."

Kiss me and find out.

* * *

Be sure to check out the previous volumes in the Man on a Mission miniseries!

Man on a Mission: These heroes, working at home and overseas, will do anything for justice, honor... and love

* * *

If you're on Twitter, tell us what you think of Harlequin Romantic Suspense! #harlequinromsuspense

Dear Reader,

When I wrote *Cody Walker's Woman*, I gave my heroine, Keira Jones, four brothers—all older, all former US Marines and all playing a role (good and bad) in shaping the woman she was.

Then I wrote *Alec's Royal Assignment*, *Liam's Witness Protection* and *Killer Countdown*, the stories of three of Keira's brothers. But Niall—the second child of five, like me—was elusive. All I really knew about him at that point was how Liam described his brother in *Liam's Witness Protection*—a onetime US Marine and now a black ops warrior. But that description alone captivated readers, who begged me for his story.

I fell in love with Niall when he showed up out of the blue in *Killer Countdown* to help his elder brother, Shane. Writing about Niall was easy after that, but I needed a woman to match him. All the Jones brothers except Niall had found exceptional women to love—Angelina, Cate and Carly. How could Niall settle for anything less?

Enter the brilliant Dr. Savannah Whitman, quietly exceptional. She's not looking for love, especially in the arms of a man who lives in the shadows. But Robert Herrick wrote hundreds of years ago, "How Love came in, I do not know." And neither do Niall and Savannah. Somehow, though, love creeps in on catlike feet when we least expect it, and Niall and Savannah are no exception in *Black Ops Warrior*.

I love hearing from my readers. Please e-mail me at AmeliaAutin@aol.com and let me know what you think.

Amelia

Award-winning author **Amelia Autin** is an inveterate reader who can't bear to put a good book down... or part with it. She's a longtime member of Romance Writers of America (RWA), and served three years as its treasurer. Amelia resides with her PhD engineer husband in quiet Vail, Arizona, where they can see the stars at night and have a "million-dollar view" of the Rincon Mountains from their backyard.

Books by Amelia Autin

Harlequin Romantic Suspense

Man on a Mission

Cody Walker's Woman
McKinnon's Royal Mission
King's Ransom
Alec's Royal Assignment
Liam's Witness Protection
A Father's Desperate Rescue
Killer Countdown
The Bodyguard's Bride-to-Be
Rescued by the Billionaire CEO
Black Ops Warrior

The Coltons of Texas

Her Colton P.I.

Silhouette Intimate Moments

Gideon's Bride
Reilly's Return

Visit the Author Profile page at Harlequin.com.

For all the US Marines I've known and the ones I haven't, men and women who place their lives on the line to keep our country safe. For Susan Kyser Frank and Harry A. Frank, who understand that US Marines are a rare breed. And for Vincent...always.

Prologue

Niall Jones's life depended on him blending into the background wherever he was. Moving through the shadows as if he was a shadow himself. And no one was better at it. Others came close, but he was the best. He'd lost track of how many disguises he'd donned. How many aliases he'd used. How many lives he'd led. When he assumed a role, he *became* the role. Until the next time.

Which was exactly what he was doing now. He watched his target through seemingly sleepy eyes, but he knew every breath she drew. Every rise and fall of slight breasts that wouldn't normally attract his attention. Her face, too, was unremarkable. Not unattractive, but not the kind of face that would automatically draw a second or a third glance.

And yet…there was something about her mouth. Something that piqued his interest and held his gaze. Sweetly curving lips that smiled more often than not, but also hinted at restrained passion. Lips that made him wonder what they'd taste like, feel like beneath his, if he kissed her.

Not that he had any intention of kissing her…unless it was necessary. Dr. Savannah Whitman was his target, and he couldn't lose sight of that fact. She might look sweet, innocent and far younger than the thirty-six years he knew her to be—that delicate skin of hers, the lack of makeup and the way she wore her hair might have something to do with it—but she could very well be a cold, calculating traitor. And if there was one thing Niall hated, it was traitors, people who would sell out their country for *any* reason.

He knew more about her than most of her friends. He knew the relevant details about her life, from the day she was born until now.

He knew exactly how much money she had in the bank, that she hadn't attended her high school senior prom, that she had three patents to her name with a fourth pending. He knew the phobia she'd struggled against for most of her life, and when and why it had first afflicted her. And he knew she'd resigned her top secret job with an international defense contractor the day after her parents' funeral.

What he *didn't* know was what made her tick. What was going on in her head. Why she'd resigned and what she intended to do now with the highly classified data stored in the memory banks of her mind. Data the US government would love to erase…but couldn't. And most important, if she really was a security risk as the government feared.

Which was why he was here, shadowing her footsteps as she took this fifteen-day land tour and river cruise through northern China. Which was why he might very well be called upon to romance her, as a way to get close enough to compile evidence that would stand up in court to convict her of espionage. Which was why…as a last resort… he just might have to kill her.

Chapter 1

Savannah Whitman stood on the ramparts of the Great Wall of China, staring up at the sea of humanity ascending and descending the steep incline to the top of this section of the wall in the Badaling Hills north of Beijing. It was a work day, so she couldn't understand why so many people were here. This was *not* the way she'd envisioned it would be when she'd spent thousands of dollars on this guided tour. She'd picked this specific tour in large part because the pictures in the brochure made it appear as if she'd be mostly on her own as she crossed several items off her bucket list of things she just had to see once in her lifetime—the Great Wall and the Forbidden City in Beijing, the terracotta warriors in Xi'an. And the Yangtze, of course, the longest river in the world that began and ended in the same country.

She sighed softly as she was jostled by those eager to pass her and begin the climb to the top of this well-preserved section of the fabled wall. She wanted to go up there, too. She did. But...

Coward, she jeered at herself. Coward, because she didn't deal well with crowds. She'd thought she'd be practically alone on the Great Wall, with only thoughts of her parents to keep her company, but now her breath came in little panicked spurts as she tried to fight back her enochlophobia. *You spent good money to see the Great Wall*, she reminded herself. *You can do this. You can! Just take a deep breath. Lots of deep breaths. Then put one foot in front of the other and climb up there, damn it!*

But the unreasoning fear had such a hold on her she couldn't move. Not even to escape by struggling through the crowd to the gondolas that had brought her and the rest of her tour group this far.

Then from above her head she heard a warm, deep voice speaking English. "Just breathe," the man said gently as he herded her away from the crowd and against the stone railing. "Breathe deeply."

When he said that, she realized somehow she was no longer being pushed, bumped or elbowed. Her rescuer had used his body to create a tiny space for her in the crowd, and she closed her eyes in thankfulness. Yes, her back was pressed against an ungiving stone wall that had been built millennia ago, but at least she wasn't hemmed in by people. And the man wasn't squashed up against her, either—some distance separated them, as if he knew she couldn't bear to be touched at this moment.

She opened her eyes and stared at a broad chest wearing a light, khaki-colored jacket. And on the jacket she spotted a familiar badge, exactly like the one she was wearing but with his name on it instead of hers—he was one of her tour group. "Oh, thank God."

He must have heard her fervent whisper because a laugh rumbled out of him. But she knew instinctively he wasn't laughing at *her*. At least, he wasn't laughing at her fear. He was laughing because she'd amused him somehow.

Her eyes focused on the name written on his badge. Niall

Johnson. "Thank you, Mr. Johnson," she managed, now that she could breathe again. Then her gaze moved up. And up. And up. Until she reached his face and she blinked. *Holy cow!* she thought. How was it she hadn't noticed him before? Because beneath the shaggy light brown hair was a face that was indubitably memorable, with nearly classical features. And his eyes... His eyes were such a deep, dark brown she could almost see herself reflected in their depths.

"Niall," he said now. "Just call me Niall. And you're..." He peered down at her nametag. "Savannah Whitman. May I call you Savannah?"

"Oh yes. Please do." Then her tongue tied itself into knots and she couldn't think of a single thing to add. Which was nothing new where the opposite sex was concerned.

In all modesty, Savannah knew she was a brilliant engineer. Top in her field of missile guidance, navigation and control, with three patents before she'd reached the midpoint of her thirties. She could talk for hours without notes when it came to such esoteric subjects as time to go, field of view and line of sight. She could teach classes on those subjects, too, and had. She could write complex algorithms that maybe a thousand people in the world could easily decipher. She'd been so valuable to the US government and her previous employer they'd practically begged her not to resign, even playing the "you owe a duty to your country" card.

But when it came to men in a social situation—especially handsome men like Niall Johnson—words escaped her. Her tongue stuck to the roof of her mouth. Her hands shook. And she felt as if she were standing there naked. Defenseless.

But then something remarkable happened. Niall smiled down at her. And his eyes held such understanding Savannah knew she had nothing to fear where he was concerned.

His eyes lingered on her mouth and she knew he was attracted to her. Maybe not as attracted to her as she was to him—he was an assault on her senses, so tall and solidly male he practically oozed testosterone—but apparently he felt she could hold her own with him. Unusual and refreshing. So refreshing she believed it for some reason she couldn't fathom.

He was a total stranger, and yet she felt as if she knew him. As if she could be comfortable with him, the way she was with the next-door-neighbor boys she'd grown up with in Vail, Arizona. Boys who had become men, but not men she looked at as *men*. And they saw her as a friend and colleague, not as a woman.

But that wasn't how Niall Johnson was looking at her. The warm interest in his dark eyes was as tangible as a caress. Savannah shivered slightly under his steady gaze, her nipples tightening. As if…as if…

"I don't know about you, but I really want to climb to the top," Niall said, indicating what he meant by a motion of his thumb. "Now that you've caught your breath, how about we do it together?"

She loved how he made it sound as if her panic attack earlier was nothing more than shortness of breath due to exertion. His eyes told her he understood the true cause, but they also conveyed a rock-solid belief she could conquer her fear *and* conquer the wall at the same time. And that belief made her willing to risk it.

"Tell you what," he said. "Why don't you lead the way? Then you can set the pace…whatever you're comfortable with. I'll be right behind you, making sure no one bumps into you. How's that?"

No one would dare jostle him, she acknowledged silently. She didn't know how he knew her fear wasn't so much of people, and not even of those behind her, but rather of people coming up behind her unseen. People touching her when she wasn't expecting it. Feeling trapped. But somehow, he seemed to know.

"You don't mind?" She hated the hesitant tone in her voice, but she had to ask. It was patently obvious he could get to the top much faster alone than accompanying her, even though she desperately wanted to go up there with him keeping the crowd at bay.

His smile grew, and Savannah's abdomen quivered under the blatant male interest in his dark eyes. She'd never had a man look at her as if she was Little Red Riding Hood and he was the Big Bad Wolf waiting to gobble her up. And she was shocked to realize this was another item on her bucket list, one she hadn't realized was there until this instant. *Just once in my life I want a man to—*

She cut that thought off before she could put it into words…even though they were only in her head. But for the first time in her thirty-six years of always being practical and playing it safe, she let go of her hold on reality and snatched at the fantasy that miraculously appeared to be within her grasp. This whole tour and cruise was a dream come true. Why couldn't Niall Johnson be part of it?

She wasn't crazy enough to believe in love at first sight. And she wasn't having rosy visions of happily-ever-after. But no man had ever, *ever* made her body meltingly aware of every breath he drew the way Niall Johnson did. And she decided then and there that if he planned to seduce her into his bed, she was totally on board with that idea.

It's almost too easy, Niall thought as he stood behind Savannah, protecting her from the crowd while she gazed in rapt wonder at the view from the top of the wall. *Like shooting a stationary target.*

"Where's your camera?" he asked abruptly, wanting to

distract himself from thoughts that were making him uncomfortable…but shouldn't. She was his assignment. He needed to remember that.

"Oh." She glanced up at him over her shoulder. "I wasn't thinking…" Her right hand fumbled in the pocket of her padded vest and pulled out a camera. He noted the make and model effortlessly—noticing things, logging them into his brain for future reference, was second nature to him. He couldn't *not* be aware of everything around him… including the expression on Savannah's face that she had no idea conveyed how absolutely vulnerable she was to his brand of charm. Charm he had no business using on an innocent victim.

Whoa! Where did that thought come from? he berated himself. Dr. Savannah Whitman could very well be a traitor. And if she was, she deserved every bad thing he might do to her, up to and including taking her out. If absolutely necessary. He couldn't allow her to reveal what she knew to his country's enemies. He *wouldn't* allow it.

Savannah gazed out over the rolling hills, then snapped a few photos. "The GPS doesn't work in China, you know," she told him, a trace of regret in her voice. "I bought this camera for this trip specifically because of that feature. I wanted a permanent GPS record of every place I visited. But…" She sighed. "I'm not exactly sure why, but it doesn't work. It worked just fine in the US—I tested it. Do you think the Chinese government is somehow blocking the signal?"

"Could be," he said cautiously. He knew the answer. But he wasn't about to reveal to her that he knew or *how* he knew.

She chuckled suddenly, taking him by surprise. "And you couldn't care less, one way or the other." She turned within the frame of his arms, her face alight with humor. "Sorry. I'm babbling. I have a bad habit of blurting out what's on my mind. Even worse, my mind tends to jump around a lot—that's the engineer in me. So carrying on a normal conversation with me is a challenge."

"A challenge?" he murmured. "I love a challenge."

He would. She didn't know how she knew that about him, but she did. He wasn't talking about carrying on a conversation with her, of course. She wasn't that naive. He was talking sex, plain and simple. She caught her breath, then shook her head. "I won't be much of a challenge," she said before she could think about how unwise it was to admit it.

He didn't move closer, but somehow it felt as if he had. And instead of the choked-up feeling that always overcame her whenever she feared she couldn't escape, this time her shortness of breath had nothing to do with fear and everything to do with excitement.

"You're no pushover," he told her, that tantalizing smile in his eyes matching the one on his lips. "Damned if I know what you are, but I know that much."

Kiss me and find out.

Savannah was aghast at herself, until she realized she hadn't actually uttered those words out loud. But then Niall's head came down, shortening the distance between them, and his lips brushed hers. Just a delicate touch, but she trembled. Made an inarticulate sound deep in her throat. And her hands came up of their own volition to clutch his arms. To hold him right where he was. To keep him kissing her.

Then he deepened the contact, and Savannah lost any grasp she had on reality. Being kissed by Niall, feeling his body rock-hard against the softness of hers as he held her with male intent, sent her into an alternate universe, one where she could only cling to him for safety. She couldn't escape but she didn't *want* to escape. Not from him.

Suddenly, Savannah realized a little sound of arousal and surrender was coming from her throat. She tried to break away, to free herself from his powerful spell…and he let her go.

It was only a slight movement on her part, but he responded immediately. And that impressed the hell out of her. Most men she knew wouldn't have. Most men would have tried to overcome what they thought was merely token resistance on her part. But not Niall. He had incredible self-control…and a will to match.

"Seen enough?" he asked eventually, after her heartbeat slowed…as if they hadn't just spent the last few minutes *not* taking in the magnificent view at all. "We still have to fight our way back down to the gondolas and make it to the tour bus before eleven. And our tour guide warned us to allow forty-five minutes for that, to be on the safe side." He glanced at his watch. "It's ten after ten now."

Savannah couldn't believe how the time had flown. And Niall must have read her crestfallen expression, because his eyes held understanding as he turned her gently to face outward again. "We have five minutes," he said in his deep voice. "Make the most of them."

Gratitude washed through her. Not just that he seemed to get how much this meant to her, that she was actually here on the top of the Great Wall the way she'd dreamed of being since she was a little girl. But also for the fact that he was here with her. Holding her safe. Sheltering her from the crowd.

"It's amazing," she managed in wistful tones. "I've seen pictures of course. My mom and I used to—" She stopped abruptly, afraid she'd be overcome with emotion if she continued that line of thought. She sighed a little to herself, suppressing the pang, and said instead, "The sheer immensity of it is unbelievable." She glanced at him over her shoulder. "Don't you think so?"

He nodded slowly. "Unbelievable." But he wasn't looking at the view. And Savannah knew he was talking about her.

The steep walk back down passed in a blur. A comfortable blur where she didn't panic once. The gondola ride, too. Savannah scurried into the slow-moving car when it was her turn, but Niall took so long entering after her no one else managed to crowd in with them. Then he sat down next to her, when he could have had the entire opposite seat to himself, and Savannah knew he'd deliberately maneuvered things this way, something he confirmed with, "I'll bet you're glad for a little privacy."

She wanted to express her thanks, but the words wouldn't come. She just gazed at him instead. But he seemed to get her message, because one corner of his mouth twitched upward in a half grin. "Yeah. Can't say as I know what it's like, being afraid of crowds. But I do enjoy privacy myself. At home—" He broke off suddenly, and Savannah wondered what he'd intended to say. And why he'd stopped himself from saying it.

Savannah and small talk in a social situation didn't normally peacefully coexist. But she suddenly wanted to know everything she could about Niall, so she asked softly, "Where's home?"

"Washington, DC." That alpha male smile was back in full force. "And you?"

"Vail, Arizona. Just east of Tucson."

"Born and raised?"

She nodded. "I've lived there all my life, except for my college years. What about you?"

He shook his head. "Denver. Then four years in the Marine Corps, stationed all over hell and gone."

"What made you decide to settle down in DC?" The question tumbled out before she could stop herself.

His expression didn't actually change, so Savannah didn't know how she knew but somehow she did—this wasn't a question Niall was going to answer in detail. And she was right. "Work," he said briefly. "And you? Where do you work?"

"I don't, actually."

He raised his brows. "Lady of leisure?"

She shook her head vehemently. "I should have said I don't work right now. Although I'm sure I'll go back to it after this year."

"What's so special about this year?" When Savannah hesitated, he said, "Sorry, don't answer if it makes you uncomfortable. I have a bad habit of asking questions I shouldn't."

She tore her gaze away from his and realized their gondola was almost at the terminus. "It's a long story," she finally admitted. "And—"

"And now's not a good time for a long story," he finished for her. "How about over dinner? Dinner tonight is at our hotel, as I recall. We can find a quiet spot and you can tell me all about it." His hand reached out and cupped her cheek, gently turning her face to his. His gaze lingered on her mouth for a moment before he added, "And at the same time, you can tell me what's lacking in the male population of Vail, Arizona."

Bewildered, she let her eyes ask for elucidation. His voice was deep, male and sent shivers of awareness through her as he said, "You can explain how it's even remotely possible a woman like you is traveling on an excursion like this alone."

Chapter 2

Savannah surveyed the contents of the closet in her hotel room with disfavor. As if something incredibly eye-catching and seductive would miraculously appear if she stared long enough, but she knew that wasn't going to happen. She didn't *own* anything incredibly eye-catching and seductive. And if she did, most likely she wouldn't have brought it on this trip anyway. Slacks, blouses, sweaters and jeans were all she'd packed. Not a single dress. Well, there was that dressy tunic to be worn over slacks, which she'd packed for the Welcome Reception on the river cruise portion of the tour. But it wasn't nearly sexy enough for a dinner date with Niall Johnson.

Then she took herself severely to task. "It's not a date. It's just…dinner."

But dinner with a man who looked at her the way she'd dreamed of having a man look at her. As if she was irresist-ible. As if he wanted to do unspeakably wonderful things to her body…all night long.

Her imagination immediately went into overdrive and her nipples tightened unbearably. Unexpected heat in her core sent the blood rushing to her cheeks, and all of a sudden she grabbed her purse off the bed and headed for the door. There were at least two elegant shops on the first floor of this five-star hotel. And she had time…if she didn't dawdle.

Five hundred seventy-three dollars poorer, Savannah opened her hotel door at Niall's knock, and he literally did a double take. "Wow. I mean…" He seemed at a loss for words, and the stunned expression in his eyes conveyed that every penny had been well spent. "Wow," he said again.

"Thanks." She thought about adding, *Just a little something I packed at the last minute*, but she didn't think she could pull it off. Instead, she admitted, "I kind of got carried away in the stores downstairs." Which she had. The peach-colored frock, with its frothy, layered-chiffon skirt and coyly plunging neckline, was one she'd never even imagined trying on. But the saleswoman in the shop had known her business, and before Savannah had realized it, she'd bought the dress, sheer stockings and silk-and-lace wisps of panties and a bra.

Then, because she'd already splurged, she'd headed for the drugstore and the cosmetics counter there. Peach lip gloss to match the dress, of course, and eye shadow to make her gray eyes smoky and mysterious—it was amazing what a little makeup did to change a woman's appearance. Not to mention what it did for a woman's self-esteem in a social setting.

She didn't wear makeup as a general rule, because she'd always wanted to be taken seriously as an engineer. Not as a *woman* engineer. So she'd never worn it at work, but that didn't mean she didn't know how to apply it. She'd experimented in middle and high school like most girls, and she knew what suited her. But it had been a long time.

Niall looked fantastic in gray slacks and a long-sleeved

white dress shirt, but then he had this morning, too, in much more casual clothes. His slightly-too-long brown hair would have looked ungroomed on another man, but on Niall…it was perfect. Out of the blue, she thought of Kurt Russell as Wyatt Earp in the movie *Tombstone*, and realized she'd hit the nail on the head. She could *so* envision him as a gunslinger in the Wild West.

He was watching her mouth again. Something about that intent stare thrilled Savannah to no end. She would normally be flustered by male attention of that sort—not that she'd had all that much of it in her life, in large part because she'd eschewed it—but still…

It was different with Niall, though. He made her feel desired, but safe…in an unsafe sort of way. In other words, as safe as she wanted to be.

But she didn't want to be. She'd spent all that money on this dress and everything else, for one reason and one reason only. She wanted to throw caution to the winds. She wanted to be reckless for once in her life. She wanted to be wild and wanton. And she had every intention of letting Niall teach her how to be wild and wanton, things at which she was absolutely sure he was an expert.

Which was why she'd bought something else at the drugstore. She'd hidden the little box in the nightstand by her bed, but she was acutely aware it was there. And if she played her cards right tonight, Niall would be using its contents. Multiple times.

Niall told himself it was just the dress and the makeup. *Fine feathers make a fine bird*, he reminded himself cynically. But he was lying to himself…and he never did that. Which meant it wasn't the dress, and it wasn't the makeup. It was the woman he was attracted to. He'd been entranced by her lips earlier today, and there hadn't been a trace of lip gloss on them then.

Desire had tugged at his loins when he'd created that little space for her on the Great Wall, and he'd wanted to pull her into his arms and possess that mouth with a single-mindedness that made a mockery of his assignment. Desire that had flared out of nowhere. Desire that now threatened to get out of hand.

She's your target. The reminder helped, but not enough. Not nearly enough.

"So tell me why this year is so special," Niall invited. They'd filled their plates at the buffet, then reseated themselves in the secluded corner booth he'd charmed the hostess into seating them in.

He watched as Savannah swallowed a bite of the excellent shrimp in lobster sauce he'd already sampled. His brain took a quick detour as he considered pressing his lips to the delicate hollow of her throat, clearly visible in that temptation of a dress. He dragged his attention back with an effort when she said, "My parents died three months ago."

He blinked. He knew that fact—of course he knew. He knew just about everything there was to know about her. But he'd never have thought their deaths would be something she—

"They were booked on a round-the-world cruise," she continued softly, her eyes filled with shadows. "To be followed by a series of cruises along ancient waterways—the Nile, the Amazon and the Yangtze Rivers, among others. It was the dream of a lifetime for them. It's not as if they'd never travelled before, but not like this for many, many years…mostly because of me."

"Because of you?" He knew why, but he wanted to encourage her to confide in him. To trust him.

She hesitated. "My parents used to travel a lot during Christmas and summer breaks from teaching, mostly in the US. And they continued doing that when I came along. But…" She glanced down at her plate, then back up at Niall. "The summer I turned four, we flew to Hawaii—Oahu, actually. I loved it, right up until I got separated from my parents in a Waikiki open-air tourist market. *Masses* of people. All strangers. All crowding around me. And when I started crying, everyone tried to help. But that only made things worse. People kept coming up behind me, touching me. I panicked and began hyperventilating. I passed out eventually, collapsing into a little ball on the ground. By the time my parents found me…"

"So that's why you don't like crowds."

"Not crowds so much," she explained, "although I prefer not to be in them. It's more people coming up behind me. Touching me unexpectedly. Like today at the Great Wall."

"I understand." He didn't have to fake the empathy.

"I had therapy, of course. And I don't panic nearly as often as I used to. But for the rest of my childhood and adolescence, we never traveled anywhere that might bring on one of my crowd-induced panic attacks. Which pretty much ruled out most tourist destinations. It wasn't until my parents no longer had to worry about me that they were free to travel again, but…"

She paused as if her thoughts were a million miles away, and Niall asked, "But…?"

"Then my mom got sick. Kidney failure. Which meant she was tied to a dialysis schedule that wouldn't allow her to travel far from home, especially overseas. You *can* arrange for dialysis someplace other than your home hospital here in the US, but she was also on a waiting list for a transplant. I don't know if you know how that works, but when you're on the list they give you a beeper. You have to be at the ready the instant a kidney becomes available, because there's a very limited time window. Otherwise it goes to someone else, the next blood-and-tissue match on the list.

"And my mom had a somewhat rare blood type, which meant the odds of a match weren't all that good to begin with. She wasn't about to risk missing out on a kidney transplant, so they never went anywhere they couldn't return from at a moment's notice."

She sighed softly. "My mom finally got her transplant two years ago. But my parents had been planning for the day they'd finally be free to travel again long before that. They were going to take a spectacular trip to make up for all the trips they hadn't been able to take over the years, first because of me, then because of my mom's health. And they were going first class all the way. They'd planned what they would see and do at each port of call, in minute detail.

"They had to wait, somewhat impatiently, to make sure my mom's body didn't reject the donated organ, but the trip was all they talked about, especially toward the end, when it was finally going to be a reality. They'd both arranged sabbaticals so they didn't have to worry about how long they'd be gone—they were professors at the University of Arizona, you see. My father in mathematics, my mother in ancient history," she explained unnecessarily, although she didn't know it.

"And...?" Niall prompted when she fell silent.

"And they were on the way to the airport to embark on their grand adventure, when a trucker fell asleep at the wheel. At least...that's what the police theorized. His truck jackknifed on the I-10 freeway, then flipped over, pinning my parents' car beneath it."

Even though Niall already knew all of this, hearing the words from Savannah, hearing the grief in her voice, did something to him, and his brows drew together in a frown.

He reached across the table and touched her hand briefly. "I'm so sorry."

She drew a shaky breath before continuing. "It still hurts," she said in a tight little voice. "But it's not as bad as it was at first."

"I lost my dad some years back," Niall admitted before he could stop himself. "And yeah, it still hurts. It will always hurt. That old 'time heals all wounds' saying is a load of crap. But it does get easier. Trust me on this."

She smiled mistily at him, and Niall had the sudden, eerie sensation of falling.

Five tables away—not close enough to hear the conversation, even though they strained their ears—a couple posing as husband and wife covertly watched the other couple. Both wondered what Savannah Whitman was saying to put that steely eyed expression on her companion's face. And both wondered just who the hell he was, what he was doing with their target and…whether or not they'd need to take him out. Things were going to be tricky enough as it was. They didn't need some stranger throwing a monkey wrench into the works.

"She was supposed to be on her own," the woman muttered. "Isn't that what Spencer told us?"

"Yes." Just the one word, but it conveyed a wealth of meaning.

"How are we supposed to—"

Her pseudo-husband cut her off. "I'll think of something. I always do."

"Yes but—"

"Quiet!" He cast her a quelling glance. "I'm trying to read their lips." He cursed under his breath. "But the angle is all wrong, damn it! Why did you allow the hostess to seat us in this out-of-the-way table? If we were closer, I might be able to hear what they're saying or at least read their lips."

"Why did I— It was you. *You* were the one who—"

He brought his hand up sharply, and she fell silent. "Let's go the buffet," he said, standing abruptly. "Maybe we can maneuver into getting close enough to hear something. At least find out who the hell he is."

Niall shook his head and the eerie feeling went away, but he wondered what it meant. He'd never suffered from vertigo before, but then, deep down, he knew it wasn't vertigo. He just didn't want acknowledge the real cause. To distract himself he said, "So your parents were killed in an accident. And then…?"

"At first I was in shock. I mean…they weren't that old. I just didn't expect it, you know?"

He nodded.

"Not both of them at the same time. But as I was picking out clothes for them to be buried in, it came to me with such cruel irony that they never fulfilled their dream. They'd planned this trip for so long, and then—boom! They never got to take it. They never saw the Egyptian pyramids except in photographs. They never stood on the Acropolis and felt history all around them. They never gazed at the ceiling of the Sistine Chapel in awe and wonder. All the things they'd promised each other they'd do someday."

Her voice was little more than a whisper at this point, and Niall sensed she was talking more to herself than to him. She swallowed hard, and he knew she was holding back tears.

"Someday never came for them. Death cheated them out of the someday they'd promised each other. I stood at their graves after the funeral, and I swore I wasn't going to wait another day. I was going to do all the things I'd dreamed of doing, and I was going to do them *now*."

Niall saw it all then, and the relief that rushed through him was out of proportion to what she'd said. But it wasn't out of proportion to what it meant to him.

"I resigned the very next day. Everyone thought I was overreacting to my parents' deaths, and would change my mind once I came to my senses. I knew that wasn't going to happen, but they tried to convince me anyway. They wanted me to postpone my decision until I'd had time to think about it. No amount of thinking was going to make a difference, though. Does that make sense?"

Niall nodded again.

"I gave them a month's notice, but I agreed to extend it to two because I still had to settle my parents' estate, sell their house. Stuff like that. And I needed time to arrange some of the trips I wanted to take anyway, so…"

She paused for a moment, then continued. "But I… I couldn't explain the real reason I'd resigned to the people at work. They didn't want to listen, and I'm not very good at talking about personal issues with them, anyway, especially my section hea—"

She cut off the rest of what she'd started to say, and Niall filled in the blanks. *Section head*, by which he knew she meant her immediate supervisor at the internationally famous defense contractor—one of the top five in the US— where she'd worked up until a month ago.

Her sudden reticence in discussing her job made more sense to him than it might have to someone who wasn't in his line of work. Employees of defense contractors were strongly urged never to talk about what they did with outsiders, for fear of security leaks. Savannah had been a missile guidance, navigation and control engineer. She'd held a top secret clearance granted by the Department of Defense and had designed weapons the US relied upon to stay ahead of its enemies militarily.

But he'd bet anything she'd resigned because she was fulfilling some kind of vow she'd made to herself and to her parents. *Not* because she was a potential traitor.

Between her confession and everything he'd learned by hacking into her computer and searching her hotel room last night, it all boiled down to one thing: his assignment was most likely a total bust. Whoever had gotten it into his head that Savannah planned to sell what she knew to the Chinese government and had dispatched him here was way off base.

If he didn't need to worm his way into her confidence and compile evidence to arrest and convict her of espionage…if he didn't need to worry about her betraying his country, either…that meant she wasn't a security risk. Which also meant, even as a last resort, he wouldn't have to kill her.

And considering his reaction to kissing her earlier, that revelation was a godsend.

Chapter 3

"**O**ops!" said a voice behind Savannah as someone bumped into her chair. "Sorry about— Well, hey there!"

She looked up and saw a face she recognized from their tour group, but she couldn't immediately put a name to the face and searched in vain for a nametag.

"Savannah Whitman, right?" the vivacious blonde said. "I'm Mary Beth, remember? Mary Beth Thompson. And this is my husband, Herb." She turned to the man who'd come up beside her, holding a full plate. "Herb, you remember Savannah, right? We were on the same plane from San Francisco."

Mary Beth chattered away about the crowded conditions at the Great Wall. "All that pushing and shoving! So rude, too! Why, I could barely take a picture without someone walking right into the frame." She moved on to discuss the factory they'd visited afterward. "Wasn't that jade factory incredible? Did you buy anything? I could have spent a fortune. Good thing I had Herb with me," Mary Beth said with a laugh, "or I'd have put a major dent in my credit card for sure! But I have to say, the food in the factory restaurant was just so-so, don't you think? Not five-star like this restaurant."

Savannah couldn't get a word in edgewise. But apparently Mary Beth didn't need an answer to any of her questions. She just kept rolling on, and Savannah was terribly afraid at any moment Mary Beth would suggest she and her husband join them for dinner. Savannah didn't want to—not only was she already getting a headache listening to Mary Beth's incessant chatter, she also wanted Niall all to herself. But she didn't know how she'd say no if...

"Well, hello," said another woman, stopping by their table, accompanied by a smiling man, both of whom looked familiar. "Weren't you in our cable car going up to the Great Wall this morning?" she asked Savannah.

"Oh. Oh yes, I think I was. It's..." Savannah surreptitiously looked for a nametag she didn't find, then searched her memory. "It's Tammy and...and Martin, right?" she said triumphantly. "I'm sorry, I don't remember your last name."

"Williams," the man threw in.

"That's right. Sorry, I'm really bad with names."

Niall had risen when Mary Beth and her husband had stopped at their table, and had stayed standing. But after one quick glance at Savannah's face, he politely but firmly made it very clear the other couples were de trop.

Savannah smiled admiringly at Niall when they were alone again. "How did you do that?" she asked, leaning forward to make sure she couldn't be overheard. "I mean, you weren't rude, but you managed to get rid of them in no time at all."

He shrugged, but a tiny smile tugged at the corners of his mouth. "Just something I picked up at my mother's knee."

"I want to meet your mother."

His smile deepened. "You'd like her. And what's more to the point, she'd like you."

A sudden, sharp pain stabbed through her, so unexpected, so real she was afraid to look down in case she'd see blood somewhere. She tried not to let her smile fade away, but she wasn't completely successful. Niall watched her for a moment, then said in a quiet voice, "Just tell me."

The words slipped out. "My parents would have *loved* you."

He didn't say anything, just took her hand in his and stroked his thumb back and forth in a move that was both comforting and somehow erotic.

"I miss them so much," she whispered in a desperate undertone. "My mom—she's the one who got me interested in ancient history. I was thinking of her when I was standing on the Great Wall. Remembering lying on my bed, poring over books on ancient China with her. And my dad—he's the one who introduced me to the pure beauty of mathematics. But I didn't want to be a mathematician, like him. I wanted to be an engineer because it was *applied* math. I wanted to make a difference. Wanted to help keep the world safe. That's why I became a—"

She stopped short because she suddenly remembered her numerous security briefings. *Don't tell anyone what you do*, she'd been warned. *You can say who you work for, but nothing more than that. And* never *mention your security clearance.*

But Niall's eyes held such understanding, she added, "I know people mock ideals these days. And patriotism seems passé, but that's how my parents raised me. When I graduated college, I was recruited by..." She mentioned the name of her former employer, knowing Niall would probably recognize the name and make the connection to the Department of Defense. "Microsoft and Google recruited me, too, and a half dozen other companies. But I wanted to do my part in keeping my country safe."

His hold on her hand tightened. "I understand, more than you can possibly know." His voice dropped a notch. "That's how my parents raised me, too. There's this quotation from Edward Everett Hale my dad carved in wood before I was born, and hung over the fireplace mantel in the family room at home. It's still there. *'I am only one, but I am one,'*" he recited softly. *"'I cannot do everything, but I can do something. And I will not let what I cannot do interfere with what I can do. And by the grace of God, I will.'"*

She gazed wonderingly at him. "Would you believe I've read that saying before? Not exactly those words, but close."

"Yeah. I've seen variations on it, too. But it influenced me from the time I was old enough to understand what it meant. And I joined the Marine Corps when I turned eighteen. So did all my brothers and my baby sister when they were old enough. Not that my parents pushed us into it. It was just…" He seemed to search for the words. "A way of giving back, I guess. I know our country isn't perfect. We've made mistakes. Grievous ones sometimes. But I wouldn't trade the US for any other country in the world."

Savannah smiled tremulously at Niall. "You *do* understand."

"Yeah. I do."

They gazed at each other in silence for endless moments, and Savannah had never felt closer to another human being than she did right then with Niall. But eventually she tore her gaze away and glanced down at her largely untouched plate. "Oh rats," she said for something to say. "Our food's cold."

"It's a buffet. You could get a new plate."

"And waste good food?" She shook her head at him and picked up her fork. "I'm not going to perpetuate the stereotype of the 'ugly American.' Not if I can help it. It's cold, but it's still edible."

They made small talk as they ate. And Savannah couldn't believe this was really her. Where was the woman who was tongue-tied in the presence of the male of the species in a social situation? But everything seemed natural with Niall, as if she'd known him forever instead of meeting him for the first time this morning.

She frowned as she acknowledged the truth of that thought; she really knew nothing about Niall.

"Are you still a marine?" she blurted out.

He shook his head. "Four years was enough for me. My older brother made it his career, though, until—" He stopped abruptly, and Savannah wondered what he'd intended to say.

"Until...?"

"Until he was wounded and they gave him a medical discharge. Now he does something else."

"If you didn't make the Corps your career, what do you do?" She almost missed his slight hesitation.

"Security."

She wondered about that infinitesimal pause, but didn't ask him about it. Instead she said, "What made you decide to take this trip? I mean, it's mostly couples. And it's mostly people who are..." She cleared her throat. "Well, retired. I know why *I'm* here, but..."

He smiled at her. "I'm forty. Not retired yet, but not so young, either. And I have a bucket list, just like you. Everything seemed to dovetail with work, and so..."

He wasn't being completely truthful. She didn't know how she knew that; she just did. But she wasn't ready to call him on it. Yet. *Someday*, she vowed, *he'll trust me enough to tell me the truth, the whole truth and nothing but the truth.*

As soon as that thought occurred to her, another thought crept into her consciousness. What made her think there was going to be a someday with Niall?

They strolled leisurely through the hotel's vast lobby afterward, in companionable silence for the most part. When they passed the shop where Savannah had purchased her dress, she stopped momentarily to look at the others in the window. "I almost bought that one," she murmured, pointing to a red silk sheath with the most gorgeous gold embroidery in a very Chinese design.

"Red's not your color." Niall turned, and when his gaze traveled over her from head to toe, Savannah felt it as a caress.

"No?"

"No. It's all wrong for you."

She didn't know what made her say it—she *never* flirted—but she teased, "I didn't know you were a connoisseur of women's clothing."

A short huff of laughter answered her. "I'm not. But I'm a connoisseur of *you*." His voice dropped. "And what you're wearing is perfect…for you."

She caught her breath at the blatant desire in his eyes, kindling an answering desire in her. And all at once she remembered this morning, and her determination that if Niall wanted to make love to her, she wasn't going to say no. Except for that one time she'd fallen in love in her teens, she'd played it safe all her life where relationships were concerned. How many chances like this would come her way? How many opportunities would she have to live the fantasy?

You even planned for this, she reminded herself. *There's a box of condoms waiting upstairs.* But she couldn't make her lips form the words to invite him up to her room. She wanted to. But she couldn't.

Niall saw Savannah safely back to her hotel room on the thirty-eighth floor. He leaned in and kissed her lightly, not trusting himself any further than that. If he kissed her the way he wanted to—the way she deserved—he wouldn't have been able to walk away at all. And he needed to. The shy invitation in Savannah's eyes was an indictment of him. Of his assignment. And of what he'd actually—for a brief period—considered doing. *How do you make love to a woman you'd convinced yourself you could kill?*

He could have done it yesterday, if absolutely necessary. He could have slept with a traitor without a qualm and gone after the evidence to convict her, or kill her, when she was still his target. But not now. Not when he knew his assignment was most likely pure BS. He'd done things for his country that kept him up at night, things he wouldn't necessarily want his mother or sister to know about, but he'd never done anything of which he was ashamed...until now.

"Lock your door," he whispered when he raised his head.

"Lock my door?" Bewilderment shone from her gray eyes.

"I want to hear that lock click behind you. Then I'll know you're safe...from me."

She caught her breath. "What if I don't want to be safe?"

The sound that issued from his throat was nothing more or less than a growl. "Damn it, Savannah! You don't know the first thing about me."

She stared up at him, an enigmatic expression on her face. "You're wrong," she said quietly. "I know you better than you think." A tiny smile tugged at the corners of her lips. "The fact that you have no intention of following me into my room despite what your body is saying tells me all I really need to know about you." She reached up and touched two fingers to his cheek. "Good night, Niall. Thank you for a lovely evening."

Then she was gone, closing the door in his face the way he'd told her to do. And the click of the lock was audible.

He walked next door and inserted his keycard in the slot. Savannah didn't know it, but he'd arranged to have the room right next to hers. She was also unaware he'd broken into her room last night while she was at the lavish three-hour Peking duck banquet outside their hotel, which Niall had missed.

He'd searched everything Savannah had with her and had found nothing. No incriminating papers. No CDs, DVDs or thumb drives that might contain top secret files. He'd hacked into her laptop, too, and copied her data files for perusal back in his hotel room, which he'd done into the wee hours of this morning. He'd also installed worm software on her laptop. Every keystroke she made, every website she visited, every email she sent—Niall would know about it.

And he'd planted nearly invisible voice-activated cameras and listening devices, all of which weren't necessary if she wasn't a traitor or a security risk. He wouldn't turn off the electronic monitoring system yet, just to be on the safe side. But they were checking out of this hotel day after tomorrow. When she went down to breakfast that morning, he would retrieve the equipment he'd installed last night, then install it at their next hotel. Assuming he didn't get called back to the US in the meantime.

Her laptop was a little more problematic. The worm he'd introduced into her operating system wasn't as simple to remove as the cameras or audio devices. It could be done, but it would take hours. He'd have to wait for another time, and there wasn't a rush to uninstall it. And if he was re-called, well...the worm would stay where it was.

That didn't mean he had to review the data logs, though. He'd have to see what his boss had to say. And he wouldn't watch the voice-activated video, either. Listen, yes. Just to make *sure* she didn't meet with someone she shouldn't in her hotel room. And if he heard something suspicious, the video would still be there. But otherwise Savannah's pri-vacy would be inviolate. That was the least he could do, now that he knew she was probably innocent.

But not watching Savannah on video didn't mean he'd turned off his imagination where she was concerned. He lay on the top of the covers, his arms beneath his head, and closed his eyes.

He could see her clearly in his mind as she'd first ap-peared when she opened her hotel door. She'd brushed her mousy brown hair until it shone, then piled it on top of her head. Even with that and her two-inch heels, he'd still tow-ered over her. But then, at six-two-plus, that wasn't unusual for him. She'd done something different to her eyes, too—mascara on her lashes and that shadowy stuff women used to make their eyes appear larger. But it was her mouth that had nearly poleaxed him. He wanted that mouth on him.

"Damn it!" He was fully aroused now, and he had no one to blame but himself. "Stop thinking of her," he ordered, but it was easier said than done.

He unbuckled his ankle holster, which contained his totally-illegal-in-China-and-he'd-serve-hard-time-if-he-got-caught-with-it Beretta M9, and laid it on the nightstand. He'd carried a Beretta since his days in the Marine Corps, and he loved it. It fit his hand as if it had been made for him, and he always felt naked without it.

Then he turned up the volume on the electronic moni-toring system—although nothing in Savannah's hotel room had set off the voice activation so far—before stripping to the buff and padding into the bathroom. He'd already taken one shower this evening, before he'd knocked on Savannah's door at dinnertime, but he needed another one now.

Preferably cold.

Two shivering minutes later his arousal was tamed… barely. He fished his toothbrush out of his travel kit, squeezed on toothpaste and was just about to slide it under the tap when he remembered. He cursed himself softly for almost making what could have been an error his body would pay for later. He cracked open a fresh bottle of water, shaking his head at his near stupidity and the necessity.

Not that this was new to him. It wasn't. He'd been stationed places where bottled water was necessary for everything during his years in the Corps. He'd traveled on assignment to the jungles of Africa and South America, where the sanitary conditions were much worse. But it still bothered him.

He turned out the bathroom light, then crawled naked under the covers…where his thoughts stubbornly returned to Savannah. Wondering what she was doing at this very moment. Was she already in bed on the other side of the wall? Did she wear nightclothes—a gown, a T-shirt, PJs? Or did she sleep in the nude as he did?

Crap! Stop thinking of that, you pervert.

Then he remembered he hadn't done what he'd intended to do the minute he returned to the privacy of his room. He rose and grabbed his secure laptop from the safe, brought it back to bed with him, then turned it on. It took a few minutes to boot up—the security precautions installed meant jumping through a few extra electronic hoops. Then, of course, he had to log onto the Virtual Private Network. And since he had to access it through a satellite feed, it took even longer. But eventually he was connected securely.

He'd already composed the email he would send while he was waiting for his laptop to be ready, so now his fingers flew over the keys as he typed. Finished, he scanned what he'd written, then hit Send and left the computer on.

The twelve-hour time difference between Beijing and Washington, DC, at this time of year meant he could expect a fairly prompt response. It was—he glanced at the clock on the nightstand—10:06 p.m. So it was just after ten in the morning in DC, which meant he might hear back in a few minutes.

He pushed the laptop to one side and lay back against the pillows, waiting. Hoping to receive the "stand down" command he'd requested, because he didn't want to waste another day on this meaningless assignment.

There was another reason he wanted to leave China sooner rather than later, and it had nothing to do with wasting his time. He wanted out of here because being around Savannah was dangerous to his peace of mind and to his closely guarded heart. She'd already elicited things from him he *never* talked about. Like how his dad's death had affected him. Like his brother's medical discharge from the Corps.

He was just dozing off despite telling himself to stay awake—*too little sleep last night*, his body was telling him in no uncertain terms—when he heard an odd thump from the room next door, followed by Savannah's voice, which he could hear clearly on the monitor, saying, "Who is it?"

Chapter 4

"Housekeeping."

Savannah frowned. She hadn't called housekeeping for anything, and she remembered the warning given to women traveling alone—*never* open your hotel door unless you know who's on the other side. And even then, be on your guard. She peered through the peephole but couldn't see anyone, and that alone roused her suspicions.

She was just about to tell whoever was on the other side of her door that she was calling hotel security when she heard the oddest noise, followed by what sounded like the thud of running footsteps on the carpeted hallway floor. Then nothing.

She raced to the phone and was poised to dial the operator when there was a light tap on her door, followed by a deep voice she recognized. "Savannah? It's Niall. Are you okay?"

She dropped the phone back into its cradle and made a mad dash for the door. She threw it open without even checking the peephole, something for which she'd berate herself later, but at the moment seemed utterly unnecessary.

A barefooted, shirtless Niall stood in her doorway, as

if he'd somehow divined she was in trouble and had only bothered to pull on his jeans before coming to her rescue. "Are you okay?" he repeated, running his gaze over her from top to bottom as if he needed to reassure himself.

"I'm fine." Then her curiosity got the better of her. "How did you know I needed help?"

He hesitated. "My room's right next door. I heard something and came to investigate. I didn't want to intrude, but better safe than sorry, my mother always says."

A tiny pang went through her at the familiar phrase. "My mom used to say that, too." Only then did she realize blood was trickling from Niall's forearm. "Oh my God, you're hurt!" She dragged him by his uninjured arm into her room and closed the door behind him. Then turned him so she could examine the wounded area. "What happened?"

She didn't wait for an answer, just darted into the bathroom for a clean, dry washcloth and her toiletries case, which also contained her little emergency kit.

"Sit," she ordered, when she came back. Niall glanced at the foot of the bed, then pulled the desk chair out and swiveled it around before taking a seat. Savannah pressed the washcloth against what was little more than a six-inch scratch, which was a good thing. It wouldn't need stitches, just disinfecting and a gauze bandage. "What happened?" she asked again as she efficiently applied first aid.

"There were a couple of masked—I guess you could call them intruders—outside your door when I stepped into the hallway. Not sure exactly what they were after, but the masks were a dead giveaway they weren't there for a legitimate reason. They took off like bats out of hell as soon as they saw me, but I gave chase. I had my hand around the arm of one of them when the other produced a knife and lunged for me." He didn't even wince when she applied the alcohol wipe against the cut.

"I turned to avoid the thrust," he continued, "and the blade grazed my forearm. But I had to let go of the other intruder, and that was all she wrote. They vanished through the fire door and did something to it so it wouldn't open from this side. Which reminds me," he said as an aside, "I need to call hotel security, have them clear the blockage just in case there's a real fire and people need to escape that way."

"Good idea," Savannah said, but her mind wasn't really on what Niall was saying about the fire door. She was laser focused on patching him up. "There," she said with satisfaction as she patted the last piece of adhesive tape into place. "Almost good as new." She smiled down at Niall, but her smile soon faded as her gaze slid farther down and she noticed for the first time a devastating scar near his heart, a bullet wound if she hadn't missed her guess, and the surgical scar bisecting his chest. "Oh, my God," she breathed. "What...?"

She automatically went to touch it, but he caught her hand in an iron grip and prevented her. "Sorry." His voice was brusque. "I know it's offensive, but I was in a hurry and didn't take time to put on a shirt. I'll go back to my—"

He started to rise, but she pushed him back down. "Not until you tell me how it happened," she insisted, quietly but firmly. "I'm not offended. And I'm not disgusted. What I am is appalled you think I would be."

When he didn't say anything, she nodded to herself as understanding dawned. "Someone told you it was offensive. A woman. A woman you cared about. A woman you... loved?"

Not by the flicker of an eyelid did he betray she'd guessed correctly, but she knew she was right. "Oh, Niall," she whispered, her eyes filling with tears. "I'm so sorry."

This time she didn't try to stop him when he rose. "Don't

pity me, for God's sake," he rasped. "That's the last thing I want from you."

"Not pity. Empathy. Because human beings can be so cruel to one another. Intentionally cruel. And it's those intentional cruelties by those we love that inflict the most damage because we have no defenses against them." It had been twenty years, but she still remembered when someone had done that to her, and she breathed raggedly. "Please tell me what happened."

At first she thought he wasn't going to. But then he admitted in a low voice, "I took a bullet meant for another man. That's all."

"That's all? That's *all*?" Without even thinking about it, Savannah reverently pressed her lips against the scar, wishing with all her heart she could "kiss it and make it better" the way her mother used to do when Savannah scraped her knee or cut her finger. Wishing she could draw the poison from Niall's soul that way, poison planted by the woman he'd once loved, the one who'd told him the scar on his otherwise beautiful body was disgusting.

Then one muscled arm closed around her, dragging her against a body that had no give at all, and his free hand tilted her chin up. His mouth descended on hers, completely obliterating any memory she'd had of any other man's kiss. The kiss went on and on, until surrender was the only possibility. Until every nerve ending in her body was inflamed. When he finally raised his head, she stared up at him, mutely pleading for more.

His face hardened. "Don't look at me like that."

"Like what?"

"Like you want me."

"But I do." Savannah had never—*never*—been this upfront with a man about what she wanted, what she needed. Which was quite possibly why her few sexual relation-

ships could be summed up in one word: *Meh.* But she had
no reservations about telling Niall. And she was sure right
down to her bare toes that sex with Niall would be anything but *meh.*

"Savannah…"

The rejection in the way he said her name stung, but not
as badly as it could have if it wasn't patently obvious by
the impressive bulge in his jeans that he wanted her, too.
And despite the need that hummed through her body, she
understood.

"'Not tonight, dear, I have a headache,'" she murmured
in a teasing fashion, and was rewarded by his masculine
chuckle.

"No headache, just a hard-on I'd give anything to bury
deep inside you." She gasped at his forthright language, although she wasn't offended. "But there are reasons I can't
share with you why that would be a very bad idea."

"Why can't you share them?"

He laughed again, defusing the sexual tension. "Trust
me, you wouldn't want to know. And besides, there's another, even more important reason why not."

"And that is?"

"Because my parents raised me to be a gentleman. And
a gentleman doesn't take advantage of a lady when she's
vulnerable." He kissed the tip of her nose. "And you, Dr.
Whitman, are definitely vulnerable. Not to mention one
hell of a lady."

It wasn't until Niall had returned to his own room and
Savannah was snuggling under the covers alone that she
suddenly wondered how he knew she held a doctorate. She
cast her mind back over their conversations, but she
couldn't remember ever having mentioned it to him. And
her name badge only said "Savannah Whitman," not "Dr.
Savannah Whitman," or "Savannah Whitman, PhD."

That's odd, she thought, meaning to ask Niall about it the next day. Then her brain shut down as she slid into sleep, and the question completely slipped her mind.

Niall picked up the phone the minute he was back in his hotel room. He called the operator, who transferred him to hotel security. He didn't mention Savannah's name or that masked intruders had tried to gain entrance to her room, because he was fairly sure this was no random attack. He merely reported that he'd seen the perpetrators and tried to give chase, but they'd escaped into the emergency stairwell on his floor and had apparently jammed the fire door from the inside. Could security look into it?

Then he checked his email. Sure enough, his inbox contained the recall he'd asked for, a recall he no longer wanted.

He quickly considered his options. One, he could meekly acquiesce to his orders, pack his bags and head back to DC. He dismissed that idea immediately.

Two, he could tell Savannah his suspicion that someone was trying to kidnap her. He didn't know who, but he was pretty sure he knew why—the highly classified data in her brain. And though the obvious suspect was the government of the People's Republic of China, he didn't think so. Someone had convinced the Department of Homeland Security and the Department of Defense that Savannah was a security risk. Why? If a foreign government was behind the kidnapping attempt, getting Niall dispatched here was contrary to their interests.

Which meant someone was deliberately trying to make it *appear* as if the PRC was involved, so that when Savannah disappeared the US government would either think she'd defected or the Chinese were behind her disappearance. Suspicion would be diverted from the true culprit either way.

But unless he confessed everything, he doubted he'd be able to convince Savannah she was in ongoing danger. And if he couldn't convince her, no way would she go back to the States with her bucket list unfulfilled, not with the motivation driving her.

Three, he could ask to have his recall rescinded and instead be assigned to guard Savannah while she was in China. Bodyguard would be a divergence from his usual role, but not completely outside the realm of things he'd done in his career.

Could he keep her safe for the next two weeks? There were no guarantees in this world, but he had faith in himself. Hell yes, he could keep her safe. *Would* keep her safe, or die trying.

But he'd have to word his request carefully if he went with option number three.

He clicked Reply and started typing. He read back through what he'd written six minutes later, modifying a word here, a phrase there. Satisfied at last he was conveying the message that would get him the result he wanted, he clicked Send.

He lay back against the pillows, one arm beneath his head. He had no qualms about what he'd done. No second thoughts about telling his boss Savannah was in danger…and potentially an unwitting security risk. He hadn't come right out and said it, but he'd implied that if the PRC was trying to kidnap her in a way that wouldn't cause an international incident, then his original assignment still applied—he had to prevent Savannah from revealing the top secret military defense information she possessed to the enemy, even if she didn't intend to do it. And the only way to do that was to guard her 24/7.

And how are you going to do that, hotshot? How are you going to guard her 24/7?

The only answer that came to him was the one he was most afraid of—becoming Savannah's lover for the remainder of this trip. Afraid, because he wanted this deep down in the secret recesses of his soul. Not just to keep her safe, but because he wanted her. Plain and simple.

But he didn't just want her in his bed. He didn't just want to sate himself with her body, although that urge was getting stronger by the minute. He wanted the woman who'd kissed the scar on his chest as if it were a sacred badge of honor. He wanted the woman who'd cried for his pain.

And that scared the hell out of him.

Savannah woke early and was dressed and downstairs before the hotel restaurant opened for breakfast at six. She was hoping she'd run into Niall and invite him to join her. But though her eyes searched everywhere, she didn't see him.

Her attention was caught by the waving arm of Mary Beth Thompson, who was sitting with her husband, Herb. She didn't want to eat breakfast with them, but she didn't think she had a choice. Then she saw Tammy and Martin Williams at a table near the front door. She waved back at Mary Beth and shook her head, pointing toward the Williamses as if to indicate she had a previous assignation with them. Then she carried her tray over to their table.

"Mind if I join you?"

Tammy smiled. "Please do."

Savannah sat with a sigh of relief. "Thank you so much. Don't take this the wrong way, but I just couldn't bear Mary Beth's brand of chattiness at breakfast."

Tammy laughed and signaled to the waiter. "Coffee?" she asked Savannah.

"Yes, please." She smiled at the waiter. "No cream."

Tammy reached into her purse. "Do you need some no-sugar sweetener? I have some here."

"Oh no. I brought my own. I did my research before I came on this trip. 'Don't drink the water. Don't even brush your teeth with it,'" she intoned, checking items off her fingers as if ticking them off a list. "'Bring your own no-sugar sweetener, because very few places will have it. Lock everything you don't want stolen in the safe in your hotel room.'" She made a face. "That last thing applies everywhere, unfortunately, not just here in China. I had my iPhone charger stolen out of my hotel room in Washington, DC, one time."

"What were you doing in DC?" Martin asked, buttering a roll.

Mindful of her security warnings, Savannah merely said, "Oh, I was there on a business trip." She didn't mention that, except for a cab ride around the city to see a few of the monuments from a distance, all she'd really seen was the view from her hotel—she wasn't about to go into her fear of crowds with mere acquaintances. Which hammered home the difference between them and Niall. She hadn't hesitated to confide in Niall her deepest secrets, because... well...because she felt as if she'd always known him. As if she could trust him.

And one other thing. She was falling for him. Hard.

Was she going to get her heart broken? Probably. But she didn't care. She wasn't foolish enough to think he was Mr. Right. But if she played her cards well, he could be Mr. Right Now.

She looked up from her plate suddenly, and there he was, standing in the entrance to the restaurant. So tall. So ridiculously fit. So reassuringly male. And all at once she remembered how he'd kissed her last night, then left her because he was a gentleman.

Their eyes met across the short distance, and she beamed at him. Her gaze slid to the empty chair next to hers, a blatant invitation. One he seemed to have no hesitation accepting.

"Mind if I join you?"

Savannah just smiled her welcome, but Tammy said, "The more, the merrier. Grab a plate of food. Want me to order coffee for you?"

"Sure. Black." He glanced down at Savannah's now-empty plate. "Come keep me company," he invited. "You can tell me what was good."

He didn't really need her recommendations, but he wanted her company. That was all Savannah could think of as she followed him to the buffet. She took an empty plate and added some fruit, watching while Niall piled his plate high with protein, no carbs and no fruit. "Is that how you stay in such great shape?" she asked. "Mega protein?"

He smiled lazily down at her. "I eat things other than meat. But not where you can't trust the water that comes out of the tap."

"Oh." She glanced at the cut fruit on her plate.

"You think they wash the fruit in bottled water?"

"Oh," she repeated blankly. "I never thought of that." She mentally reviewed what she'd already eaten, and felt slightly queasy. Her expression must have given her away, because he said, "It's probably not an issue, so don't start second-guessing yourself. Just keep it in mind going forward."

Niall and Savannah left the restaurant together. "Don't forget the tour bus leaves at eight," Tammy called after them. "And the tour guide said they wouldn't wait for us if we weren't on the bus. You don't want to miss the Forbidden City."

"We'll be there," she assured her new acquaintance. "No way would I miss that."

Niall steered her toward the front door. "Let's go look at the fountain," he told her. "There's something I want to discuss with you in private."

"That sounds ominous."

"It's not meant to be," he began, then amended, "Well… maybe it is. It's about last night."

"You mean the attempted break-in?"

"I don't think it was a break-in, Savannah," he said, his voice very deep. Very serious. And obviously very concerned. "I think you were targeted. And I don't think they planned to rob you."

"Why would you think that?"

"I talked with hotel security last night and this morning—that's where I was before breakfast. This hotel has extensive security cameras at all the entrances, and they reviewed the tapes. No one wearing the clothing I saw entered or left the hotel last night, with or without masks. Which means they didn't leave the hotel. Which means they either work here…or they're guests." He paused, then added softly, "And if they're guests, my money says they're on the tour."

Chapter 5

Savannah stared up at Niall, an arrested expression on her face. "Okay," she said slowly. "Maybe they work here. Or maybe they're a sophisticated gang of thieves who're masquerading as guests, maybe even on the tour. But how do you get from that to thinking they weren't just planning to rob me?"

Niall chose his words carefully. "What did they say when they knocked at your door?"

She shook her head, her brow furrowed, as if she wasn't seeing his point. "All they said was—" Then she got it. "Housekeeping," she whispered. "But no Chinese accent."

He nodded. "I don't see them speaking English like an American if they were there to rob you. It's possible, of course, but not very likely. Which means you were probably targeted for some other reason. And the only reason that comes to mind is…the job you used to have."

"How do you know what my job used to be?" Her face had lost some of its color. "I never told you."

"I can put two and two together, same as you. You told me you're an engineer. You told me who your employer was, and you told me they tried to convince you not to quit." He smiled faintly. "Doesn't take a rocket scientist to figure out you were a rocket scientist. And, therefore, vitally important to the defense industry in some way. Which makes me think…"

"I'm not *that* important. Not enough for someone to, to—"

"Kidnap you?"

She swallowed hard. "It's like something out of a spy novel. Things like this don't happen in real life."

"Maybe not. But give me another reason why someone would target you." She couldn't and he knew it, and his heart went out to her. "I work in security," he reminded her, although he wasn't about to tell her what kind of security. "It's my job to be suspicious. To question everything." He waited for that to sink in, then asked, "I don't suppose you'll agree to cancel the rest of this tour and go home."

She blinked at him as if she couldn't believe what he was suggesting. "Go home?" she asked, clearly stunned. "I've wanted to take this trip practically my whole life. I finally— *finally*—get up the courage to do it after my parents—" She stopped abruptly, and the stricken expression on her face told him she couldn't finish that sentence without breaking down. But she didn't have to say it for him to know what was in her mind. "And you want me to go *home*?"

Her voice had risen in intensity, but then she glanced around to make sure she hadn't drawn attention with her outburst. She lowered her voice when she continued. "No way," she said fiercely, but with a tearful edge that made his throat ache. "I saw the Great Wall yesterday, but that's not nearly enough. I'm going to see the Forbidden City, Niall. And the Xi'an terracotta warriors, too. I am. I'm going to cruise the Yangtze River, visit the Three Gorges Dam and the Goddess Stream. I'm not giving that up. I'm not. I'm *not*!"

He cradled her face in his hands. "Okay," he soothed. "Okay." He slid his arms around her and pulled her close. "I understand, Savannah. I do. You're not just doing this for you, but for your parents, too. I understand."

He felt the shudder that traveled through her entire body when he mentioned her parents. Well, he'd known what her answer would be, hadn't he? Which meant his options had just dwindled down to one. Protect Savannah for the next two weeks. Keep her safe so she could visit all the sights she'd planned to see, for herself and for her parents.

And to do that—to be with her 24/7—he just might have to accept the invitation she'd extended last night and become her lover. A sacrifice in one way, because any more time in her company would push him right over the edge. He knew that. And when they returned to the States, when he had to let her go—how could she ever forgive him once she discovered why he was there in the first place?—it would be like taking a bullet to his heart again.

But in another way, it wouldn't be a sacrifice. Because part of him acknowledged he had to have her, just once. He had to know what it was like to make love to her. To feel her body arch beneath his and make her cry his name. To see the smile of a woman who'd been well and truly loved on her face when she looked at him.

He didn't know how he'd managed to go from contemplating killing her to needing her like he needed his next breath in less than twenty-four hours, but he had. And he knew his life would never be the same again.

Damn, damn, damn! the man told himself as he closed the email and logged off his computer. The fourteen-hour time difference between Alamogordo, New Mexico, and Beijing meant he'd only learned of last night's failure to kidnap Savannah Whitman early this morning, and his encrypted, coded reply with further instructions for his agents hadn't been read until they'd woken this morning in Beijing. Phone calls back and forth wouldn't be any better time-wise, and he would run the risk that the National Security Agency might be listening. His emails could be intercepted, too, but the encryption should make it nearly impossible for the NSA to crack them, and besides he was using coded instructions.

No, encrypted emails were far more secure, and his frustration had nothing to do with the method of communication. Just with the execution…or lack of it.

He'd tried for years to lure the quietly brilliant Dr. Savannah Whitman to work for his company to no avail. But now he had no choice. He'd lost too many competitive proposals to the company that had employed Dr. Whitman, because the damned DoD trusted her and her work. Which meant his company had been teetering on the brink already. And the breakthrough missile design she'd just come up with this summer? The one that had made the missile his company had been supplying to the DoD for years obsolete?

He'd cursed her, but he'd also known he had to gain possession of her to stave off bankruptcy. And he could no longer afford to wait the two years demanded by the non-compete agreement she'd signed, either. Not that that would prohibit her from working for his company those two years; it would just forbid her from working on something directly related to a previous project…which was exactly what he wanted her to do. And he knew she was just too ethical to try to skirt the strict interpretation of that non-comp.

So he'd had an epiphany when he'd learned she was taking a year off after the deaths of her parents and traveling the world, beginning with China. This was his perfect opportunity to kidnap her…and throw suspicion on the Chinese government.

His secret glee had known no bounds when he'd cast aspersions on her character with the US government—payback for the many times she'd turned down his job offers—and he'd pretended to be greatly reluctant about revealing the "true" reason behind her resignation from her former employer. It had been so easy to manipulate suspicion, because certain high-ranking individuals within Homeland Security and the DoD were paranoid about the government of the People's Republic of China. A private word here, a calculated disclosure there and he'd succeeded beyond his wildest dreams.

But he still had to kidnap her and make it appear to be the work of the PRC. Everything depended on it. Which meant this man who'd suddenly turned up on the tour and befriended Dr. Whitman, this man who'd unwittingly interfered with the brilliant plan, had to be eliminated. One way or another.

Savannah stared in wonder at the vast expanse in front of her that was Tiananmen Square, across the street from the Forbidden City. So vast, it literally dwarfed the tens of thousands of people assembled there. The tour guide was droning on and on about the history of Tiananmen Square in her electronic earpiece, but she turned off her little receiver because she didn't need him to tell her. She *knew*.

She could see the row of tanks in her mind's eye, see the lone man confronting them. You could debate the rights and wrongs of what happened that day in 1989 and everything that led up to it, but the bravery of the man confronting the tanks was beyond question.

She turned to Niall, standing quietly at her side, and blinked away tears. "He *believed*," she whispered.

Niall seemed to be able to read her mind, because he said, "Yeah. He had the courage of his convictions. He didn't die that day, you know—he was pulled to safety. But no one knows what ultimately happened to him. There are conflicting reports. Some say he was later arrested and executed, some say he escaped and went into hiding."

"I believe in fighting for democracy, too," she blurted out. "With all my heart. I have friends who ask me how I can do what I do for a living and still sleep at night. And I tell them they don't understand. The work I do—the work I *did*," she corrected, "it's vital to national security."

She drew a quick breath. "Guided missiles are so much better than anything we used to have. It's my job to make sure our missiles are as accurate as possible, so they hit the military targets they're aimed at, and civilian casualties are minimized."

He didn't say anything for the longest time. Then he leaned down and brushed his lips against hers in a chaste kiss. "Eloquently put," he murmured when he raised his head. There was an expression in his eyes she couldn't interpret. It almost looked like remorse. But what about her words would make Niall feel remorseful?

More proof—if he needed it—that Savannah wasn't a traitor, Niall realized. But someone had deliberately set out to convince the US government she was. Why?

Her words also made him extremely glad he worked for a government that didn't automatically assume guilt and act accordingly. Yes, he'd been dispatched to prevent Savannah from betraying the US by whatever means necessary. But his first assignment had been compiling proof of her guilt that would stand up in a court of law. Killing her would have been a last resort, only if he couldn't stop her any other way.

He didn't want to dwell on what might have been, because it wasn't going to happen. Not now. But what she'd just revealed only added to his determination to find out who had made Savannah his target, and why. And to bring that person to justice.

The couple posing as husband and wife watched from a hundred yards away as Savannah and Niall walked hand in hand through the Forbidden City. Savannah, they were quick to notice, was completely oblivious to the danger they posed. Niall, not so much. His gaze was constantly moving, moving. Checking out the crowd, almost as if he were cataloguing people for future reference. They smiled and waved when his eyes met theirs, then they turned away to enter one of the small courtyards to deflect suspicion that they had Savannah and Niall under observation.

"Spencer was right," the man said. "He's a complication we don't need."

The woman froze, then glanced left and right to make sure no one was close enough to overhear. "You're going to kill him?" she whispered, obviously appalled. As if to say she'd signed up for kidnapping, but not for murder.

"I'd rather not if I don't have to. Don't want to bring official scrutiny on the tour if I can help it. But if I can arrange a little accident..." He shrugged. "A broken leg, maybe. Something to put him in the hospital or at least incapacitate him. We'll see."

Hours later, Savannah was exhausted. She'd walked for miles, it seemed, had ascended and descended countless broad stairways in her determination not to miss anything, had poked her nose into numerous courtyards, had peered into glass-walled rooms depicting homey little scenes of family life in the royal palace. She'd taken hundreds of photos with her camera that would be a pictorial diary she'd look back on years hence.

And she'd reveled in Niall's company. She'd been surprised at how knowledgeable he was about Chinese history, both ancient and modern, and had thoroughly enjoyed every moment they'd spent discussing the pluses and minuses of life in China's glorious past.

"Not so great for women, of course," she stated after long discussions about Chinese contributions to art and science, the Silk Road and commerce, gunpowder, the invention of paper and life in general under the Chinese emperors.

"Yeah, but not really all that different from what life was like for women in England or Europe at that time, either," he countered.

"True." She stopped and drew a deep breath, conscious that her leg muscles were about to revolt.

"Tired?"

"A little," she admitted, then amended, "Okay, a lot. But very happy I came here. It's just so much to cram into a small span of time. I could spend days here and not see everything."

One corner of his mouth twitched into a half smile. "Yeah, but you've seen the highlights, same as at the Great Wall. And you can always say you've been here." He gestured to her camera. "Want me to take your picture for you?"

"Ye…yes…"

But he'd apparently noticed her slight hesitation. "You *don't* want me to take your picture?"

"That's not it." *Just spit it out*, she told herself firmly. "Could I take one of the two of us?" She raised her camera. "I've gotten pretty good at taking selfies. Would you mind?" Then she held her breath.

"The pictures you already took of me aren't enough?"

She stared at him. "You knew? You didn't say anything."

He laughed. "You'd make a lousy spy—you weren't all that surreptitious."

"Oh." Nonplussed, she asked, "You don't mind?"

"Mind that you want memories of the time we've spent together?" His lips quirked into a smile. "What do you think?"

"I wasn't… It's just that… Well, yes," she confessed. "But I'd like at least one photo of the two of us together. Please?"

He slid an arm around her shoulders. "My pleasure."

Savannah held her camera out away from the two of them and snapped a couple of shots, looking at the screen after each one to make sure she hadn't cut off the top of their heads or anything stupid like that. "One more," she pleaded.

Niall flashed her a smile. "Why sure, darlin'."

His smile went right through her, and she felt it all the way to her toes. She sighed softly, then smiled at the camera and pressed the button. "Thanks."

"Now one for me…to go with my collection."

Her smile faded. "Collection?" she faltered, unsure what he meant by that but not liking the sound of it. Was Niall referring to a collection of women he'd been—?

"Pictures of you," he added, as if he'd suddenly realized how she'd interpreted his statement. He whipped his iPhone out of his pocket to show her, scrolling through what appeared to be a dozen or more photos of her taken today. Candid shots, not posed, but each one clearly conveying her excitement at being there.

"When did you… How did you take these without my knowledge?"

"Because unlike you, I *am* good at taking pictures surreptitiously." He drew her back against him, held the iPhone out and *click*! Then *click* again.

He held the phone for her to see without even looking at them himself. "Okay?"

The first picture was typical tourist fodder—they were both smiling at the camera, and in the background you could clearly see the Hall of Supreme Harmony. The second picture, the one she hadn't been expecting and therefore wasn't posing for, was troubling. Because she'd turned in that split second between the first and the second clicks, and was staring up at Niall with an expression that could easily be called…yearning.

She wanted to insist he delete that photo because it was too revealing, but she didn't want to call attention to it, either. So she just nodded and handed him back the phone, then watched in silence for his reaction.

"Not bad," he said judiciously, reviewing the first one. When he swiped a finger over the screen to view the second one, however, he said nothing at all. But his eyebrows twitched into a frown before he shut the phone down and pocketed it.

"Come on," he said, grasping her hand and drawing her willy-nilly after him toward the northern end of the Forbidden City. "There's still time to visit the Imperial Garden. I've heard the rockeries there are not to be missed."

Savannah had signed up for one of the few optional side tours, the Peking opera, so Niall had, too. But unlike Savannah, whose gaze was fixed on the stage practically the entire night, Niall spent most of the evening watching her. Wondering if he wasn't making a bad mistake.

The photo from this morning bothered him. A lot. It was one thing to become Savannah's lover—which he had every intention of doing. It was another thing entirely to make her fall in love with him—which he had *no* intention of doing.

He had a healthy libido and an active sex life. He'd long

since gotten over Francine, the one and only woman he'd ever asked to marry him, back when he'd been young and stupid enough to fall for a woman so shallow her only reaction to his being shot was disappointment that his body was no longer perfect. Back when he'd still been in the Marine Corps. He wasn't carrying a torch for his "one true love" or anything like that—he'd said goodbye and good riddance in the same breath. And he wasn't nursing a wounded heart, no matter what Savannah might have thought last night. He'd had nineteen years and a plethora of women to make sure of it.

He'd broken no hearts over the years because he'd never settled into a long-term relationship, which was just fine and dandy with him. He'd cared a couple of times more than the rest, but he'd never let himself fall in love again for one reason and one reason only: the job that meant more to him than anything.

Problem was, the woman sitting next to him didn't know it. Didn't know him. Didn't know she'd been his target as recently as yesterday.

He'd never gotten involved before with a woman who didn't know the score. Who didn't know the rules of the game going in. Who didn't know it *was* a game. Which meant he'd never spent time with anyone as naïve as Savannah.

He considered this carefully and concluded, yeah, that word applied to her. But there were other words that came to mind. Words he shied away from, because they only added to the guilt he was carrying over how he'd met her in the first place.

And if he wasn't careful, he could hurt her. Badly.

Chapter 6

Niall sat with Savannah as the tour bus drove through the crowded streets of Beijing away from the old section of the city. This trip to the *hutongs*—the narrow, ancient alleyways that had once dominated Beijing—along with a rickshaw ride and tea tasting at an ancient temple, had been designed to give them a flavor of the old days. But the entire time, all Savannah could think of was that the five-star hotel she'd slept in last night was a world away from the life experienced by the residents here.

Niall said nothing, and Savannah wondered if he was thinking the same things she was. Finally, she broke the silence, but she trailed off as she found herself unable to put her thoughts into words. "I never imagined…"

"Very few Americans do."

"This wasn't what I expected."

Niall picked up her hand and examined it. "What did you expect?"

"I… I don't really know. I mean… I wasn't thinking about the *people*," she admitted in a low voice. "Just the history. You know?"

He squeezed her hand in seeming understanding. "Yeah.

It's easy to forget much of the world doesn't live the way we do even now." He was silent for a moment. "But what you have to remember is, people often cling to the familiar. That they don't want change, even if it's change for the better from one perspective. When China was renovating the city for the 2008 Olympic Games, they bulldozed a lot of these older neighborhoods. But many people fought to keep them, to keep their traditional way of life. The daughter of a historian should understand the importance of cultural heritage. So don't feel bad for them, and don't feel guilty. They're living the life they want."

"How'd you know I was feeling…guilty?"

He smiled that faint smile she was coming to recognize. "You have a very expressive face."

Their flight to Xi'an that afternoon went off without a hitch, although Savannah wondered how Niall had managed to secure a seat next to her. All the married couples had, as a matter of course, been assigned seats together. She hadn't expected to have him as her seatmate for the relatively short flight because they weren't a couple as far as the tour knew. But she was glad anyway, and especially grateful to have him at her back during the boarding process—no one would dare to shove *him*.

She didn't think anything of it at first when he gave her the window seat, but then she realized he hadn't asked her preference, aisle or window; he'd just shepherded her into that seat. That's when she realized this was part and parcel of what he'd done all day yesterday and today. As if no one was going to cross the protective shield with which he'd surrounded her.

"I wanted to ask you," she began softly after the airplane had taken off. "You mentioned yesterday morning you work in security." She hesitated. "Is there something I should do to protect myself? I mean, I'm not going home, but I'm not planning to just ignore the potential threat."

"For starters, don't go anywhere alone." He smiled that faint smile she was fast coming to recognize. "But you don't have to worry about that—I've been sticking to you like glue, and I intend to keep doing it."

Disconcerted, all she could think of to say was, "Oh." Then she added, "You're not responsible for me, Niall. I'm grateful, of course, but—"

His smile grew. "Won't be a hardship, if that's what you're thinking. Especially if your invitation still stands."

"Invita—" She broke off as she realized what he meant, and a hot tide of warmth invaded her cheeks.

He slid his hand beneath the hair at the nape of her neck and gently but firmly drew her head toward his as his lips descended for a kiss that drove every rational thought out of her mind. She gasped for breath when he finally released her, only to have his lips take hers again, and she melted.

She found herself free eons later, with no memory of having been released. She touched a shaky finger to her swollen lips, then whispered, "How do you do that?"

"Do what?" he asked, tongue-in-cheek, but his knowing smile told her he knew damn well what she meant.

"I'm not a virgin," she blurted out, then was aghast at herself.

All Niall replied was, "I never expected you were." His expression was enigmatic. "I'm not, either."

"Of course you're not," she asserted with a hint of exasperation. "But I'm not… That is, I haven't… What I mean is, I already told you I won't be much of a challenge."

He ran a finger along the curve of her cheek. "I'm not looking for a conquest, if that's what you were thinking," he assured her. "And I don't put notches on my bedpost. But I will admit I have every intention of making love to you, if you're willing. Tonight. Tomorrow night. And every night for the rest of this trip." His deliberately seductive voice made her shiver uncontrollably. "And once we get on the boat, I'm thinking love in the afternoon sounds pretty damn good, too."

She closed her eyes and swallowed hard, then looked at him again and confessed ever so faintly, "I'm not that good at it."

His eyes softened as they gazed at her, as if he understood how difficult it had been for her to reveal this to him. How humiliating. "Don't worry, Savannah. You will be." He brushed her lips with his. "Don't take that the wrong way. I'm not some arrogant, boastful son of a bitch who thinks he's God's gift to women. But you and I both know you're an incredibly responsive woman...with me. Last night..."

He'd left her again at her hotel door last night. But unlike the first night, this time he'd kissed her until they'd both been breathless. Until her whole body had trembled with longing and she'd mutely pleaded for more. Until he'd taken her keycard from her hand, unlocked her door and growled, "You're hell on my good intentions," before forcing her inside and closing the door—with him on the outside.

She dragged her attention back with an effort to what Niall was saying now.

"I don't give a damn about your past, what you have or haven't done in bed. All I know is last night proved we have something special together. Chemistry, with a touch of magic thrown in. Which means your sexuality is just waiting to be tapped." His voice was little more than a whisper of sound when he said, "And I want to be the man who taps it."

Her pulse accelerated like a bottle rocket because this was what she'd been telling herself she wanted. But some little demon of fear of the unknown suddenly possessed her, and she gripped his shirt in panic, not sure she could go through with it. "Niall..."

"Trust me," he soothed. "It'll be all right. You'll see."

The rest of the flight passed in a daze for Savannah. Niall held her hand the entire time. Reassuringly. Protectively. But not possessively. And he didn't try to seduce her with words again, either. He was just...there.

She gazed eagerly out the window at the city below just before they landed, but was disappointed it looked no different from the air than any other modern city. She couldn't help but hear her mother's voice in her head, nevertheless, reminding her that Xi'an, under a different name, had at one time been the capital of China, rivaling the centers of other major ancient civilizations. Somewhere down there were the two-thousand-year-old terracotta warriors she'd come to see. She wouldn't be disappointed then.

But that was tomorrow's agenda. Tonight...tonight there was Niall.

Savannah had never understood what all the hoopla was about where sex was concerned. She'd lost her virginity at sixteen to the captain of the football team, a painful, less than fulfilling experience in a relationship that had lasted little more than a month. He'd said he loved her and she'd been dazzled into believing him. But once he'd talked her into sleeping with him, he'd dropped her like a hot potato... and then bragged about it. Humiliating her unbearably.

She'd wised up after that and had been more selective, eschewing "chemistry" and going for men she liked and respected. But after two tepid affairs in college, she'd decided sex was vastly overrated. Either she was undersexed or she had the misfortune of picking men who didn't do it for her. Or some combination in between. She'd envied other women in college when they'd talked about their incredible sex lives, but she'd kept quiet. She'd had no intention of revealing her woeful inadequacy where that was concerned.

She'd dated sporadically in grad school, but once she'd attained her PhD and had accepted the job with her former employer, she'd stopped doing even that. No way would she date someone she worked with; if the relationship didn't work out, she still had to see that person on a regular basis. *Not happening*, she'd told herself on more than one occasion, vividly remembering her excruciatingly humiliating experience in high school.

And she'd been so focused on her career she'd had little time for anything else. Little time to meet anyone other than the men she worked with. And she'd consoled herself with the thought that she wasn't really missing anything anyway.

But that was before she'd met Niall. Before he'd looked at her with that certain something in his eyes, before he'd touched her and set off sparks that made her quiver with anticipation. And she knew—*she knew*—sex with Niall would be anything other than tepid. Sex with Niall would rival the best she'd ever heard about from other women, the best she'd ever read about in the romances she'd sneaked from her mother's bookshelves when she was a teenager.

And all she had to do was let it happen. All she had to do was overcome any latent inhibitions that might crop up at the last minute. All she had to do was—

"Everyone else is off the plane, Savannah. I think the flight attendants would like us to leave, too."

"Oh." She blinked and came back to the here and now, realizing Niall was right. The cabin was empty except for them. He probably thought she'd wanted to wait until after the crowd had deplaned, and had stayed at her side. She wasn't going to tell him she'd been so lost in thought she'd never even realized they were on the ground.

Niall rose and moved into the aisle, shouldering his knapsack and pulling their carry-ons from the overhead compartment, then waiting patiently. Savannah gathered up her purse and the light jacket she'd brought with her and pointed to her suitcase. "I can carry that."

He gave her a look that spoke volumes, then started up the aisle, carrying both his and hers. She scurried to keep up with him.

They claimed their checked luggage inside the terminal, then boarded the tour bus that would take them to their hotel.

"Dinner's at our hotel tonight," Niall reminded her. "May I have the pleasure of your company?"

She couldn't help but smile at the old-fashioned courtesy, especially since he'd already expressed his intentions about tonight in no uncertain terms. Still… "You're right," she said. "Your parents raised a gentleman. And I'd love to have dinner with you."

Niall was grateful the operators of this tour handled checking into the hotel for their guests, because that meant keys to the rooms were handed out in the hotel lounge, along with corresponding room numbers. He quickly memorized a dozen of these and paired them with the couples who were occupying those rooms, including those of the Williamses and the overly friendly Thompsons. Not that he suspected anyone in particular, but still. If someone was targeting Savannah, what better guise than guests on the same tour?

He'd already set in motion background checks on all thirty-six of his and Savannah's fellow tour-bus occupants, quaintly called Michael's Family after the English name of their Chinese tour guide. The designation was a convenient way for each of the tour guides to keep track of the people in their group when they were dispersed in crowds.

Niall knew very well whoever was targeting Savannah didn't have to be someone in their tour group. There would be close to five hundred passengers on the river cruise portion of this trip, and *all* the passengers were suspects, since they were all housed in the same hotels. Not to mention the tour guides. But…he was playing the odds. And the odds were, someone in their little tour group had their sights set firmly on Savannah.

Which meant he couldn't leave her unprotected. Not on this land tour, and not on the river cruise. Because the same thing that had made his government wary, the same thing that had caused him to be dispatched, still put Savannah at risk—the highly classified data in her brain.

No one was going to take advantage of that. Not if he had anything to say about it.

Savannah unpacked and debated with herself over whether she should wear the same dress she'd worn the first night with Niall or go buy something new, then regretfully decided she didn't have time to shop—Niall was coming to get her in less than an hour. Besides, much as she wanted to dazzle him with another killer outfit, she wasn't sure she could carry off something more enticing than the dress he'd already said was perfect for her, which she'd had dry-cleaned at their last hotel. She'd pair it with other jewelry and do something different with her hair, but underneath she'd wear the same wisps of lace and silk she'd carefully washed out after Niall had left her at the door to her room the first night.

He'd already promised he wouldn't do that tonight, and she wanted to…well…she wanted to be particularly sexy to make up for the things she'd admitted earlier.

"Awkward," she muttered as she stripped and stepped

into the shower. "Did you have to make a complete fool of yourself?"

But Niall had taken it in stride. Hadn't seemed to find her wanting in some way because of her admission. In fact, he'd seemed to think whatever had been lacking in her previous sexual relationships wasn't her fault at all, which had a particularly freeing effect on her now.

She was dressed and ready far too early, so she grabbed her laptop out of its case and booted it up to check her email. She frowned when her computer seemed to take an unusually long time to start up, but quickly forgot all about it when she checked her email and found a long chatty letter from Nancy. Her next-door neighbor, with her husband, Rick, was looking after Savannah's house while she was gone.

She replied with a quick note about everything she'd seen and done so far, including visiting the Great Wall with "a million of my closest friends" and the trip to the Forbidden City yesterday. She said nothing about Niall, however. She wasn't quite sure why.

She'd just hit Send when there was a rap at her door. She logged off quickly, slipped on the heels that didn't even come close to making her as tall as Niall, then took one last look in the mirror.

"Smile," she reminded herself. "Breathe. It's just dinner. Dinner and sex. Dinner and hot, steamy sex. Dinner and hot, steamy sex with a man who pushes all your buttons and sure as hell knows what he's doing."

Chapter 7

Niall thought he'd been prepared for the reality that was Savannah all decked out—he'd seen her in the same dress the first night, after all, not to mention the makeup that once again enhanced her delicate loveliness. She'd done something different with her hair this time, swept her wavy tresses up in a classical chignon that made his hands itch to take them down, but that wasn't it. No, she had a certain glow that hadn't been there either of the last two nights, almost as if she were lit up from within. As if she were eagerly anticipating what he'd promised her this afternoon—to-die-for sex.

Savannah wasn't beautiful the way his sisters-in-law were beautiful. She wasn't drop-dead gorgeous as Carly was, or a tall, slender Valkyrie like Angelina, or even fragilely angelic like Cate. But she had a physical appeal all her own, and something more. A frighteningly powerful intellect that could easily intimidate a man who wasn't completely secure in his masculinity.

Could she think rings around him? Probably, especially in math and engineering. He'd tested out of a bunch of classes in college after he'd left the Marine Corps and had finished in three years, but he'd never even considered going for a higher degree—he'd wanted to be *doing*, not studying, and had doggedly pursued his bachelor's degree only because it was a requirement for the job he'd wanted all those years ago. And those three—nearly four—patents she held put her head and shoulders above most people in terms of creative thinking.

Despite all that, though, they'd found common ground and had never had a shortage of things to talk about. And the sparks that flew between them? The sexual chemistry neither of them could hide?

He shoved those thoughts aside for a moment. "You look lovely." His voice was husky with repressed desire that had unexpectedly surged to the fore when Savannah had opened the door and smiled at him. He would have given his next paycheck to forget all about dinner and move right on to dessert.

But that's not an option, hotshot, the gentleman he'd been raised to be whispered in his mind. A gentleman didn't pounce. A gentleman wooed a woman. Dinner. Small talk. Little gifts, such as flowers. Which reminded him…

"I thought you'd like these," he said, bringing his hand from behind his back, holding three long-stalked tiger lilies in not-quite-full bloom, surrounded by ferns in a crystal vase, wrapped in silver-gilt tissue paper. He'd scoured the hotel's flower shop for the perfect offering, shaking his head against the more traditional roses, carnations, orchids. But when he'd seen the tiger lilies in a vase in the corner of the refrigerated case, he'd immediately known they were the ones.

They were Savannah—lovely and unusual. Maybe not the way she saw herself, but the way she could be…if she let herself go. And he was going to make sure of that tonight.

The hint of vulnerability that came over Savannah's face

made him wonder if no one else had ever given her flowers before. It didn't seem possible, but…

"Thank you," she said in a voice that confirmed his suspicion. "I should put them in water but I don't—" She stopped abruptly when she took the flowers and realized they were already in a vase.

"Hotel and all, I figured you wouldn't have a vase handy," he explained.

She looked up at him. "Do you always think of everything?"

He allowed himself a small smile. "I try." He wasn't thinking of the flowers in that moment. He was thinking of the other things he'd bought this evening but left in his hotel room, where he'd stop on their way back from dinner.

The hotel restaurant lived up to the tour brochure's promise of first-class dining for the discriminating traveler. White linen tablecloth and napkins, fine china, silverware and crystal wineglasses set the stage for impeccable service and haute cuisine. Niall didn't usually patronize high-end establishments, but thanks to his mother's training and a job that had taken him all over the world and required he fit in everywhere, he felt comfortable in that rarified element.

Wine, on the other hand, was something he knew well. He perused the wine list and ordered a little-known but highly rated organic merlot from the choices offered.

Savannah waited until the wine steward left before reminding Niall, "Alcohol is only included in the base price on the river cruise portion of this tour."

Niall smiled at how she seemed to be concerned for his wallet. "I know. They'll charge it to my room. But I think you'll appreciate this one."

They chatted easily throughout the meal, which consisted of lamb stir-fried with ginger and scallions for Savannah and Chinese roast pork for Niall, with salads on the side, all of which had been preceded by soup that seemed to accompany every meal in China.

Savannah sipped at her merlot. "You're right," she told Niall. "This is wonderful. How do you know so much about wines?"

He shrugged. "It's a hobby of mine. I picked up the habit of drinking wine with every meal when I was in Europe. And since I'm single with no children, I can afford to indulge without putting a crimp in my budget. What about you?" The question was one to which he already knew the answer, but he was curious to see what she would say.

Savannah shook her head. "I rarely drink. Neither of my parents did, and somehow that rubbed off on me. I'm not a teetotaler," she was quick to add. "It doesn't bother me when other people drink in reasonable amounts. I just can't stand drunkenness."

"Same here. And not just because they're a danger to others when they get behind the wheel of a car. A man who's drunk isn't in control of himself or the situation around him. That could be fatal in my line of work. And usually is."

"So what exactly do you do?" she asked. "You mentioned security a couple of times, but…"

Niall had already decided what he'd answer if she asked for more details. "I guess you could say I'm a trouble-shooter. I plug security leaks." He smiled lazily, as if it was no big deal, and deflected her attention by focusing it on her. "What about you? I know you were an engineer working for—" he named her former employer "—doing what exactly?" It wasn't until he'd asked it that he realized it was a trick question. But now that he had, he was curious what she would answer. If she was following strict security protocol she shouldn't tell him.

An expression of discomfiture crossed her face. "Does it really matter? I don't work there anymore. Maybe I'll go back after this year, or maybe I'll do something different. I don't know. All I know is my job is no longer going to be the be-all and end-all for me. I'm going to have a life outside of work. I'm going to do the things I want to do *now*, and not wait for 'someday.'"

Niall finished his excellent roast pork, then asked, "Other than traveling, what are some of the things you want to do?"

Her face grew solemn. "I always thought I'd be a good mother—mine was a great role model—but it just never happened. I wasn't willing to marry someone I didn't love just to have children. So I've been giving a lot of thought to becoming a Big Sister through the Big Brothers Big Sisters of America program. I never did it before because it's a substantial time commitment, if you do it right. But I've come to realize you have to make time for the things you really want."

He raised his wineglass to her in a sincere salute. "Noble cause and a worthy goal. I hope you follow through. What else?"

"Well... I used to sing in a choir all through school, something I really enjoyed. And I'm told I have talent. But ever since I started working I've neglected my singing. I'd like to go back to it, join a choir again. But like Big Brothers Big Sisters, that takes time. Time I thought I didn't have to spare before my parents died."

She'd just revealed something else Niall already knew about her. He'd viewed video of her in her high school and college choral groups, and she was right—she definitely had talent. Which made her something of a Renaissance woman. Multifaceted, not just brilliant in engineering and math.

He nodded approvingly. "So you want to be a Big Sister and you want to sing again. What else?"

Her gaze dropped to her now-empty plate, then back up at Niall. In a low voice, she confessed, "I'd like to…well… I'd like to find someone to fall in love with. To grow old with. I don't want to live the rest of my life alone. I've left it rather late, I know. Statistics are against me. By the time a woman reaches my age, her chances have decreased dramatically. But I'm not giving up."

He hadn't seen it coming. And all he could do was curse himself for encouraging Savannah in serious introspection. Because she was doomed to disappointment if she was thinking he might be that person. He wasn't long-term relationship material. Make love to her? Yes, of course. Help her unlock her sexual potential, teach her everything he knew in that area? Absolutely. But he was not a man any woman should fall in love with, especially her.

For one thing, he could never share anything about his job with a woman. Any woman. What kind of basis was that for the trust necessary in building a relationship?

He'd killed people, for another thing. Yes, he'd done it at the behest of his government in order to save lives, much as a soldier on the battlefield. But still…

And then there was the job he'd originally been sent to do, which he didn't even want to think about now.

If he was looking for a long-term relationship, however— *which you're not,* he reminded himself firmly—it would be with someone like Savannah. Loving. Caring. Smart as a whip. And with a latent sensual streak he couldn't wait to unleash.

She wasn't the first woman he'd wanted, not by a long shot. But he hadn't wanted anyone the way he wanted her in…well…in forever. There was one thing about Savannah that put her in a totally different league from the women with whom he'd had discreet liaisons in the past nineteen years. Every other woman he'd gotten naked with had avoided looking at the scar over his heart, although he'd caught a few of them casting surreptitious glances at it when they thought he wasn't looking. Followed inevitably by aversion, disgust or worst of all, pity.

Savannah had done none of those things. She'd kissed the scar with a kind of reverence, as if acknowledging the physical manifestation of his act of courage was a badge of honor, which was how Niall thought of it when he thought of it at all. Which was why he'd never had cosmetic surgery to minimize the scar's visibility.

So what did all this mean? If he was honest with himself, he had a huge problem. He was dangerously close to falling for her. After knowing her for three days.

Niall took Savannah for a walk after dinner. Xi'an was a beautiful city at night; darkness and twinkling lights hid a lot of faults, just as they did with many American cities. She visibly relaxed as they walked and talked, which had been his goal. He hadn't missed how she'd slowly tensed up as the evening wore on.

He waited for a pause in the conversation, then said casually, "It's okay to change your mind, you know."

She halted abruptly and raised startled eyes to his. "Change my— What do you mean?"

"I'm not going to pounce, so you can stop worrying. Do I want to make love to you?" He smiled down into her upturned face. "Absolutely. More than you can imagine. But I can wait until you're truly ready."

"I am. I mean… Well…I thought I was, but…"

"But you're having second thoughts." His smile held

understanding and reassurance. "I'd never hurt you, Savannah. But you only have my word for it. So if you want to wait, that's okay by me."

Savannah stared up at Niall, wondering how it was his reassurances about waiting made it seem completely unnecessary. "Would you kiss me?"

An enigmatic expression crept into his dark brown eyes. "I'm not going to seduce you into bed. That's not how this is going to work between us."

"Not that." She scrunched her face with frustration, trying to think how best to word it. Finally, she said, "I've never been all that good at expressing what I want in my personal life, in bed or out. But with you, I… I don't seem to have those same reservations. I want you to kiss me because when you do I know exactly what I want. And what I want is…you."

Niall held her hand all the way back to the hotel, and in the elevator up to their floor. He only spoke once. "Your room or mine?"

The condoms she'd once again secreted in her nightstand drawer were definitely on her mind when she said firmly, "Mine."

"Okay," he nodded, then stopped at his room. "Hold on a sec."

He was in and out of his room in less than a minute, carrying a black leather case when he came out. "A few essentials," he explained briefly.

Savannah figured one of the essentials was probably condoms. She considered mentioning she'd already thought of it, but chickened out at the last minute. As they moved to her room, she wondered what else the leather case contained. She didn't have to wait long for her curiosity to be satisfied. Once the door closed behind them, he unzipped the bag and removed the contents, placing them on the nightstand. A miniature music player. A box of condoms as she'd expected, although she couldn't help noticing these were extra large. And a tube of—

"Oh. I never thought of that."

"Not saying we'll need it." His voice was deep and soothing. "But just in case…"

Her nervousness returned out of the blue, but before it could take hold Niall switched on the music player. He held out his hand to her as swirls of soft, dreamy music filled the room. "Dance with me."

Then he smiled at her, a smile so filled with tenderness and understanding her nervousness dissipated, and she moved unselfconsciously into his arms.

She couldn't really call what they did dancing. More just swaying back and forth to the music as one emotionally evocative tune blended into another. Niall dipped his head and his lips found hers from time to time. Long, drugging kisses she gave herself up to without a qualm.

She was so caught up in just enjoying the experience of being held in his powerful embrace, so taken with his kisses and the music, she scarcely noticed when he unzipped her dress and slid his hands inside the opened edges. Once that happened, however, she *did* notice, because his hands stroked. Caressed. And set off sparks that heated her blood and sent streamers of desire everywhere.

She shivered with longing, then stopped swaying and leaned back a little while still in the cradle of his arms. Her hands moved of their own accord, and she began unbuttoning his shirt with fingers that weren't quite steady.

His hands closed over hers for a moment. "I can stop any time," he informed her, his face serious. "I want you to know that before we go any further. It might get a little tricky toward the end, but everything stops when you say stop."

"Don't stop," she whispered. "Please don't stop."

Afterward, Savannah could never clearly recall how they'd ended up on the bed, naked and—in her case—trembling with anticipation. Niall's hands—*oh, God, his hands!* she thought disjointedly, when she could think at all—seemed to be everywhere, coaxing a response out of her she'd never imagined she was capable of giving. And when one large hand settled at the juncture of her thighs and he murmured, "Open for me, Savannah," it seemed the most natural thing in the world.

The first orgasm took her completely by surprise. She'd been floating, listening to the romantic music and Niall's whispered words of encouragement as his fingers created magic, when all at once her body arched against his hand and tension wound tighter and tighter inside her. She clutched his arms and gasped his name as he drove her up and over with seemingly effortless ease.

But he wasn't done. He'd donned a condom before she realized it and had positioned himself between her thighs, his erection nudging for entrance. His breathing was erratic, but he demanded, "Say the word." And she knew he was giving her another chance to change her mind.

"Yes. *Please*, yes." She clutched at his hips to pull him into her, then moaned when he did just that. Pressing deep, deeper, until he filled her completely, and she came apart in his arms. He withdrew slowly, and all she could think of was "no." No, she couldn't bear the emptiness. Couldn't bear the loss of heat and fullness and—

She caught her breath again and her eyes closed in wonder when he surged back in, his chest rubbing against her nipples until they ached and formed hard little peaks.

"Look at me, Savannah," he demanded, as if he wanted

her to be sure who it was bringing her body to life. As if it was important to him somehow. And when her eyelids drifted open, he said, "Say my name."

"Niall," she whispered dutifully. Then, "Oh, Niall," as he rebuilt her desire slowly. A steady rhythm of in and out, creating a firestorm of longing and need for more. And more. Until the slow pace was almost agony because she was nearly there, and she begged, "Please, Niall."

He ducked his head and captured one nipple, suckling until she couldn't bear it, until she exploded again, rocking her hips up against his as his thrusts increased in intensity, throbbing tightly around him until he joined her in what the French called the little death.

Her heart was beating, beating, beating, and her lungs were gasping for air. But so were his. A sense of oneness filled her as he rolled them over to take his weight off her, but keeping the connection. And all she could think of in that moment as Niall's arms closed tightly around her and she nestled against his chest was that he'd been right. She *was* good at this…with him.

Chapter 8

The shower Niall insisted they take together was another revelation for Savannah. She'd never imagined her body could be so attuned to another human being's that she could be brought to the brink again so easily...especially after two orgasms that far eclipsed anything she'd ever experienced. But when Niall's mouth took hers, when his soapy hands slid over her arms, her breasts, her waist, her hips, she shivered with longing that was only assuaged when the fingers of his right hand slipped between her legs and set up a thrumming rhythm that devastated her. And all she could do as the warm water cascaded over their bodies was cling to him and shudder her release.

Her legs were so rubbery afterward that Niall had to dry them both off. Then he swept her into his arms over her faint protest that she could walk, and carried her back to bed.

They lay there in silence for what seemed like forever, as Savannah tried to marshal her thoughts but couldn't. Niall's heart beat beneath her ear—a steady thump, thump, thump that mirrored her own pulse now that she'd come down from her multi-orgasmic high.

Finally she broke the silence. "We didn't need the lubricant after all." Then she could have kicked herself that she'd picked those words out of the jumble in her brain to say to him.

Niall's chest reverberated with soft laughter. "Uh, no, we didn't," he agreed.

She tugged the covers over her face to hide her embarrassment. "I didn't mean to blurt that out," she mumbled.

"You didn't say anything I wasn't already thinking," he consoled her. He drew the covers away from her face and placed a finger beneath her chin to lift it, to force her eyes to meet his. "And I was never more grateful for anything in my life."

She searched his dark eyes, but they held nothing but the truth. Then she admitted, "Me too," a smile creeping across her face. One that was met with an answering smile of satisfaction and something else that surprised her— admiration. Because she'd let her inhibitions go? she wondered. Because she'd responded to him wholeheartedly? Because she'd taken him as high as he'd taken her?

"Whatever you're thinking behind those serious gray eyes is probably right."

She blinked, then shook her head. "How can you possibly know what I'm thinking?"

His smile deepened. "When a woman thinks a man can walk on water..."

"I never said that!"

"You didn't have to. It was in your eyes."

She blushed, but she didn't look away. "So okay, yes. It was pretty fantastic. *You're* pretty fantastic."

He shook his head. "You're the fantastic one, Savannah. All I did was unlock the door. After that it was all you."

Niall woke with an armful of soft, warm woman who smelled amazing draped bonelessly across his chest. And an unforgettable evening burned into his memory. He'd told Savannah nothing less than the truth last night—it had all been her. He'd been blown away at how responsive she was to his slightest touch. She hadn't shied away from anything, either, had let him take her on a magic carpet ride from start to finish.

Afterward she'd gazed at him as if he were her hero, and his early-morning semierection hardened in a rush at that memory. Was there any better aphrodisiac than having a woman look at you as if you could work miracles?

But as soon as that thought came to him, another one crowded in. One he didn't want to deal with, but was going to have to: *Whatever you do, don't let her fall in love with you.*

No, he wasn't arrogant enough to think all he had to do was give a woman a few orgasms and she'd fall hopelessly in love with him. That wasn't it at all. But they'd connected in other ways, too, not just in bed. And that had disaster written all over it, because sure as shooting he'd break her heart when she found out who and what he was. No way could she ever forgive him for that.

And if he fell in love with her, something in his heart of hearts he admitted he was already in the process of doing? Something he'd never imagined was even remotely possible, because he hadn't thought he was still susceptible to the softer emotions, not since Francine knocked them out of him nineteen years ago. But with Savannah…

Suck it up, Jones, he told himself harshly, excising those thoughts with the precision of a surgeon with a scalpel. *A woman like Savannah isn't for the likes of you.*

Savannah woke alone. At first she couldn't believe it— she dragged the T-shirt she wore as a nightgown out of the drawer and over her head, then checked the bathroom, but no. No tall, incredibly fit man with shaggy brown hair, dark chocolate eyes and hands that should be licensed as a lethal weapon where women were concerned. She looked on the nightstand and on the desk, but there was no note, either.

A cold, sinking feeling settled over her as second thoughts made an unwelcome visit. Was this what was known as a one-night stand? Was this how a woman felt when she'd shared what she'd thought was an incredibly intimate evening with a man, only to find he didn't feel the same?

She sank onto the edge of the bed, her arms crossed over her middle to try and stop the shakes that surfaced from nowhere. *Sex,* she reminded herself savagely. *That's all you asked for, remember? Incredible sex. Mind-blowing sex. But just sex.*

A sound at the door brought her head up sharply, and she suddenly remembered the other night and the masked intruders Niall had chased away. She grabbed the first thing she could reach that could be used as a weapon—the lamp on the desk—and hefted it over her head to bring it down sharply on whomever walked through the door.

Only to drop it with a carpeted thud when Niall appeared in the open doorway, her electronic keycard in his hand.

He took in everything in a single, comprehensive glance, and said levelly, "I should have woken you to let you know I was just going next door to change clothes."

She picked up the lamp and returned it to the desk, glad to see it wasn't broken. She plugged it back in and straightened the lampshade before saying just as levelly, "That probably would have been a good idea."

Niall came up behind her but didn't touch her, for which she was grateful. But she couldn't bring herself to look at him, either. Instead, she kept fiddling with the lampshade, trying to remove the dent.

"I'm sorry," he said in a deep rumble. "Sorry I scared you. And even sorrier I let you wake up alone." Remorse colored his words. "Look at me, Savannah." But she couldn't until he cupped her cheek with one hand and convinced her to turn around. "I can be an SOB at times, but I'm not *that* much of an SOB. I was only planning to be gone a couple of minutes, and you were sleeping so soundly I didn't have the heart to waken you. But I'd never walk away without a word on the morning after the night before. Is that what you thought? That I'd just left?"

"It occurred to me."

His hands tightened around her arms, and pain slashed across his face. "I guess I deserved that."

Part of her wanted to reassure him, to say he didn't deserve it. But another part of her wanted to lash out and hurt him as she'd been hurt when she'd woken up alone, and cauterize her own wounds at the same time. "You don't owe me anything," she said through stiff lips. "I threw myself at you—I admit that. I wanted to know what it was like, and I wasn't disappointed. Thank you very much. But we don't have to pretend it was anything more than a—"

He shook her suddenly, cutting her off. "Don't say it." His jaw set so tightly her own jaw ached. "Don't attribute motives to me that are untrue," he said through clenched teeth. "Whatever you think happened here last night, you're wrong. You think it was just sex? Think again. You're not like that, and believe it or not, neither am I. I don't sleep with just any woman who will let me—that's an insult to both of us."

His head slanted down without any warning at all, and he took her mouth with an intensity that shook her to the core. But his lips softened almost immediately, and instead of demanding a response, he was coaxing one.

When he finally raised his head, they were both breathless. "*That's* what happened here last night," he insisted. "Something neither of us can deny. You wanted me, Savannah, and—God help me—I wanted you. You. Not a convenient body. *You*. I wanted the woman who fought down her fear of crowds to climb the Great Wall. I wanted the woman who stood on the ramparts of the Forbidden City, her face aglow with excitement. I wanted the woman who wouldn't throw away good food just because it was cold." He kissed her again, but oh-so-gently this time. "Tell me you wanted me, Savannah. Tell me."

She couldn't lie. "I wanted *you*, Niall. I wanted the man who helped me conquer my fears. The man who wouldn't take advantage of me that first night. The man who took a bullet for someone else."

His eyes closed and his arms enfolded her as a sigh shuddered out of him. "Okay then," he said, stroking her tousled hair. "I am so sorry you woke up alone. And I swear I'll never leave your bed again without letting you know where I went. But you have to promise me something, too."

"What?" Her question was muffled against his chest.

"You have to promise to trust that I'll never just walk away without a word. Without a backward glance. When the time comes, when you return to your world and I return to mine, I'll leave a piece of myself behind with you, the same way you will with me."

Everyone piled into the tour bus after breakfast, excitement mounting. Like Savannah, the Xi'an terracotta warriors were a must-see item for most of the people on the tour, and there was a lot of happy chatter among them. Many of the couples had made friends by now, so there were cries of "sit here!" and "I snagged an extra bottle of water from the front. Do you need one?"

Niall herded Savannah toward the back of the bus, as

he'd done yesterday and the day before. The front seats had gone quickly, but that was okay with him. Sitting far in the back allowed him to keep a wary eye on the rest of the occupants. Not that he expected trouble on the bus in front of dozens of witnesses, but he held by the maxim to always sit facing the door. He couldn't be taken unaware that way.

"Got your camera?" he asked Savannah.

She patted her vest pocket and nodded. "Batteries charged, extra battery pack and extra SD card, too, just in case. I plan on taking hundreds of pictures today."

Niall smiled. Savannah's enthusiasm was contagious, and even though he'd been here ten years ago on another assignment, he couldn't help feeling a vicarious sense of excitement.

Mary Beth Thompson and her husband, Herb, were the last to board, and for a moment he feared the overly gregarious couple would join Savannah and him at the back if there were no seats near the front. He heaved a small sigh of relief when another couple halfway back called out, "Mary Beth! Herb! We saved seats for you!"

His eyes met Savannah's, and she whispered, "Oh, thank God!"

"I guess there is such a thing as being too friendly," he murmured.

She chuckled. "I don't think Mary Beth has ever heard that silence is golden."

"I pity her poor husband."

She gasped and choked on laughter. "Oh, so do I! I was just thinking the same thing."

They didn't talk much after that. Once the bus pulled away from the hotel, the tour guide got on the microphone and began his spiel on everything they would see that day.

"Qin Shi Huang, the first Emperor of China, who also built a portion of the Great Wall, commissioned the thousands of terracotta soldiers, archers, horses and chariots more than two thousand years ago," he intoned. "And each face is unique. Archaeologists theorize the faces are those of actual persons serving in the emperor's court."

"As if we didn't already know that," Savannah murmured in Niall's ear. "Even if I hadn't researched it on my own, it's all in the tour company's brochure. Who doesn't read the brochure ahead of time so they know what they're going to see?"

"Most people. Now shhh," he cautioned. "Just pretend you're suitably impressed."

"We will spend four hours at the museum, after which we will have lunch at a terracotta factory nearby, where you can purchase fine replicas of the statuary you will see this morning."

"I'll bet he gets a kickback on the sales," Savannah whispered.

That did it. Niall choked on laughter he quickly turned into a pretended coughing fit, and Savannah solicitously handed him an unopened bottle of water. After he'd taken a couple of swallows and wiped his streaming eyes, he told her severely, "I'll bet every dime I have you were a holy terror as a child. Did your parents ever spank you?"

Her eyes danced with humor. "I was a model child."

"Yeah, I'll just bet."

"Okay, maybe once or twice," she admitted. "You?"

He assumed a pious expression. "I was a model child."

"Uh-huh." Her skepticism was obvious.

"Well, there *was* this one time…but it was all Shane's fault."

"Shane?"

Quick as a flash, he mentally reviewed what he'd been about to say and revised it slightly. "My older brother."

"The one who was medically discharged from the Marine Corps?"

"One and the same."

"So tell me what happened. What did you and Shane do?"

He winced in exaggerated fashion. "We stole a car."

"What?"

"Well, we didn't actually steal it. We just sort of borrowed it without permission."

"You stole a car." She blinked at him and repeated, "You stole a car."

"It belonged to our dad. Did I mention that?"

"You stole your dad's car?"

"Yes, but it was Shane's idea."

She hesitated. "But you went along with it."

"Yeah."

"Oh."

He winced again. "Yeah. Oh. I was sixteen. Shane was a year older. Our dad had this red Corvette he rarely took out of the garage. Drove Shane and me crazy. But we paid for our crime, believe you me. Our dad tanned our hides when he found out. Taught us a lesson, that's for sure. Shane and I have trod the straight and narrow ever since."

"You really stole your dad's car? You're not making this up?"

"We really did. But we've been model citizens ever since. So what's the worst thing you've ever done?"

"Nothing like stealing a car." She still seemed stuck on that concept.

"Come on, fair's fair. I've revealed my criminal past. What about you?"

She thought for a moment. "Well, the statute of limitations has long since expired. And the store owner said he wouldn't press charges, so..."

"Shoplifting? You?"

"I know. I *know.* I was seven. Old enough to know it was wrong."

"What did you steal?"

She bit her lip.

"Come on, Savannah, confession is good for the soul. What did you steal?"

She winced much as he'd done. "A miniature Bible."

He would have burst out laughing if he hadn't already created a scene earlier, so he strangled his laughter and covered his face with his hands, his shoulders shaking. When he finally had himself mostly under control, he wheezed, "You stole a *Bible*?"

"The irony, I know. I'd never seen a book so tiny it fit in the palm of my hand, and I was fascinated. I just *had* to have it. Somehow, before I knew it, it ended up in my pocket."

"So what happened?"

"My mom found it." She shivered suddenly. "I can still remember the humiliation when she made me take it back to the store and turn myself in. Almost twenty-nine years ago, but that lesson is burned in my memory. I'll never forget it." All at once her eyes filled with tears, and she blinked hard to keep them from falling. "I didn't realize it at the time," she whispered, "but my mom stood behind me as I walked up to that counter and confessed my crime, sharing my guilt…the mother of a thief. Some mothers might have let it go. Some might have punished me by grounding me or something like that, but not mine. She made the punishment fit the crime. Made sure I'd never forget it."

She gulped. "She was such a good mom. My dad, too. Wonderful parents. I look back at my childhood, and I realize all the ways they helped shape the woman I am. I miss them so much."

His arms closed around her without conscious thought, and he pressed her face against his chest as she sobbed once, then lay quiescent. "It's okay, Savannah. It's okay to grieve."

"I told myself I wasn't going to cry anymore," she breathed, clinging tightly. "It's just…"

"I understand." And the damnable thing was, he did understand, because his parents had raised him the same way Savannah's parents had raised her, and he loved them just as deeply. And when his dad had died relatively young? He'd grieved for the longest time. Still did, on occasion, though he tried not to dwell on it. But he still loved his father and all the wonderful growing-up memories he would take to his grave.

Savannah's loss was still so fresh. And she'd lost both parents, not just one. Added to that, she had no siblings to share her grief the way he did. It just about killed him that she had no one to hold her and love her and tell her it was going to be okay, that there was light at the end of the tunnel.

That was the moment he realized he was dangerously close to falling in love with Savannah, if he wasn't already.

And wasn't that a kick in the teeth for a man like him? A man with zero chance of being the kind of man she needed long term. *You can tell yourself that until you're blue in the face,* he thought savagely, *but that doesn't change the truth.*

Because the truth was, he wanted to be that man. Fiercely.

Chapter 9

Just as at the Great Wall, there were hordes of people pushing and shoving to get close to the railing near the entrance for an unimpeded view of the row upon row of terracotta warriors. Savannah didn't know how Niall had accomplished it, but somehow he'd managed to squeeze through the crowd and make a place for her at the railing, then stood at her back, his arms wrapped protectively around her, holding the hordes at bay so she wouldn't suffer a panic attack.

She had her camera out and was snapping picture after picture, thankful her camera was highly rated for the low light inside the cavernous museum.

"Ready to move on?" Niall asked when she stopped taking pictures.

She'd been so focused on getting to the railing for her first glimpse of the terracotta army she hadn't realized what she was doing. But now she turned her head to the left and right and shuddered. Masses of people surrounded them. How were they going to escape the press of bodies?

Niall must have felt the shudder, must have realized she was starting to panic, because he leaned down and spoke quietly in her ear. "Trust me, Savannah. I'll get you out safely if you'll just trust me and follow my lead."

"O...kay..." she said, but her teeth were already chattering.

"Tuck your camera away—don't want to drop it." And when she'd done so, he swung her into his arms and shouldered his way through the crowd.

"Niall! What are you— You can't carry— Oh my God!"

Before she knew it, they were out of the press of people struggling to get to the railing, and the crowd thinned. He lowered her feet to the floor when they reached the ramp on the far left side and smiled down into her still-startled face. "I told you I'd get you out of there."

"Yes, but I... I didn't want to make a scene."

"If you'd slipped into a full-blown panic attack at the railing—which you were just about to do—you'd have made a hell of a scene. More than what I did."

"You're right," she acknowledged after a moment.

"And if you look around, no one gives a damn. It's done. It's over. And no one cares."

"You're right," she repeated as she glanced from side to side and realized no one was paying them the least attention.

"So..." His smile deepened, and a devilish gleam entered his eyes. "How are you going to thank me?" He waggled his eyebrows in exaggerated fashion.

She laughed, and the laughter dispelled the last of her panic, obviously something Niall had done with that goal in mind. "Oh, you..." She cuffed him playfully on the arm, but then an upwelling of gratitude made her reach up and pull his head down to hers. "My hero," she whispered, brushing her lips against his. "Thank you."

* * *

Fifty yards away, still at the railing, pretending to take photographs, the pseudo-couple focused their cameras on Savannah and Niall. The woman leaned over to the man, as if in a romantic gesture, and pressed her lips against his ear. "I thought you were going to get him out of the picture somehow."

His mouth barely moved. "No chance so far. He's amazingly careful of his surroundings. Might have to wait until the boat."

"What does Spencer say?"

He snorted. "Spencer wants what he wants, when he wants it. But he's not the one in the field. And I'm not taking any chances just because he's impatient."

"Okay. You're the boss."

His eyes were cold when he faced her. "Yes. And don't you forget it."

Niall's gaze was sweeping back and forth through the crowd, checking for the slightest betrayal of a hostile action toward Savannah, while at the same time achingly aware of every move she made. He wished—how he wished—he could sweep her into his arms again and take her someplace safe. Someplace where he didn't have to constantly be on his guard. Someplace like his condo in Washington, DC, a miniature fortress.

But he couldn't convince her to leave China with the balance of her bucket list unfulfilled. *Been there, done that, bought the T-shirt and was shot down before I got to wear it*, he thought with a touch of mordant humor. And he couldn't take her out of here against her will, either. Which meant constant vigilance while in public.

They were ahead of most of their tour group, he saw. Their tour guide was standing halfway up the ramp they'd

come down, holding his sign for Michael's Family high
enough for everyone to see it above the crowd. A gaggle of
faces he recognized were huddled around the tour guide,
listening to what he had to say. Niall could hear him, too,
although he'd reduced the volume on his electronic receiver
until the voice was little more than a whisper in his ear. He
didn't need the history lesson; he just needed to know when
it was time to move on so they didn't become too separated
from the rest of their group.

Savannah turned a flushed and ecstatic face toward him.
"Isn't it amazing? Have you ever seen anything like it?"

"No. Never." But he wasn't talking about the rows of
statues. He was talking about Savannah herself, and the
glow that mimicked the one on her face last night when
she'd answered the door at his knock.

Beautiful, he realized with a sense of shock. Beautiful
the way a piece of music could catch at your heartstrings
and make you ache for something just out of reach. And
just as he couldn't really compare two completely different
songs that were both heart-wrenching, he couldn't compare
Savannah to any other woman, either. Her beauty would
never fade because it had nothing to do with her features
and everything to do with her loving heart.

And though he'd already acknowledged and accepted he
could never be the man in her life long-term, in that moment he fell a little deeper under her spell.

Niall accompanied Savannah on the last of the optional
side tours that night: dinner and a live theater show featur-
ing one of China's most glorious dynasties. "I don't want to
miss a thing," she'd explained artlessly on the bus back to
their hotel, so he'd ponied up the extra five hundred yuan—
not quite seventy-five dollars—and signed up, as well. He
wouldn't put it on his expense report, however. Some agents

would do that without a qualm, and he knew no one would question the expense if he did. Savannah was no longer his target but she *was* under his protection. Which meant he needed to guard her whenever she was out and about, including this side tour. But like the flowers he'd given her, tonight was personal. Very personal.

She wasn't wearing the peach-colored dress she'd wowed him with twice with now, but she *was* looking particularly fetching in a silky, navy pantsuit that clung in all the right places. And Niall's fingers itched to take it off her. Slowly.

His imagination of what he planned to do later that night didn't distract him from being vigilant. Vigilance came as natural as breathing. But so far, other than that first night, there'd been nothing. No threats. No danger.

He wondered about that now. He'd turned in his daily activity reports—leaving out any mention of the personal, of course—but he was afraid if there wasn't another incident soon that indicated Savannah still needed protection, he might get pulled off the assignment. And that was *not* going to happen. He had plenty of vacation time on the books and the entire land tour/river cruise was already paid for. So if he had to take vacation to stay with Savannah, that's just what he'd do.

The bus was dark and Savannah kept eyeing Niall whenever his attention was focused elsewhere. He'd been—well, not *distant*; perhaps *introspective* was a better word— introspective, ever since they'd left the museum.

He'd let her take pictures of him as a terracotta warrior at the factory, and had done the same for her. He'd smiled that devastating smile when she'd asked him to. He'd even joked and laughed with the other guests at their table in the restaurant above the factory. But she'd known something was on his mind. She just didn't know what. And the little demon of insecurity that hit in social situations reared its ugly head.

She comforted herself with the memory of this morning, when he'd apologized for letting her wake up alone. *He said he'd leave a piece of himself behind when it's over, and that he'll take a piece of me with him when he goes*, she thought, which had certainly been reassuring to hear.

That's when it hit her. She didn't want Niall to leave. She didn't want it to be over. Ever. Because—*stupid, stupid, stupid!* she railed at herself—she was falling in love with him. With his banter. His smile. That way he had of reading her mind. Not to mention the way he'd coaxed not one, not two, but three overwhelming orgasms out of a body she'd once thought was undersexed. Not anymore. Not with him.

I'm not that good at it, she'd confessed miserably. And what had been his response? *Don't worry, Savannah. You will be.*

And she had been good at it…with him. Had she already been falling in love with him? Was that why? Or was it just that despite the self-deprecating words that had followed his assertion that she would be good at sex, he *was* God's gift to women?

She didn't know. But one thing she did know. It would break her heart when he walked away when this trip was over. And there was absolutely nothing she could do about it.

They flew to Chongqing the next morning, where they would board the river boat for the cruise portion of the tour: six days and five nights on the Yangtze River. Then they'd finish up the tour on shore again, in Wuhan and Shanghai.

Savannah dozed on the flight, her head pillowed on Niall's shoulder. She'd gotten very little sleep last night, but she didn't regret it. Niall had surpassed himself, taking her to new heights time and again. He'd taught her things about herself she'd never known, and had taught her things about his body she'd always been curious about.

"It's okay, Savannah," he'd told her when he'd used his mouth on her. "You'll enjoy it. You'll see." And she had. So much so he hadn't even needed to coax her to do the same to him. His reaction had been off the charts, and had filled her with a sense of accomplishment akin to the one she'd felt when her company had told her they were applying for her first patent. She'd *loved* doing that for him.

When she slipped deeper into sleep, she began dreaming of Niall. But not of him making love to her. Of him saying, *I don't think it was a break-in, Savannah... I think you were targeted. And I don't think they planned to rob you.*

Why would someone want to kidnap her? Niall thought it was because of the job she used to do. It was a terrifying idea, and one she'd dismissed out of hand. As she'd told him, it sounded like something out of a spy novel, not something that happened in real life. But could he be right?

She jolted awake, then subsided back onto the solid cushion of Niall's shoulder and tried unsuccessfully to go back to sleep.

For no reason at all she suddenly thought of the annoyingly persistent Spencer Davies, of Davies Missiles and Fire Control in Alamogordo, New Mexico, and the last conversation she'd had with him. He'd been trying to lure her to leave her current employer and come work for him, something he'd done several times before, constantly sweetening the pot with each offer. Stock options this last time. *Stock that will shoot up in value if we have you on board, Dr. Whitman*, he'd cunningly worked into their phone conversation.

She'd turned him down, she remembered, as she'd turned him down each and every time he'd made her a job offer before. Not just because she was content with her work in Tucson and living close to her parents in Vail, but because there was something about Spencer Davies she didn't trust.

He seemed like the kind of man who'd take shortcuts, who'd rush a missile into production before it had been thoroughly tested. Yes, the testing her company did added considerably to the cost, most of which was borne by the US government and ultimately the taxpayers. But men and women in the military were relying on the missiles they produced, not to mention the civilians who could be severely impacted if something went wrong. Lives were on the line. Shortcuts were shortsighted.

Savannah drifted back to sleep without realizing it, but her thoughts followed her into the dream world.

She'd never had any intention of working for Davies Missiles and Fire Control, in large part because she could never work for a man she didn't respect. And who could respect Spencer Davies? But one never burned bridges, not in her industry. Today's competitor could be tomorrow's joint venture. So how had she answered his latest offer? Something about being honored, as usual, but...

I'm quitting for the foreseeable future, Mr. Davies, and you won't even be able to contact me.

You're quitting? His disbelief had been evident even through the phone. *But you're too brilliant at your job, Dr. Whitman. How can you possibly quit?*

She hadn't told Spencer Davies the real reason any more than she'd told her section head or the head of her department when she'd given notice. It was too personal, and she'd been afraid she'd break down and cry if she talked about her parents, something that—as a woman in a company still predominantly composed of male engineers—she couldn't fathom doing. So she'd said the same things she'd written in her resignation letter.

I want to travel, Mr. Davies. And having a top secret clearance makes it problematic to visit some of the places I want to go, like Russia and the People's Republic of China. I'm quitting rather than taking a leave of absence so it won't be an issue. I'll worry about my security clearance when and if I—

"Savannah?" A voice broke into her dream, and a strong hand gently squeezed her arm. "We're here, Savannah. Time to wake up."

She opened her eyes to see Niall bent over her, then blinked several times to clear the dregs of sleep from her brain. She yawned and quickly covered her mouth, then blinked again. "Sorry. I must have been more exhausted than I thought."

His expression turned wicked and knowing. "Did I wear you out last night?"

Heat flashed through every part of her body—including her cheeks—at the memory of everything they'd done last night. At the way she'd moaned his name and clutched his arms...shoulders...hips... At the way she'd pleaded with him to put out the blaze he'd ignited. And the way he'd done just that. She wanted to respond with the same lighthearted banter, but she couldn't think of a single, solitary thing to say other than, "Yes." Then she tacked on, "Yes, you did."

The heat concentrated in her core when he leaned over and whispered in her ear, "Good. Because you wore me out, too. But now I'm completely recovered, and remember what I said about love in the afternoon? I can hardly wait."

Niall escorted Savannah to her stateroom on the aft end of the boat. "You're 508, correct? I'm in 510, right next door. Wait here."

He unlocked her door, then went inside and gave the room a quick once-over before he let her enter. "Mind if I leave these here for now?" he asked, indicating his back-pack and carry-on suitcase, in which he carried his laptop and a few other pieces of equipment he didn't want in his stowed suitcase. "I need to check out the boat before we sail, and I don't want to leave them in my room unattended."

"No problem."

A sudden knock at the door heralded her luggage, which Savannah confirmed and Niall carried in for her.

"Luggage for 510, too?" he asked, flashing the keycard for the room next door, still in its paper case displaying the cabin number. "Thanks," he said, adding, "Here you go," as he deftly slipped a tip to the porter.

He closed the door and hefted his suitcase as he asked Savannah, "Okay to leave this here, as well?"

"Of course."

She started for the door to the balcony, but he snagged her arm and tugged her gently back toward him. "Hang on a minute." When he had her attention, he rested his hands on her hips and said, "You have a double room."

She flushed. "Not because I...not for the reason you think."

"You have no idea what I'm thinking."

"I'm using my parents' tour credit, and they'd reserved this kind of stateroom. Taking something else would have meant losing money, because I needed to use up their entire credit with this tour company on one trip. So I opted for the bigger stateroom and more space, even though I didn't really need it." She swallowed and added faintly, "Not be-cause I expected to...to share my room with someone."

"The thought never crossed my mind. Honest." It re-ally hadn't. All he'd been thinking was hallelujah that one of them had a double, because it wasn't him. "I don't want to assume, so I have to ask. I have a perfectly good single room next door I can use if that's what you prefer." Not that he had any intention of leaving her unprotected, but he'd long ago learned women could be touchy if a man assumed too much. He could thank Francine for that lesson—the one thing she'd taught him he'd put to good use in his subsequent relationships with women.

Delicate color tinted Savannah's cheeks, and Niall realized she felt shy about inviting him to move in for the duration of the cruise. So he brushed a strand of hair away from her face and tucked it behind one ear, then turned on the humor.

"I don't snore, at least I don't think I do. And I'm fairly housebroken—I rinse out the sink after I shave and I remember to put the toilet seat down when I'm done." A smile tugged at her mouth and he knew she was leaning toward yes. So his voice dropped a notch. "Ask me, Savannah. Please ask me."

"Please stay with me," she whispered.

Intense emotions speared through him, including longing and gratitude that she wanted him. At least for now. "My pleasure." He leaned in to murmur in her ear. "And yours."

Niall left Savannah with the stern warning not to leave her stateroom until he returned, and not to open the door for anyone except him.

She snapped him a half-mocking salute. "Sir, yes, sir!"

"I'm serious."

"Were you an officer in the Marine Corps?" she asked in the manner of someone who really wanted to know. "Because you act like I'm a soldier under your command."

"Marine, not soldier," he corrected her. "Never call a marine a soldier. And no, I wasn't an officer. But until we catch whoever wants to kidnap you, you'd better believe you're under my command."

"Now wait just a minute," she started to say, but he cut her off with a kiss that left him stunned at how quickly passion flared between them. And from Savannah's reaction, he could tell she felt the same way.

He touched his forehead to hers, closing his eyes for a moment as he fought for control. "To keep you safe, Savannah. This is what I do for a living, remember? Security? Please trust that I know what I'm doing."

She drew a quick breath. "Okay. I do...trust you, that is. And I'll do as you *ask*," she said, emphasizing the word, as if to say *command* was not and never would be acceptable.

Savannah adored everything about her stateroom, from the compact bathroom, to the two double beds, to the balcony, on which resided two chairs. She could already envision floating down the river with Niall sprawled in relaxing fashion on the seat opposite hers.

And, of course, she was ecstatic she had a double with all that extra space, which meant Niall would be sharing her cabin most of the time. If she'd opted for the single when she'd booked this cruise...well, she wasn't even going there. And when her brain remarked it was curious his room was next door to hers, the same way his hotel rooms had been, she brushed that thought aside as immaterial. *It's serendipitous*, she told herself. *Fate. Kismet. Meant to be.*

She wasn't going to think about the end of this tour, either, she decided as she unpacked and hung her clothes in the closet. She wasn't going to worry about having her heart broken when Niall said goodbye. She was just going to live each day as it came. Enjoy every moment spent in Niall's company.

She'd sworn on her parents' graves she wasn't going to miss out on anything because of something that might or might not happen in the future, and she was sticking to that vow. When she was old and gray, she'd take these golden memories she'd stored up out of the treasure chest. And as she'd resolved the day she'd met Niall, she'd glory in the knowledge that once upon a time there'd been a man who'd made her body meltingly aware of every breath he drew.

Chapter 10

Niall traversed the entire boat before it left the dock, checking every foot from stem to stern, memorizing the location of every safety feature, from inside and outside stairways, to life rafts, to the emergency cords. But that wasn't all. He located the bar, the lounges, the exercise room and the computer room. He went up to the top deck, with its romantic swings for two, and down to the bottom deck where the crew rooms were.

He was standing on the prow, his arms akimbo and his hands on his hips, thinking Savannah would probably get a kick out of a *Titanic* moment in this spot when they finally got underway, when he had the eerie sensation of being watched. He didn't turn sharply to see if he could catch whomever it was, because he didn't want that person or persons to know he'd sensed them. Didn't want them to know he was on guard against them, that he was anything other than a tourist.

He stood there for one minute, then two, until the feeling went way. Still, he was careful to signal his intention to turn around before he actually did it, glancing around and upward in a seemingly casual move.

"Hi, Niall!" Mary Beth Thompson waved from the sundeck above him to get his attention. Herb waved, too, after a moment, and Niall waved back.

"Hey there," he called up. "Do you know when we're supposed to set sail?" He glanced at his watch to give the impression he wasn't sure, even though he had the entire itinerary memorized and already knew departure was set for midnight.

"Sometime after dinner is all I know," Mary Beth called back. "And speaking of dinner, it starts at five. Herb and I would love it if—"

"Thanks," he replied before she could get the invitation out, heading for the door into the lounge. "I'd better go unpack before dinner."

Niall carefully considered the Thompsons as suspects as he headed toward Savannah's stateroom. He'd received a preliminary background report on them as well as all the others on the tour, but so far they seemed to be exactly as they came across: affable, wealthy, not that smart. And friendly to a fault. That overabundance of camaraderie kept them on his suspect list, because he could easily see how someone might befriend Savannah as a way to cozen her, to earn her trust and get close enough to kidnap her. And he did find it suspicious they were on the deck above him when he felt he was being watched. No one else had been around.

But the Thompsons weren't his only suspects, not by a long shot. It could just as easily be Tammy and Martin Williams, although their preliminary background report had also come back clean. But that didn't mean anything. It just meant that *a* Tammy and Martin Williams existed. It didn't mean this couple hadn't assumed those identities.

The same could go for all the others on the tour. They might be who they said they were, but then again they might not. *Someone* was after Savannah—he hadn't imagined those masked intruders, hadn't imagined the slash on his arm.

He needed something more to go on. First on the agenda? Fingerprints. Which meant, despite Savannah's aversion to Mary Beth's company, it looked as if dinner with the Thompsons tonight was in the cards.

Savannah finished her own unpacking, then stared at Niall's suitcase, carry-on and knapsack, wondering if she should—*No!* she told herself firmly. Not only would it be an intrusion on his privacy, but it would smack too much of something a wife would do. And though part of her thrilled to the idea of being Niall's wife, another part said, *Whoa! Don't get carried away by the fantasy. You and Niall aren't dating. What you have is a sexual relationship based on high intensity chemistry and liking on both sides. The fact that you're falling in love with him is irrelevant to the equation.*

Thinking of equations started her down another path, one related to her previous job. With nothing else to do, she got out her laptop and opened the file where she'd been jotting down random notes and equations—nothing classified, nothing that would make sense to anyone but her— just things she wanted to remember when and if she went back to being a GNC engineer.

She stared at one of them for the longest time, puzzling over something she knew wasn't quite right but couldn't figure out why. Then it came to her, and she changed one sign in the equation from positive to negative. "That's it!" she whispered, excited she'd resolved the problem.

A rap at the door and Niall's voice calling her name made Savannah quickly log off and slip her laptop back in its case, then hurry to open the door.

* * *

"You can't possibly be serious." Savannah was staring at him as if he'd lost his mind. "Dinner with the *Thompsons*?"

"And as many of the rest of the couples from our tour group as we can fit at our table. Tomorrow at breakfast, we'll pick different couples. Same goes for lunch and dinner tomorrow, too."

"But…" She cast him a pleading look. "This is our first night on board. Do we *have* to ruin it with Mary Beth's incessant chatter?"

"I need fingerprints. If you know of another way, I'll be happy to try it." He knew there wasn't, but he had to at least pretend to give Savannah a choice. He drew her into his embrace, rocking her a little in comfort. "If it wasn't crucial, I wouldn't ask, but it is." He crooked a finger under her chin, forcing her to meet his gaze. "And I'll make it up to you, I promise." He waggled his eyebrows the same way he'd done the day before, forcing a reluctant chuckle out of her.

"Money?" she asked with a pretend hopefulness.

"Better than money."

"Ahhh…" She nodded wisely. "You're bribing me with sex. That's illegal, you know."

He grinned because he knew by her teasing tone she accepted the necessity of dinner with Mary Beth and Herb. "Yeah, I know it's illegal," he murmured, sliding his hands up to caress the sides of her breasts. "But only if you turn me in."

She shivered, but he knew it was in a good way, so he kept going, slipping his fingers between them to toy with her nipples until they peaked for him. She wasn't ready to surrender, however, and he loved that about her. "A man who would steal a car from his own father…" she began with fake self-righteousness.

"Says the woman who stole a Bible."

"Hey!" She feigned shock and dismay. "You said confession was good for the soul. You can't use that against me *now*!"

He couldn't resist—he kissed her. Once he started, it was nearly impossible to stop, because she kissed him back. Because she rocked against what had instantly become hard, and moaned in the needy way she had that drove him crazy.

And just like that he had to have her.

He tumbled her onto the bed and tore at his belt buckle. The button on his jeans. The zipper. And Savannah was doing the same with her own clothes. He freed himself and reached for her, then stopped cold and cursed.

"Don't stop," she pleaded. "Please, Niall."

"Condom."

"Oh, damn!" He actually thought she was going to cry.

"Hang tight." He scrabbled in his pants pocket until he came up with his wallet and extracted the condom he'd put in there yesterday. He held the packet between his teeth and ripped, then sheathed himself in record time. "Say the word," he managed when he was poised at the threshold.

"Yes. Please, yes."

He thrust deep as she arched into him. For just a second, he rejoiced that never once had they needed lubricant, and they still didn't. Then he couldn't think at all, just feel this incredible woman throbbing all around him. So close to coming just from wanting him, which was a *huge* turn-on. Meeting him thrust for thrust. Clinging to his hips with frantic hands as if she were afraid he might stop…and she couldn't let him stop.

It could have been over in no time, but Niall gritted his teeth and held back with an effort. No way was he flying solo. Savannah was coming with him or he wasn't flying at all.

He reached between their bodies and stroked the heart

of her desire, and that was all it took. She bucked beneath him and came hard, sobbing his name. A handful of thrusts later, he came, too, her name on his lips.

Niall surfaced when the soft, warm body at his side suddenly vanished. "What..."

But she was already gone. He heard the shower running and acknowledged he needed one, too. One-handed, he stripped over his head the shirt he hadn't managed to get off earlier, and tossed it to one side. He jackknifed off the bed and nearly tripped when he tried to stand, which was the moment he realized he'd been so desperate he hadn't managed to get his pants completely off.

"Crap." That had never happened to him before. He'd never needed a woman to the extent he'd needed Savannah this afternoon, more proof she was unique in his experience. More proof his attachment to her was strengthening by the hour.

He shucked his jeans and reached the bathroom just as the water cut off. "Uh-uh," he told her when she started to step out of the shower, and he crowded her back in. Then, "Damn," as he realized two things. First, the shower stall was barely wide enough to accommodate one body, much less two. Second, he couldn't possibly stand erect in the cubicle; it hadn't been designed for a man who topped six foot two.

Savannah was laughing, which made him laugh, and she squeezed past him, her wet, naked body rubbing against him. *Deliberately?* he wondered, then answered, *Hell yes*, when she smiled and ran teasing fingers over his abs as she stepped out.

Two minutes later, after some awkward gyrations, he was finally done and he turned off the water. He maneuvered out of the shower stall and found a towel waiting for him. A towel and a very amused woman in panties and a bra.

"You were watching?" he growled.

"You bet. And I enjoyed every minute of the show."

She trailed one hand over his pecs and down. Down. Over his abs, then grasping his—

"Hey, none of that," he told her, interposing the towel between her hand and its target.

She laughed in what could only be described as the gloating tones of a cartoon villain, and he chuckled softly, but for a totally different reason. This Savannah was a world away from the woman who'd told him she wasn't very good at sex. This Savannah knew damn well she *was*... with the right man.

He loved her sexual banter, loved her teasing, because it proved beyond a shadow of a doubt her confidence in herself as a woman had been restored. *Your doing*, he acknowledged with a flash of pride he couldn't quite suppress.

He took a step toward her, but she was already gone, calling, "Want me to get some clean clothes out of your suitcase for you?"

All humor fled as he realized he couldn't possibly let her look inside his suitcase. "That's okay," he said quickly, his heartbeat increasing until he remembered. "It's locked anyway."

A muffled voice answered him. "Oh, you're right." She reappeared in the bathroom doorway, still dressed in nothing but her underwear, apparently no longer shy about letting him see her body. Another triumph. "It's casual for dinner, right?"

"Considering I only have one pair of dress slacks with me, I damn well hope so."

"Good. I mostly packed casual clothes, too. And strong walking shoes."

Savannah turned toward the closet and Niall dropped the towel, sliding his arms around her from behind in a hug of easy intimacy, wanting to let her know how happy he was she didn't feel the need to be shy with him any longer. But when she froze, he cursed internally, released her instantly and stepped back. "God, Savannah, I forgot. I'm so sorry."

Her face was paler than usual when she turned around, but otherwise she was composed. "It's okay," she reassured him. "I only panicked for a second. Then I realized it was you and I…" She reached up to cup his cheek. "Really, I'm okay."

Remorse swamped him. He knew. He *knew* about her psychosis. Hadn't he carried her out of the crowd yesterday so she wouldn't panic? "I don't know what the hell I was thinking," he admitted. "I just…"

"I *want* you to feel you can touch me anytime," she said in a low voice. "Any way you want. I've been fighting this stupid fear for so many years now, you'd think I'd be over it. But no. I'm a coward." The self-loathing was biting, and Niall couldn't bear to hear it in her voice.

"That's enough of that." His voice was stern. "You're not a coward, so don't let me hear you say that again about yourself. You've made great strides. You have. You're here, aren't you? You faced the crowds at the Great Wall, the Forbidden City, the terracotta army museum."

"Yes, but—"

"But nothing. Maybe someday your fear will be banished for good, but in the meantime it's my job to remember and respect that fear. It's my job to help you any way I can, and I will. Because the last thing I want is for you to be afraid of me in *any* way. I won't forget again, I promise."

It wasn't going to be as easy as he'd hoped to retrieve the wineglasses, Niall realized once he and Savannah were seated at a table for eight with the Thompsons and two other couples from their tour bus, ostensibly from Australia and England. He figured he'd have to settle for one set of prints this evening, maybe two, when the appetizer trays were brought to the table. And that's when he realized the glossy surface of the china trays would hold fingerprints just as well as wineglasses. He watched the trays being handed from one person to another until they'd made the rounds. And when the waiter came to remove the now-empty appetizer trays, Niall excused himself, saying, "Forgot my stomach medication in my room. I'll be right back."

He squeezed Savannah's hand in a warning, and she rose to the occasion. "Don't you hate when you forget something like that?" she commiserated, glancing from Niall to Mary Beth, who was verbally off and running practically before he'd left the table.

"Don't I know it!" Mary Beth exclaimed. "Why, one time I forgot my high blood pressure medicine and Herb had to take a cab back to the hotel to retrieve it, because I'm supposed to take it at the same time every day. And then there was that time I…"

He could still hear her as he passed through the service door after the waiter bearing the dishes from their table. Five minutes and a hundred yuan later, he carried the trays up to his cabin on Deck Five. He quickly retrieved a small leather kit from his carry-on suitcase in Savannah's stateroom, then returned to his own cabin and went to work.

"I'll have the pork medallions and asparagus," Savannah told the smiling waiter. Niall still hadn't returned, so she pointed to his empty chair and said, "And he'll have the beef tips in wine with the baked potato." *Can't go wrong with beef and potatoes*, she thought.

"Yes, ma'am. Butter and sour cream on the potato?"

Not willing to guess and guess wrong, she asked, "Could he have them on the side?"

"Of course." The waiter moved on to the next guest, and Savannah let out a tiny sigh of relief.

A movement out of the corner of her eye made her turn, and suddenly Niall was there. "Sorry I took so long," he told the table as he seated himself. "I was heading down when I passed a display of the most incredible pearls I've ever seen. I stopped for what I thought would only be a minute, and the saleswoman latched on to me like a piranha and just wouldn't let me go." He paused, then added in a droll tone, "Her commission must be pretty substantial." A statement that was greeted with laughter from everyone at the table, because they'd all endured the hard sell at the jade, silk and terracotta replica factories.

"Did you buy anything?" Mary Beth asked.

He shook his head. "I escaped with my wallet intact, but…" He glanced at Savannah and winked. "I promised her I'd be back."

More laughter ensued, but that was the end of that.

No one remarked on just how long Niall had been gone, although Savannah had agonized the entire time. The meaningful hand squeeze he'd given her before he left had tipped her off something was up, although she didn't know what. And she wasn't about to ask him at the table now that he'd deflected everyone else's curiosity; she'd find out when they returned to her stateroom.

The other couples at their table had said their goodnights an hour later, leaving Savannah and Niall the lone occupants. She'd deliberately dawdled over her dessert to make that happen, and now that the dining room was nearly empty, she reached over to Mary Beth's place at the table and curled a finger around the stem of the wineglass there.

The plates and much of the silverware had been removed earlier, before dessert was served, but not the wineglasses.

Niall reached out to stop her. "Is that why you ate your cheesecake a miniscule bite at a time?" he asked.

She frowned. "I thought you needed fingerprints. Isn't that why I had to spend the evening with Mary Beth?"

He grimaced. "Yes, well…about that."

"If you're going to tell me I *didn't* have to, I might have to hurt you," she warned, and he laughed softly.

"I'm trembling in my boots," he teased.

"You don't wear boots," she reminded him. "So tell me why you don't need fingerprints after all."

"I do need fingerprints. But I already got them."

Just that quickly, she realized how. "The appetizer trays."

Admiration for her perspicacity filled his eyes. "You're quick. I like that."

"It wasn't that difficult. You left right when they did, so…"

"Let's hope no one else made the connection."

She shook her head. "I don't think so. Everyone else bought your story."

"But not you."

"I probably would have, if you hadn't squeezed my hand right before you left." She was silent for a moment, wondering how best to say what she suddenly wanted to say to him, what she'd been thinking about ever since he'd returned to the table. "You're a very convincing liar, Niall," she said finally. "You mix bits of the truth with your lies, which makes it easy to believe you."

Chapter 11

Niall went completely still, his face a frozen mask Savannah didn't recognize. That's when she realized his expression was usually quite animated, and he exuded an innate charm it was nearly impossible to resist. The charm had vanished along with the animation, and she wondered why. Had he taken her words as an insult? She hadn't meant them that way, so she struggled to explain.

"That wasn't a criticism. Truly. It's just that I'm a fairly honest person. I know I told you about my one foray into a life of crime…" She smiled faintly and he smiled back, but she sensed it was an effort. "But that was a long time ago and I learned my lesson." She stared at his hand, which was still laying on hers, then turned her hand to clasp his. "I want you to know I'll never lie to you. And I wouldn't even begin to know how to deceive you. What you see is what you get where I'm concerned."

"And you're telling me this why?"

She breathed deeply. "Because you've been honest with me from the start. You're not looking for anything more than a vacation fling, and I get that. I thought that's what I wanted, too."

"But…"

"But I'd be lying if I said I wasn't looking for more. Not from you," she rushed to add when his hand tightened on hers. "I'll settle for whatever you're willing to give me for as long as that lasts. And when you walk away…" She swallowed hard. "I'll take that piece of you that you said you'll leave behind. And I'll gladly give you a piece of me to take with you when you go." She smiled again because she had to smile. Or cry. "Someday I'll find a man who wants more—I believe that with all my heart. But I'll never regret this time with you." She drew her hand away gently. "That's really all I wanted to say."

The bullet he'd taken to his heart all those years ago hadn't hurt this bad, Niall admitted to himself, shaken by the force of his desire to vehemently deny her words. But he couldn't. Because everything she'd said was the truth, save for one thing. He hadn't been honest with her…except that he was temporary man material only.

He scoured his mind for something—anything—to say that would walk the fine line between what he wanted and what he knew he could have under the circumstances. But he couldn't think of anything other than, "Thank you for telling me." Which, when you got right down to it, was pretty much the coward's way out.

"You're welcome." The polite way this was delivered, and the tiny crinkles at the corners of her eyes told him exactly what it had cost her to reveal these things to him. *And all you can say is thank you?* he berated himself.

He couldn't tell her he was falling in love with her. That was out. And no way could he come clean about why he'd crashed into her life in the first place. Even if he was given the green light by his boss to tell her, he couldn't risk being banished from her side, not while she still needed his protection. *Not to mention you're nowhere close to being ready to give up sharing her bed*, his conscience piped up at the worst possible moment. But he had to tell her something.

"You *will* find someone, Savannah. Someone far better than me." Thinking of her with another man, admitting it couldn't be him, was like tearing a bandage off in one fell swoop—you knew it would hurt, but it was better to get it over with quickly rather than dragging the pain out.

She rolled her eyes in response to his heartfelt words, taking him by surprise. "Oh please. Not the 'it's not you, it's me' line. That's so cliché, Niall. And frankly, I thought better of you than that."

"It's not a line." He bit the words out, anger springing out of nowhere. "I told you before, there are reasons I can't share with you why I'm the last man with whom you should get involved."

"But I am involved, and it's too late to go back and change it."

"Savannah..."

"It's okay. It's just physical. I understand." She stood up and unhooked her purse strap from the back of her chair, then slipped it over her shoulder. "You promised me the best sex of my life, and you've delivered so far. In spades. I don't want to give that up. So please forget I said anything, and let's just focus on what we *do* have for the rest of this trip."

Niall made love to Savannah that night as if he could lay his heart at her feet without saying the actual words. As if he could show her how precious she was to him by taking her higher and further than he'd ever taken her before. If all he could give her was sex, he reasoned, he was going to make it so damn good for her she'd never forget him. The way he'd never forget her.

And she gave back to him with every sigh, every moan. Every rasping cry of fulfillment that culminated in his name.

He loved the smoothness of her skin beneath his fingertips. The taste of her on his tongue and the way she clung to him when he drove her up and over the peak time and again. But most of all he loved being buried in her body. So tight. So deep. Torturing himself by moving slowly, drawing her pleasure out until she couldn't take any more and pleaded for release. Then giving her that release. Finding it together. Being the man she needed, if only in this way.

They dozed when sleep overtook them, then woke and picked up where they'd left off. They writhed on the bed late into the night, until he sensed and heard the rumble of boat engines that indicated their midnight departure. Then he donned a condom one last time, and thrust deep.

In the wee hours of the morning, Savannah lay sprawled naked beneath the bedclothes in total abandon, her chest rising and falling in the slow cadence of deep sleep, like the princess in a fairytale. He'd worn her out, in the best way possible. He'd carried her into the shower the last time because her legs just wouldn't support her, and had held her upright while he'd rinsed them both off as best he could in the close quarters. Then he'd dried her with gentle hands, carried her back to the bed and tucked her in. She'd been asleep in seconds.

His body was exhausted, too, but his brain wouldn't shut down. He kept hearing Savannah saying, *Someday I'll find a man who wants more—I believe that with all my heart*.

How he wanted to be that man. The one who would give her the *more* she deserved. But no matter how he tried to resolve things in his mind to give them the outcome he wanted, he kept coming up short. Even if he quit his job for her, how could she ever get past his initial assignment? He couldn't see any way around that.

Finally he gave up trying to sleep. He dragged some clothes on, scrawled a note and left it on the nightstand: *Back soon.*

The entire boat appeared to be sleeping, except for the pilots in the wheelhouse. Niall climbed all the way to the top deck, but he saw no one. The night pressed in all around, and the stars seemed to mock him as he stood at the stern watching the moonbeams reflected in the rippling water the boat left in its wake.

He stood there a long time, his thoughts going round and round the way they had in Savannah's bed. Finally he gave himself a mental shake. *Cut the pity party, Jones. It is what it is, and no amount of wishing will change it. You've got work to do. Focus on that. Find out who's targeting Savannah and why. Put them behind bars. Then kiss her goodbye and don't look back.*

"Don't look back," he whispered to the night. The stars. The moon. But none of them answered him.

Niall was descending the narrow, outside staircase that would take him back to Deck Five when something caught his eye and he froze midstep. "Son of a bitch!"

His sharp gaze cut from the stairs to the deck above and the one below, but he saw no one. Someone had been here, though. Someone who'd known he'd be descending this staircase, and had laid a very clever trap.

He carefully stepped over the narrow, clear plastic fishing line stretched across the stair right below him, and went down a few more steps so he could examine the trap more closely. He whistled between his teeth, then whispered, "Nice job," acknowledging he couldn't have placed this trip wire better himself. If he hadn't seen a flash of the line in the moonlight, if his reflexes had been a half second slower, he would have pitched down the staircase and broken an arm or a leg, if not his neck.

Which meant someone was trying to get him out of the way. Which also meant someone *did* want to kidnap Savannah, and saw him as a roadblock.

He pulled out the Swiss Army pocketknife he had to put in his checked luggage every time he flew but which he'd retrieved along with his Beretta and ankle holster before they'd gone down to dinner. He cut the line close to the knots on each side. Fingerprints off the line were impossible, of course. But he might get lucky if he came back with his fingerprint kit and dusted the metal bars to which the line was attached, which was why he wanted to leave the knots in place. He also took the precaution of counting the stairs above and below the step that had held the fishing line, just in case the knots loosened now that the tension had been removed, and the tiny bits of plastic fell off. *Or in case someone is watching and removes them the minute I leave.*

He shoved the fishing line into his pocket along with his knife, then continued down the staircase with a seeming nonchalance. But he remained alert and watchful all the way back to Savannah's stateroom.

She was still sleeping peacefully the way he'd left her, and he made a mental note to tell her everything in the morning, so she'd be on her guard. He unlocked his suitcase without turning on the light, and felt around for his fingerprint kit. Then he headed out again.

Savannah woke when a large male body depressed the mattress and slid beneath the covers. *Double beds aren't really made for two people*, she thought, stifling a yawn. *Unless they sleep really close.* Suiting her actions to her thoughts, she snuggled up to the naked man in her bed, then pulled away. "Wow, you're cold."

"Sorry." His voice was early-morning hushed. "I had to go out, and it's pretty cold on the river at night."

"Poor baby. I'll get you warm." She pulled the covers more securely over both of them and pressed her warm body against his cold one, trying her best to repress a shiver. Eventually the warmth inside the cocoon of bedclothes was enough to allow her to drift off again, when she suddenly realized what Niall had said and her eyelids flicked open. "What do you mean, you had to go out?"

"Shh. I'll tell you in the morning." He set one hand on the curve of her hip and pulled her even closer.

"Tell me now."

At first she thought he wouldn't, but then he said reluctantly, "I couldn't sleep, so I took a walk up on the top deck."

"You couldn't—how could you not sleep? Are you made of iron?" She playfully tested his arm, then teased, "Well, one part of you seems to be made of iron, but they can't all be," which made him chuckle under his breath.

But then he turned serious again. "When I was coming down the outside staircase, I found someone had set a trip wire across the stairs."

"What?" She sat up and turned on the bedside lamp to look at Niall. "Really?"

He nodded, punched up the pillows behind him, tugged her into his embrace, then settled back against the pillows, his arms tight bands around her. "It's not just my theory anymore, Savannah. Someone is out to kidnap you, and they need me out of the way."

"Oh my God. Someone tried to kill you? Because of me?"

"I'll acquit them of attempted murder...for now. A bro-

ken limb would have put me out of commission, too. There's
a doctor on board, but no real medical facilities. The captain
and crew would probably have transferred me to a hospital
on land, at least for a day or two, which would mean you'd
be left unprotected. Exactly what they want."

She still couldn't believe it. "Why would someone want
to kidnap me? What do they have to gain?"

"I suggested it before and you dismissed the idea, but I
really think it has something to do with your job. The job
you used to have, I mean."

"You don't think…" She trailed off, not wanting to suggest what she didn't want to believe. But the sinister im-
plications of the blocked GPS signals immediately flashed
into her consciousness. Was it possible?

"Don't think what?"

"I know the Departments of Defense and Homeland
Security are paranoid about it, but I can't believe…"

"Can't believe what?"

She reviewed her security briefings in her mind, making sure she wasn't crossing some kind of line by mentioning the possibility to Niall, and concluded it was okay.
"Ever since the fall of the USSR, the main target in most
of the battle simulations conducted by the Department of
Defense—the DoD—is the PRC. The People's Republic
of China. And a lot of the cyber warfare is aimed at them,
too, because of the computer hacking originating here."

When Niall didn't say anything, she continued. "If it's
them, it truly *is* like something out of a spy novel. But why
me? I mean, I'm good at what I do, but I'm not the only
GNC engineer out there. And besides, how could they think
kidnapping me would get them what they want? They have
to know the US government would suspect them if I dis-
appear here, and it would create an international incident."

An odd expression crossed Niall's face. Then he said,

"I think that's exactly what someone *does* want. I think whoever's trying to kidnap you wants to throw suspicion on the Chinese government, to cover up their real motive."

There was so much he couldn't tell her...yet. He couldn't tell her someone had deliberately set out to make the US government think she was a traitor. That she intended to sell what she knew to the PRC. So that when she disappeared, no one in the government would be surprised. *And no one would look very hard for her, except to catch a traitor!*

He blinked when that thought occurred to him. Why hadn't he seen it before?

"But who would want me that badly? I mean it doesn't... make...sense..."

Her sudden hesitation made his sixth sense sit up and beg for attention. Hell, not just his sixth sense, *all* his senses. "You just thought of something. What?" he demanded.

"It can't be that."

"Talk it out for me."

"Spencer Davies. Davies Missiles and Fire Control— although the company is more commonly known by its initials, DMFC. It's located in Alamogordo, New Mexico. I was thinking about him on the flight here."

"And?"

"And he's tried to hire me several times, at a substantial bump in salary. He recruited me especially hard this year. But I've always turned him down, because..."

"Because why?"

"Because I don't trust him," she said in a rush. "Because he and his company have a reputation in the defense industry for taking shortcuts, and I don't like that. Shortcuts are shortsighted in my opinion. They've never gotten caught. Well, not seriously. DCMA—the Defense Contract Management Agency," she explained as an aside, although Niall knew very well what she meant, "has never done anything more than slap their hands and impose not-very-onerous fines. We're competitors with them. Or rather, the company I used to work for is competitors with them," she said, in the manner of one who was trying to be strictly accurate.

"Keep going."

She wrinkled her forehead, as if trying to remember something important. "DMFC lost several big competitive contracts in the last year," she said slowly. "To the company I used to work for."

"Were you involved in those proposals?"

She nodded. "All of them. I even have a patent pending for the IRAD work I did leading up to one of the proposals."

"IRAD?" he asked, even though he knew.

"Internal research and development. Some companies refer to it by the initialism IR&D, but we call it IRAD." She buried her face against his neck. "But I can't believe that's the reason. I just can't."

"Does he know you quit?"

She raised her head and looked at him, then nodded again. Slowly. "I didn't tell him the real reason, though. I just said I wanted to travel and my security clearance was an issue for some of the places I wanted to go. But I still can't believe…" She trailed off, and the distress on her face told him she didn't want to believe it.

Niall let out his breath long and slow. "I know someone who can find out for sure."

"Who?"

"My sister."

"How? No offense to your sister, but if what you suspect is true, it's a matter for the US government."

He laughed softly. "Keira *is* the US government," he said, careful not to mention her last name. Not that Savannah would connect Keira's married name, Walker, to her

maiden name, Jones, but since she knew him as Niall Johnson he wasn't taking any chances. "Or rather," he continued smoothly, "Keira works for a hyper-secret government
agency with a far-reaching mandate. This sounds like it's
right up the agency's alley."

"You're kidding me. The agency?"

"You've heard of it?"

"Only because there was a security incident at my work
three years ago. It was all hushed up, and the man pled
guilty to a lesser sentence in exchange for keeping things
quiet and agreeing to be a double agent for a time. He was a
spy for the Russians, and the US didn't want them to know
he'd been 'turned.' The US funneled a lot of false information to them before the government finally shut him down
last year and sent him to a federal prison."

"If it was so secret, how do you know so much about it?"

She made a face at him. "First, he was assigned to one
of the programs I used to work on, so I was questioned
extensively by special agents from the Defense Security
Service, the FBI and the agency. Second, the operation is
over and the man is safely in jail. Third, I was one of the
engineers selected to create the false information that was
fed to the Russians. Do you know how hard that is? Deliberately sabotaging your own work?"

"I can imagine." He hesitated, but he had to ask. "Why
have you told all this to me? Isn't that... I don't know...a
security violation?"

She shook her head vehemently. "I've only talked in
general terms. I haven't named names or specified what
information was sabotaged or what missiles were involved
or anything."

"Okay. Makes sense. But let's get back to my original
point. I can ask Keira to check on this Spencer Davies and
his company on the QT. She's a whiz at research, can un-

cover things no one else seems to be able to. And before you say it," he said when Savannah opened her mouth, "I also know the man she works for, the head of the agency in DC. I'm sure he'd authorize Keira to get involved."

"How do you happen to know him?"

Uh-oh, he thought. But he didn't want to lie to her again. The lies he'd told her at the start—that was his assignment. This was different. So he told her the truth. Just not all the truth.

"My sister's husband also works for the agency…rather high up in the ranks." *Yeah, head of the Denver branch qualifies as high up in the ranks.* "And two of my brothers were major players in one of the agency's ops." Just like Savannah, he couldn't name names. Not for security reasons—that op was long since closed and the bad guy was six feet under—but because the names Alec and Liam were unusual enough they might ring a bell, especially since both had been in the news a year ago. And if she recognized Alec and Liam, the surname Jones just might come to her mind, too.

He wouldn't just contact Keira, though. He'd already scanned and sent to his own agency the fingerprints he'd lifted from the china trays this evening, as well as from the railing on the outside staircase. So he'd also turn over the name of Spencer Davies and his company, DMFC, for further investigation. Hopefully somebody would turn up something.

"I have to ask you again," he told Savannah, tightening his arm around her. "Will you go home now?" Now, meaning *now we have solid proof you're a target*.

If he hadn't been holding her so close he might have missed they way her body went absolutely still at his words.

"You want me to go home." Her voice was flat. Emotionless. Then she pulled away and slipped from beneath the covers. She dug into a drawer and pulled out an oversize T-shirt, which she tugged on over her head before turning to face him. "How would going home now make me safer?" she asked in reasonable tones, which surprised the hell out of him. He'd thought from her initial reaction she'd be upset. "If you're right, I'm just as much a target in the US as I am here. At least here I have you for security," She paused. "Unless you've changed your mind about that now."

Anger, hot and swift, flashed to life. "What the hell is that supposed to mean?"

Chapter 12

"**Y**ou don't owe me anything, Niall," Savannah said in that same reasonable tone, which conversely bugged the hell out of him for some reason. "I certainly don't expect you to risk your life for mine. Someone tried to injure you tonight, maybe even kill you, in order to get you out of the way. I'd understand if you were having second thoughts about being my lover for the rest of this cruise."

Fury bubbled through him, and he threw off the covers, stomping to the chair over which he'd thrown his clothes before climbing into bed with Savannah. "That is total BS," he said between clenched teeth as he jerked his jeans on commando.

"Is it?" She raised her chin. "Then explain why you want me to go home."

That question stopped him in his tracks, with his shirt in his hands. *She has you there, hotshot*, a voice in the back of his head jeered. And though it was an effort, he tried to look at things from her perspective. "You're right," he said finally. "You're safer here than you are in the US, because I'm here with you. But you're wrong about me changing my mind. Anyone who tries to get to you has to go through me. Period. End of discussion. You got that?"

A slow smile spread over her face. "I hear you loud and clear. I just hope our neighbors on that side didn't hear you, too," she said, gesturing to the other side of the stateroom from Niall's cabin.

Well, crap. He glanced at the alarm clock on the nightstand, which glowed two eleven in bright red numerals. He waited a minute in silence, holding his breath. And when no one rapped on the wall between the staterooms, he let his breath out slowly. "Looks like we skated on that one."

Savannah walked over and took the shirt from his hands. She smoothed out the wrinkles from where he'd clutched it tightly in his anger, then laid it over the back of the chair. When she looked up into his face, she was still smiling. "I think you care about me," she said softly.

He snorted. "You *think?*"

She moved her head in an infinitesimal nod. "I do. If I were a betting woman, I'd make book on it."

Busted. But he wasn't going to admit it. "I just don't like being thought a coward, that's all."

"I never, ever thought you were a coward."

Baffled, he asked, "Then why did you say what you said?"

"Because I was angry. And when I'm angry, I say things I don't mean."

He shook his head. "You didn't sound angry."

She laughed softly. "I know. I'm not like most people. I don't yell and curse and stomp around when I'm angry." By which she meant him, obviously. "I get… I don't know… super calm and super reasonable. I take after my dad that way. My mom was the emotional one. She'd get mad at my dad for something or other, and he'd calmly reason her out of it."

"Sounds like they were a good match."

Her eyes crinkled at the corners. "They were." Then she shook her head as if she were shaking off the memories, good and bad. "So…" She stepped into his personal space and placed her hands on his bare chest, stroking lightly. "Want to kiss and make up? I've heard make-up sex is incredible."

Make-up sex *was* incredible, Savannah thought as she and Niall strolled the decks after breakfast. She stifled a yawn, telling herself that in a contest between sex with Niall and sleeping, sleeping came in a far distant second.

They'd risen early, mainly because he wanted to get down to breakfast when the dining room opened, so he could pick out the couples from their tour group he wanted to breakfast with this morning. And when everyone had finally left, Niall had somehow made off with half a dozen juice glasses…stashed in *her* carry-on bag, which he'd had her bring down to breakfast instead of her purse. A quick trip to her stateroom later, she'd been fascinated at how efficiently he dusted, lifted and catalogued the prints, before bundling the juice glasses back into her bag for a return trip to the dining room.

It wasn't until they were walking out again that a thought occurred to her. *That's odd. Why does Niall have a fingerprint kit with him…on vacation?*

She started to ask him about it, then changed her mind. Asking him implied she suspected him of something, and she didn't want to give that impression. Besides, the concept of "need to know" had been deeply engrained in her from the day she'd gone to work for her previous employer. If Niall thought she needed that info, he'd tell her. Until then…

They took the elevator to the top deck, which Savannah hadn't visited yet, and she was delighted with the swings.

"Oh look! My grandparents had one of these on their front porch when my mom was little—I have pictures."

She dragged Niall to the closest swing and pulled him down beside her, then fished her camera out of her jacket pocket. "Smile," she pleaded, leaning in close as she took a selfie of them, then two more for insurance. She scrolled through them quickly, pausing on the last one, then returning to the first to show Niall.

"It's not fair," she said, turning off her camera and stowing it in her pocket.

"What's not fair?"

He pushed off with his foot, setting the swing in motion, and she waited a moment to enjoy the sensation before answering him. "I've taken…umm…" She cleared her throat. "A *few* pictures of you, and in every one you're gorgeous. I don't think it's possible for you to take a bad photograph."

He chuckled and continued pushing with his foot. "My mother wouldn't agree with you."

"What do you mean?"

"I hated having to hold still for pictures when I was a kid. And I especially hated those formal family portraits—you know the ones I mean. Five kids, and my mother wanted a family portrait taken every year. My dad in his USMC dress blues. That was the one given. Everything else was stage-managed by my mother, including the identical little monkey suits she wanted her four boys to wear, and the girly-girl dress she'd picked out for Keira. Hoo boy, that was a fight every year, let me tell you."

"In what way?"

"Not so much for us boys. All it took was a stern word from my dad, and we'd dutifully don our duds. But not Keira. She was his baby girl, and he never put his foot down with her. I even heard him plead her case with my mom one year."

"Plead her case?"

"Keira did *not* want to wear anything that looked too feminine. She wasn't 'sugar and spice and everything nice,' she wanted to be 'snips and snails and puppy dog tails' like us."

"Tomboy?"

Niall grimaced. "Not that, really. More like she wanted to be taken seriously, which my dad, I'm ashamed to say, never did until shortly before he died. She wanted the respect the boys in the family got automatically."

"Oh." Savannah suddenly felt a sense of kinship with a woman she'd never met. Although she'd always had the support and respect of both her parents, she'd chosen a male-dominated field and was constantly having to prove herself. So much so that she'd resigned in writing, then had been tightlipped when her male superiors tried to talk her out of it rather than risk crying in front of them.

"So what happened with Keira? How did she manage to change your dad's mind?"

He smiled as if at a particularly fond memory. "She followed every one of her brothers into the Marine Corps."

"I think you mentioned that before, but wow. More power to her."

"Yeah. She served four years, like all of us except my older brother, who'd intended to make it his career. Most of her service was in the military police."

"Good for her. What about you? You told me you weren't an officer, but what did you do in the Corps?"

"Sniper."

She blinked because she never would have guessed. Not that Niall didn't come across as a complete professional where his job was concerned, but he seemed too... too kind. Too considerate. And though he tried to hide it, too emotional, something that was especially obvious when he talked about his family. When she thought of snipers—not that she thought of them often, but when she did—she imagined steely eyed loners with no emotion. Killers.

The riverboat docked at the Shibaozhai Pagoda after lunch for the first of their side tours. You could see the pagoda from the boat, and Niall would have been just as happy to stay on board as roughly half of the passengers chose to do. But Savannah was gung ho to experience everything, so Niall would climb to the top of the twelve-story pavilion with her.

He followed her up the hundreds of wooden stairs, thankful he was in shape, pausing on every landing for Savannah to gaze out the window and marvel at the world below. A few of the climbers with them stopped when they reached the wooden ladders that would take them to the very top, but not Savannah.

He tested the strength of the ladder before he would let her proceed, then told her, "You go first. I'll make sure no one gets too close."

They finally reached the small summit, which wasn't that high as far as buildings went, but was rather up there when you realized you'd climbed the entire way to the top. Savannah peered out through the round window, exclaiming, "Look, Niall. You can see all the way to the bend in the river!"

Her enthusiasm for just about everything amused him, but it also made him wonder how he'd allowed himself to become so jaded over the years. *You used to have enthusiasm. What happened? When did you lose it?*

His introspection hadn't started when he'd met Savannah, he acknowledged. It had begun when he'd met the woman who was now his older brother's wife, and realized that—incredibly—Shane had fallen in love again after umpteen years.

He'd watched Shane and Carly together and had been filled with a sense of longing for what they had. Niall had listened to Carly's voice and had known she was frantic with fear for Shane when he decided to set himself up as a target to catch the hitman who had both Shane and Carly in his sights. Yet she'd been brave enough to let him risk his life without trying to stop him, and he'd wanted that for himself. Not that he'd wanted Carly—he'd just wanted a woman like her. Soft and gentle, yet fierce and protective. One who would love him through the good times and bad, one he could love the way Shane loved Carly, with a totality he'd never known.

Be careful what you wish for, because you just might get it.

Too late to listen to the warning, because he'd already found the perfect woman for him, and she was standing in the protective curve of his arms. He just couldn't keep her.

He'd been skeptical of his brothers and the swiftness with which they'd fallen in love with the women who were now their wives. Especially his youngest brother, Liam, who'd fallen for Cate in a *day*. But now he realized time had absolutely nothing to do with it. When a man realized he'd found the other half of his soul, he couldn't do anything *but* fall.

He loved Savannah with that totality he'd wished for, and he knew in his heart she was trembling on the brink of loving him if she hadn't already fallen. Problem was, he'd put himself beyond the pale before he'd even had the chance to know her. Love her.

And therein lay the tragedy.

She turned in his embrace to move aside and let someone else have a chance at the window, but before she could he kissed her. She melted into him the way she always did, but then she tore her mouth away.

"Not here," she breathed, and he knew she was right; they didn't need an audience. But it nearly killed him to let her go.

Once more on the ground, they strolled leisurely along the walkway, stopping frequently so Savannah could photograph the marble carvings adorning the sides of the hill upon which the pagoda had been constructed.

"Stand right there," she instructed in front of a panel displaying an ancient Chinese warrior, sword in hand. She adjusted his position slightly, then snapped off several shots. "That's you."

"I don't carry a sword," he disagreed.

"No, but the expression on his face. You can just tell he's protecting someone or something, and that's you. You're a protector."

True, he thought, thinking back over his years in the Marine Corps and the job he had now. But how had Savannah picked up on it? "What makes you say that?"

"Oh, Niall," was her amused reply. "Just how clueless do you think I am?"

"I don't think you're clueless," he protested. "Far from it."

"I knew you were a protector from the moment I met you on the Great Wall."

Back when she'd still been his target. Back when he was using her fear as an excuse to get close to her, to worm his way into her confidence. Guilt made his voice harsher than he intended. "Did it ever occur to you I might have had an ulterior motive?"

Her smile faded. "I considered it," she admitted, her face solemn and still. "For all of about ten seconds."

"You're too trusting. Didn't your parents ever warn you about strangers? And what about the job you used to do?" he added, warming to his theme. "Haven't you ever heard of social engineering? I could have been anybody for all you knew."

If anything, her expression turned even more solemn. "I've heard of it, of course. I know what it is, and what it isn't. You never asked me a single question that raised a red flag. You never pushed me to tell you anything related to my work. You were just...kind. Caring. And so understanding of a fear that has plagued me nearly my whole life that I instinctively trusted you. I knew you'd never hurt me."

That last sentence was a lash against his conscience, because she was wrong, wrong, wrong! And he desperately wanted to tell her the truth. To lift the weight off his conscience. *Confession is good for the soul*, he remembered advising her in a lighthearted exchange the other day. But he couldn't do that, and not just because he wasn't authorized to tell her. As long as she needed his protection, he needed to keep his secret.

But you don't need to continue taking advantage of her, his conscience retorted in brutal fashion. *You don't need to keep sharing her bed.*

His conscience was right. Savannah had finally accepted early this morning she was a target, which meant she'd be on her guard and didn't need him 24/7. He could move into his own cabin and watch over her from there for the rest of the trip.

His conscience lightened up on him once he'd reached that resolution, allowing him to clasp her hand and accompany her back to the boat as if nothing substantial had changed between them.

But he dreaded telling her. He had a strong suspicion she wouldn't take it well. Not at all.

"I see." The calmness with which Savannah received his announcement told him she was blazingly angry.

"You don't need me day and night anymore," he explained, hefting his backpack over one shoulder and picking up his suitcases.

"I see," she repeated. "So…all the times we wore each other out in bed, that was just…what? A form of protection?"

He dropped the suitcases with a thud. "No! God, no."

"Then why?"

"I have reasons," he insisted stubbornly. "Valid reasons."

"Those reasons you said before you can't share with me."

"Exactly."

She folded her lips into a tight line. "Okay. Go then. I'll look after myself."

The backpack joined the suitcases on the floor. "I'll still be protecting you," he gritted through clenched teeth. "Just not…"

"Right. You just won't be sleeping with me. Okay. I get it. You may leave now," she said, oh-so-politely.

"Not until you promise you won't leave this room without me."

"Oh, I see it now." She nodded to herself. "Not only am I not good enough to share a bed with, but you think I'm stupid, as well."

"I don't think you're stupid." He frowned in puzzlement. "You're probably the smartest woman I know."

"You must think I'm stupid if you think you have to secure that promise from me. Well let me tell you something, Mr. Johnson. I'm *not* stupid. You've convinced me I'm in danger, so I won't do anything to jeopardize my safety or my freedom." Her lips thinned. "And now you may take your belongings and leave. I have things to do. I was planning to attend the Welcome Reception before dinner. You know, the one celebrating our first day of sailing? So I'll call your room when I'm ready. Is that sufficient?"

Savannah managed to hold on until after Niall left and she bolted the door behind him before she broke down. She threw herself on the other bed, the one they hadn't shared last night, pulled the pillow over her head and sobbed. Just sobbed. Her heart was breaking, but that wasn't why she was crying. She was crying because the expression on Niall's face at the very end betrayed he was suffering just as much as she was by his inexplicable decision to sleep apart from her.

Which meant he cared. A lot more than he wanted her to know. Which also meant the secret he was keeping from her was so important his conscience wouldn't let him stay. She couldn't imagine what it could be. But it had to be earth-shattering.

Chapter 13

Dressed all in black, the masked man tested the rope by moonlight, grateful for the light in one way, but also hoping no sleepless passenger came up on the deck and spotted his companion and him. "You know what to do, right?" he asked the woman in a low-pitched voice.

She nodded, and her voice was just as hushed when she said, "As soon as you land on the balcony and release the rope, pull it up and get rid of the evidence. Then head down to the bottom deck and prepare to launch the lifeboat you selected."

The plan was simple. Break into Savannah's stateroom, hopefully without waking her. Chloroform her. Remove his mask; he couldn't risk having someone see him disguised in the hallways as he carried her from her room to the lifeboat. Then bind her hands and feet and apply the gag to her mouth once they were there. Launch the boat with the help of his pseudo-wife, leaving her on board to pretend he was sick in their cabin as the reason for his absence the next morning.

Assuming all went as planned, once he'd transferred Savannah to his men waiting on shore, all he had to do was make his way to the next port of call, Qutang Gorge, and reboard the boat while everyone was sightseeing in the Lesser Three Gorges. Then finish the cruise as if nothing had happened.

He'd been waiting, somewhat impatiently, for his first opportunity, transmitting instructions via cell phone to his Chinese hirelings on land to continue following the boat's path as it made its way down the Yangtze River. He'd exulted when he'd observed Niall Johnson leave Savannah at her door and head to his own cabin, after which he'd cobbled this makeshift plan together.

Good thing I planned for most contingencies, he thought, mentally patting himself on the back.

He climbed over the railing, the rope securely fastened in a sling beneath his shoulders and warned the woman, "Don't screw it up," as he walked himself down the side of the boat. The rope played out smoothly from the passive arrestor mechanism he'd smuggled on board along with the rope. It didn't take long since his target's balcony was only one deck below the top.

He landed without a sound. He slid the rope out from under his arms and tugged it hard three times to signal he was safely down, and it hissed its way back up the side of the boat. He pulled his set of lock picks from his pocket and was just reaching for the balcony door when something metal clanged off the railing behind him before hitting the water below with a splash.

Savannah woke instantly. She didn't know what the sound was she'd heard, but she knew whatever had caused it wasn't normal. Had something hit the boat? She scrambled out of bed, and that's when she saw the dark shadow of a man cast by the light of the moon through the drapes covering her balcony door.

She frantically pounded on the wall between her cabin and Niall's. Then she grabbed her robe from the foot of the bed where she'd left it and was in the corridor in a flash, even before she could put it on.

Niall met her there. Just as the first night, he was barechested, wearing only jeans that weren't fully fastened and revealed what would in other circumstances be a tantalizing glimpse of hair that arrowed downward. She was distracted from her terror for a moment by the realization that Niall must always sleep in the nude, not just when he was with her. Then she shoved that thought out of her mind. "Someone was trying to get in through my balcony door," she whispered, conscious of the sleeping occupants of the other cabins on Deck Five.

"You're sure?"

"Positive."

"Stay here." He vanished into her stateroom, but Savannah followed, determined to be his backup just in case, and struggling to drag her robe on over the T-shirt that barely grazed the tops of her thighs.

Niall had her balcony door open and was examining the lock when she entered. "Untouched," he told her. "I can dust for fingerprints, but…"

"I saw him," she insisted, thinking he didn't believe her. "Him?"

"Well, I can't swear it was a man. I just saw a shadow against the drapes. But it was taller than I am and it looked like a man, so I logically assumed it was one."

He nodded, but she wasn't sure she'd convinced him someone really had been trying to enter her stateroom. "I'm not making this up, Niall. I'm not so desperate for you I'd invent a story about a break-in to—"

He clasped his hands over her shoulders, cutting her off. "You're trembling."

She squeezed her eyes shut for a couple of seconds, then opened them again. "I was terrified. I still am."

He lifted a hand and touched two fingers against the pulse at the base of her ear. "You are," he agreed. "Your pulse is racing, and it's not because you're turned on."

She choked on laughter quickly suppressed. "Umm, no. You're right. I'm not. Turned on, that is." She looked up at him, so reassuringly male, and said, "I know it's an imposition, but I have to ask. Would you sleep in the other bed the rest of tonight? I'm not trying to…to seduce you or anything like that. I just don't want to stay here by myself. Just for tonight," she assured him when his eyes widened in disbelief.

"Are you kidding me? You think I have any intention of waltzing back to my cabin as if nothing happened?"

"I thought you didn't believe me," she said, her words a faint thread of sound.

He held his hand up as if to stop her. "Let's get one thing straight. Even if I didn't believe you—which I do, by the way, for reasons I'll explain in a minute—*you* believe it happened. It scared you so much you're still shaking. What kind of sorry excuses for men have you known that make you think a man could just walk away from a woman in that state?"

When she didn't respond, he wrapped his arms around her and pulled her head against his shoulder. "Never mind. I don't give a damn about them. But I do give a damn about you. So for as long as you need me, I'm yours." He released her, saying, "Let me just run next door for some more clothes, but I'll be back in a minute. Will you be okay or do you want to come with me?"

"I think I can survive on my own for a couple of minutes," she said with a dry twist to her tone. "But before you go, would you tell me why you believe me?"

"Oh that." He paused. "What woke you?"

She thought for a moment. "There was a noise. I can't really explain, but it sounded as if something hit the boat. Something metallic."

He nodded. "I heard it, too. I didn't see the man on your balcony, but I was already awake when you pounded on the wall."

"That's why you believe me?"

"That, combined with everything else that's happened, and yeah. I think whoever's after you saw me leave you at your door and go into my cabin, and realized that left you unprotected. Something they were quick to take advantage of."

"Which means whoever it is," she said slowly, "their room is probably on this deck."

The flash of admiration she'd noted before was back in his eyes, and he said softly, "You're always on target, Dr. Whitman."

It wasn't until Niall had gone to his cabin for his clothes that Savannah realized this wasn't the first time he'd called her Dr. Whitman. And she'd never told him she was one.

"What the *hell* happened?" the man demanded of the woman when he finally returned to their stateroom after scrambling down from Savannah's balcony to the ones directly below it in quick succession, until he'd reached the bottom deck, where there was no balcony. He'd hastily removed the mask and gloves, then surreptitiously made his way back upstairs.

"It wasn't my fault, honest. I'd pulled up the rope and coiled it in preparation for disposing of it. I was trying to unhook the passive arrestor mechanism from the railing when it slipped out of my hands. It's heavy, you know," she threw at him when his face turned accusatory.

"I told you not to screw up."

"I couldn't help it!"

"We may never have a better chance than we had to-night."

"I couldn't help it, I tell you!"

"I'm docking your share of the payoff."

"What?" she gasped.

"Don't argue with me." His voice was cold. Ruthless. "Just be thankful I'm not dispensing with your services completely."

Savannah shifted restlessly in the dark, unable to sleep for a variety of reasons. She and Niall had reported the incident to the ship's captain and purser. Even though they believed the attempted break-in was another kidnapping attempt, Niall had thought it best to go on the record with it anyway. The noise and her reaction had thankfully scared the intruder off, he'd told her, but he didn't want to give the impression they knew the true motive. So it was important to set up a hue and cry that would make their suspects think she and Niall thought it was an attempted robbery… or even a possible sexual assault.

That had been an awkward conversation, she remembered now. The captain and the purser, hastily called from their beds, had stood in her stateroom and listened to everything with impassive faces, although their profuse apologies and repeated statements that this would be looked into immediately betrayed how horrified and embarrassed they were something like this had happened on their watch. Passenger safety was of paramount importance to the cruise company, they assured her.

She and Niall had put on jackets and had gone up to the top deck after the captain and purser had left, where they'd discovered more circumstantial evidence that there really had been someone trying to break in. In the eerie blue-white moonlight, they'd found scratch marks on the otherwise pristine white paintwork on the railing right above her balcony. Something had been clamped there, and Niall had theorized it was some kind of mechanical lowering device. *Whatever it was, it was probably the thing that bounced off your balcony railing and woke us both up, before it fell into the water below.*

She'd shivered at the reminder of how nearly she hadn't awakened. If the kidnapper had managed to enter her stateroom in silence, where would she be now?

And if those memories weren't enough to keep her from sleeping, there was also the question she'd wanted to ask Niall but hadn't. How did he know? She kept turning over past conversations in her mind, but couldn't recall ever having told him she was a PhD.

Could he have assumed she was because of her previous job and the fact that both her parents had been university professors? Maybe. But it was still an aberration. And if there was one thing she could never ignore, it was an outlier data point. Yes, sometimes those outliers were just that—bizarre, one-time occurrences that shouldn't be factored into the equations. But sometimes they were indicative of a serious issue, one that needed to be taken into consideration in constructing the algorithms that were her life's blood.

She'd just resolved to ask him about it in the morning when a deep voice from the other bed asked, "Can't sleep?"

She turned over to face him, even though he was only a shape in the darkness and she couldn't make out his features. "No."

"Me, neither. I keep thinking about what almost happened…because of me."

"Because of you? That's silly. It's not your fault some-one wants to kidnap me."

"No, but it is my fault you were alone."

"Oh, Niall." She couldn't help the hint of chiding in her voice. "You're not responsible for the whole world."

"I never said I was."

"You're sure acting like it."

He laughed abruptly. "Okay, so maybe I internalize too much. Is that a crime?"

She didn't know why she did it—was it something in his voice?—but she slipped from beneath the covers of her bed and slid under his.

"What are you—" His question turned into a moan when she found him with her hand and gently squeezed, then began stroking when his body responded like a house on fire. "I can't, Savannah," he said finally, after she'd already confirmed he could.

"Really? Because that's not the impression I'm getting."

His hand covered hers, stopping her. "This isn't what you want. I'm not what you want."

"I think I can make that decision for myself, thank you very much."

He rolled them over so suddenly it took a second for her equilibrium to adjust, and she had to let him go to hang onto his shoulders until her head stopped spinning.

"I don't want to hurt you." His voice was so low she wasn't sure she heard him correctly. Then, as if the words were torn from him, he added, "Don't fall in love with me, please. I'll only break your heart."

A sudden realization jolted through her, and she briefly considered telling him it was too late, she'd already fallen. But she didn't. Instead she said in her gentlest voice, "You've given me wings, Niall. A broken heart's a small price to pay." And she kissed him.

* * *

Niall was up with the dawn. Savannah was still asleep, so he carefully disengaged his body from hers and dressed quietly. He dragged his laptop out and sat on the balcony to enjoy the sunrise and the beauty of the Qutang Gorge the boat was traversing on the Yangtze River while his laptop powered up…and while he dissected the latest kidnapping attempt.

His pool of suspects had just been winnowed dramatically. Savannah had theorized last night that the stateroom belonging to the kidnapper or kidnappers had to be on the aft side of Deck Five, where their rooms were located. He agreed with her theory, because how would they have seen him leave otherwise?

And there were no passenger rooms on the bow side—that was all taken up by the Observation Lounge and Bar. So now all he had to do was cross-reference the couples on their tour bus with their respective cabin assignments. Whoever was on their tour bus who also had a Deck Five stateroom had just moved to the top of his suspect list.

He connected to the VPN and dashed off a missive to his boss, requesting he use whatever pull their agency had with the tour company to get the list of cabin assignments on Deck Five. He knew it was very likely he could bribe someone on board to get the list—the maids probably had it, and they were notoriously underpaid. A few hundred yuan to one of them just might work. But he'd only do that as a last resort. If he guessed and guessed wrong, he'd have to answer a lot of awkward questions from senior ship personnel. And after last night's conversation with the captain and the purser, it might make them suspicious of the motive behind Savannah's report.

Then he checked his incoming email. To his surprise, there was an encrypted one from his sister. He hadn't expected results on Spencer Davies and DMFC so soon. It hadn't even been twenty-four hours since he'd emailed her, and day here was night there, and vice versa.

He decrypted the email, trying but failing to contain the little buzz of excitement. He hadn't been exaggerating when he'd told Savannah Keira was a whiz at research. What had she found?

He read her careful disclaimer with impatience. *Yeah, yeah, yeah*, he thought. *I get that this is all preliminary and you need to confirm it from other sources. Just get to the point.*

And the point was…Davies Missiles and Fire Control was in serious financial trouble. They'd lost several big competitive contracts in the last year, just as Savannah had said. But that wasn't all. Their bread-and-butter missile, the one they'd been selling to the DoD forever with just minor upgrades every year, had just been made obsolete…by Savannah. By a breakthrough design for which she'd almost assuredly receive a fourth patent.

It's not common knowledge, Keira wrote, but the DoD is scrambling to find a way to keep DMFC afloat. You know as well as I do that the government tries its best to keep defense contractors in business, to keep competition alive and prices down. But the DoD can't continue fielding that obsolete missile, especially since it has already been involved in three friendly fire incidents.

"Holy crap," he whispered. Usually that occurred when the friendly target was mistakenly identified as an enemy one. But sometimes, as appeared to be the case here, it was due to errors or inaccuracy.

Just imagine the public outcry, Keira's email continued, if it got out that the DoD knew the missile was obsolete, but used it anyway…and another friendly fire incident occurred. Bottom line? DMFC is teetering.

A four-letter word Niall never used in polite company issued from his lips. He'd thought from what Savannah had told him that DMFC was in hot water, but he hadn't realized it was this bad. Which meant it made perfect sense that Spencer Davies would want Savannah...any way he could get her. Davies had tried to hire her, wasn't that what she'd told him? And when Davies couldn't lure her into coming to work for his company, he'd concocted this scheme to kidnap her.

Hold on a sec, he told himself. *Don't jump to conclusions. How the hell could Davies think he could get away with it long-term?* But as soon as the question surfaced, something niggled at the back of his mind. Something Savannah had said about Davies. What was it?

Then it came to him... *Because he and his company have a reputation in the defense industry for taking shortcuts, and I don't like that. Shortcuts are shortsighted in my opinion...*

A cold, sinking feeling settled over him, and he cursed again. "Davies doesn't give a crap about the long-term," he whispered as the hard truth settled in. "He wants Savannah to salvage his obsolete missile somehow, some way. But he can't afford to keep her alive after that. Too dangerous."

He didn't even realize his right hand had clenched so tightly it was bloodless until he felt the nails on that hand digging into his palm. He relaxed it immediately, but stared at his hand for a moment, thinking about the ultimate fate planned for Savannah. "Not in this lifetime," he promised himself. "Not if I have anything to say about it."

A rustle from inside the room informed Niall Savannah was finally waking up. He quickly logged off his computer and shut it down. He'd have to tell her about this latest development and the conclusions he'd drawn, and they needed to make some plans. But first things first. First he needed to make love to her. *Then* he'd tell her Spencer Davies intended to kill her.

Chapter 14

There was something particularly thrilling about being kissed awake by the man you loved, Savannah thought. Even though part of her was worrying about morning breath because she hadn't yet brushed her teeth and another part of her was thinking she was going to have to visit the bathroom before too long. Still, an unshaven chin was an erotic delight when a lover nuzzled her cheek the way Niall did.

And when he whispered in her ear all the wicked treats he had in store for her? Bliss.

But eventually she murmured, "Hold that thought," and made a mad dash for the bathroom. When she returned she was disappointed to see he was still dressed. She'd hoped he would have stripped down to his birthday suit in anticipation of what he'd promised her.

But apparently he'd had second thoughts.

He'd propped himself on one arm, and his expression was serious. "We need to talk."

She sighed, but not so he'd notice, thinking, *Not again.* She really, truly had thought that last night they'd gotten past whatever it was that was bothering him. There'd been a level of tenderness in his lovemaking he'd never shown her before, and she'd let herself get carried away with the fantasy. And this morning...

She sighed again, then opened the dresser and busied herself by pulling out clothes to wear that day—jeans and a favorite dusky rose, long-sleeved sweater. With her back to him, she said, "What do we need to talk about?"

"Spencer Davies. DMFC. And an obsolete missile."

Savannah and Niall disembarked from their riverboat after breakfast and walked with the rest of the crowd toward the far docks and the small sightseeing vessels they'd take to visit the Lesser Three Gorges. Even though their riverboat was tiny compared to the large ocean cruisers that carried thousands of passengers, it was still too big for the narrow places they were going this morning.

It had rained earlier, but now the sun shone dimly through the clouds. They picked their way carefully through the puddles and over the uneven slats of the trestle bridge, and Savannah couldn't help but be touched by the solicitous way Niall held her arm the entire time. She wasn't fragile and she was perfectly capable of avoiding slick spots and rough patches on her own. But his manner indicated a certain...well...*attachment* seemed to be the most appropriate word. And she was starting to hope that maybe, just maybe, he'd realize they had something special. That the bond they shared was more than just fantastic sex.

Plan for the worst and hope for the best. She could still hear her mother saying that to her. "I will, Mom," she whispered under her breath.

Niall handed her down into boat number eighteen and followed her inside. "Did you say something?"

She smiled at him. "Just to myself." She took a seat on a bench in the front row on the other side of the boat's operator—she planned to take lots of pictures, and this way she could do so out of the front window as well as the side.

Niall sat beside her and stretched his long legs out in front of him. "Thanks for picking the seat with the best leg room."

"Oh. Sorry. I wasn't even thinking about that."

He smiled lazily. "Yeah, I figured."

"Then why did you thank me?"

"Just in case."

If she hadn't already loved him, she'd have fallen for him in that instant for what that sentence said about him. "Your parents really did raise a gentleman," she murmured, pressing her face against his shoulder for a moment because she loved him so much and couldn't tell him. But she could show him.

She'd just lifted her head when Herb Thompson ducked through the front door, followed by Mary Beth, whose face brightened when she saw Savannah and Niall. "Well, hey there," she gushed. "Isn't this tiny boat quaint? I almost backed out when I saw how small it is, but Herb insisted. He said we paid good money for this cruise, and by golly we're going to see everything! Did you take a seasick pill? I have extras if you didn't, but I think you have to take them a half hour before you—"

"Madam, please keep moving," said the pretty Chinese boat guide, who looked to be about fifteen. "You are preventing the other passengers from boarding."

Mary Beth tittered and apologized. "So sorry." She glanced at Savannah again. "We'll talk afterward, okay?" and moved to join her husband, who'd picked a seat near the middle of the boat.

"Thank God! I think I would have been seasick only if she sat near us," Savannah whispered in Niall's ear, and he chuckled.

Tammy Williams stepped onto the boat a couple of passengers later, followed by her husband. She waggled fingers at Savannah but didn't stop and didn't say anything, for which Savannah was grateful.

As the rest of the passengers boarded the twenty-person vessel, she couldn't help thinking about what Niall had told her early this morning regarding Spencer Davies. The surprising thing was that she wasn't surprised, now that Niall had figured out why. She hadn't wanted to believe it before, but the explanation dovetailed nicely with the facts, unfortunately.

And she wasn't surprised Spencer Davies planned to kill her eventually, either, which saddened her. It made perfect sense from the standpoint of someone who only cared about the bottom line. Force her to come up with an answer to his obsolete missile? Of course. But even if she could, it was a one-time solution. It couldn't be sustained long-term, especially since he couldn't let anyone know she was behind the fix he was hoping she could make. Which meant he had to kill her to keep the secret.

What would he do next time, though, a few years down the road?

"You okay? You look sad all of a sudden."

She glanced up at him. "I was thinking about what you told me this morning. And you're right, Spencer Davies has to be stopped. Because I just realized I'm merely the first. If he's successful with me, he'll do it again. And again. Like a serial killer who keeps going until he's caught." She drew a deep breath and let it out slowly. "So we have to catch him and put him away."

"We?" He shifted position. "There are federal agencies to handle this." He looked as if he might say more but thought better of it.

"I'm part of this. How are they going to catch him without me to act as bait?"

Niall's face hardened. "That's not happening, Savannah. We don't need live bait. Especially if that bait is you."

Something about his words didn't make sense, and her brow furrowed. "What do you mean, we don't need live bait? *We?*" When he didn't answer, she said slowly, "You told me you're in security. And though you didn't say it, you certainly implied you work in the private sector. But I don't think you do. Do you work for the DoD's Defense Security Service? The DSS?"

He shook his head. "No. I don't." There wasn't a shred of emotion in his voice, but his dark brown eyes held hers and she believed him. She didn't know why, but she did. Then an unwelcome thought crept in. *That doesn't mean he doesn't work for another federal agency, though.*

She started to ask him, but at that moment the boat operator fired up the engine with a throaty roar. The vessel backed smoothly away from the dock, then turned in a sweeping curve and headed for the Lesser Three Gorges with a dozen other craft.

Savannah could only stare at Niall, her thoughts in turmoil. "You called me Dr. Whitman," she whispered. "Twice. Which means you know things about me I never told you." His gaze never wavered, but he didn't speak, either. "Who are you?"

"We'll talk about that later." He took her chin in his hand and gently turned her head so she was facing the front window. "The Goddess Stream, Savannah," he reminded her. "You've come thousands of miles to see it. Get your camera ready."

She was reluctant, at first, Niall saw. But eventually the sheer beauty of their surroundings got to her, and *click,*

click, *click* went her camera. He caught her attention from time to time and pointed at some particularly scenic sight, and when the boat guide lashed the front doors open so the passengers could walk out on the bow to take photographs, he held her by the hips to keep her steady. But mostly he just watched her craning her head and gazing in wonder. And his heart ached because his time with Savannah was running out, but he had no one to blame but himself.

He'd been the consummate operative before he'd met her. An actor worthy of an Academy Award—when he assumed a role, he *became* the role. But not anymore. Not since he'd fallen in love with her. Now he was human. Now he was vulnerable.

He'd slipped up three times with Savannah and hadn't realized it. Once she'd mentioned it, he'd immediately recalled the times he'd called her Dr. Whitman and could have kicked himself for being such a rank amateur. And of course, saying, *We don't need live bait,* was a dead giveaway, since it almost certainly implied he belonged to one of the federal agencies he'd told her could handle the investigation. A stupid move that could have gotten him killed if she'd been the traitor he'd first suspected her of being. A stupid move that could get her killed if he said something like that in the presence of his suspects.

So what's it going to be, Jones? Are you going to risk Savannah's life because you love her and don't want to lie to her anymore? Or are you going to love her enough to suck it up and be a damn professional?

He already knew the answer. He just didn't like it.

Savannah's stateroom had been refreshed by the time they returned. She removed her jacket and laid it and her purse on the newly made double bed closest to the door—the one she and Niall had shared—then turned to face him.

"I should go next door for my belongings," he began, but she stopped him.

"First I need to know who you are. You said we'd talk about it later. Well, now is later."

His eyes creased at the corners as if she'd called him a liar. "I wasn't lying. I don't work for the Defense Security Service."

She thought for a moment, trying to remember Niall's exact words the few times they'd discussed his work. "You said you're a troubleshooter, that you plug security leaks. What did you mean by that?"

He grinned. "You have a mind like a steel trap. Anyone ever tell you that?"

"Yes, and don't try to change the subject. What exactly do you do?"

He removed his own jacket and turned to hang it in the closet. Then he faced her again. "Before the Corps and I parted company eighteen years ago, I looked around to see what I wanted to do with the rest of my life. When I found it, I went to college and got dual degrees in criminology and computer programming to make it happen."

"And?"

"And I went to work for a security firm after I graduated three years later."

She was distracted for a moment. "You finished your undergraduate work in three years?" She had, too, just another little thing they had in common, but... "Dual degrees?" She couldn't help but be impressed. She'd only earned a Bachelor of Science in Mathematics before she'd entered grad school at twenty-one.

"Yeah. Tested out of a bunch of GenEd classes, then took the max credit hours I could take every semester. Money wasn't the main factor—I was on the GI bill—but I was itching to get out into the real world and start doing."

She brought her focus back to her original question. "Doing what?"

He smiled faintly. "I was a hot commodity in those days. The explosion of the internet and cyber security—or rather, the woeful lack of cyber security—combined with my Marine Corps experience and my degrees meant I could pretty much write my own ticket. Heady stuff for a twenty-five-year-old. I started out earning almost triple what I'd been making in the Corps, and it was all due to Uncle Sam."

She digested what he'd said, then nodded thoughtfully. "I see. Thank you for telling me." She forced a smile onto her face. "I'm sorry for being so suspicious. Blame all the security briefings I had when I was working for my former company—you can easily get paranoid, seeing spies everywhere."

He returned her smile. "Not a problem. I'd have suspected me, too, under the circumstances." He took the two steps that brought him right up in front of her and touched her cheek. "Are we good now?"

She put her hand over his. "We're good."

"Then let me go get my things, and we can head down to lunch. Okay?"

"Okay."

"Bolt the door behind me."

"You'll only be gone a few minutes," she protested.

He held her gaze. "Please."

"All right." She followed Niall to the door and bolted it. Then sagged against it and stood there long after he left, a band of pain tightening around her heart. Because she realized, despite his long and involved explanation, he'd never told her how he knew she was a doctor, nor why he'd used the word *we*.

And though she still loved him, though she believed

much of what he'd told her was the truth, somewhere in all those details he'd lied to her. She was sure of it.

Niall checked his suitcases and backpack before he picked them up. Not just that they were still securely locked, but that they were precisely where he'd left them, and that his little markers hadn't been touched. They hadn't. His bed had been made and the towels in the bathroom changed, but otherwise the room was undisturbed.

He headed for the door, a suitcase in each hand and backpack over his shoulder, wondering if he'd dodged a bullet with Savannah. She seemed to believe him, but he couldn't be positive. Everything he'd told her was the God's honest truth, except for one thing. One lie—that he'd gone to work for a "security firm" after college—buried in the middle of his otherwise truthful story.

You're a very convincing liar, Niall, she'd told him at dinner the other night. *You mix bits of the truth with your lies, which makes it easy to believe you.*

He'd learned the art of deception so long ago it was second nature to him now. He could still recall sitting in a class he'd been sent to when he'd joined his agency, a class taught by a famous spymaster.

Try to avoid an out-and-out lie if you can. Divert attention whenever possible instead, kind of like the sleight of hand a magician does. Humor helps. When people are laughing, they're not dissecting your story word for word. And afterward, all they'll remember is the funny parts.

But if you must tell a lie, remember that listeners tend to focus on the first and last sentences in a story. To make a lie convincing, bury it in the middle of truthful statements.

Which is what he'd done with Savannah. He'd been watching her reaction closely with every word he'd said. And though she'd apologized at the end for her suspicions,

though she'd told him they were good now, there'd been
that one second when he'd thought he'd seen something in
her eyes. It had vanished so quickly he'd almost convinced
himself he'd imagined it, but...

He put one suitcase down and rapped on her door. "Savannah?"

"Just a minute."

He heard the metallic click of the bolt being pulled back
and the sound of the handle being turned, which released
the automatic lock. Then the door swung inward, with Savannah framed in the opening. And in that instant before
she composed her face into a welcoming expression, he
knew she knew he'd lied.

Chapter 15

"Do I need to bring my carry-on bag?" Savannah asked Niall after he'd moved into her room and put his gear down. "Are you planning to steal more glasses at lunch?"

"Steal?" he joked. "I don't steal, I just borrow. I always return things after I lift the fingerprints."

Her answering smile came and went quickly. "Borrow, then. Do you need me to be your partner in crime again? Should I bring my carry-on bag to stash them for you?"

He shook his head. "Let's hold off on any more fingerprints for now, until we cross-reference the lists. We have quite a few sets already."

Why did you even pack a fingerprint kit anyway? It's not something one would usually bring on vacation."

He skirted that land mine by shrugging and saying, "Habit. And the possibility I could always be called back if there was an emergency. I have a bunch of stuff I carry with me when I travel for work, and I automatically packed it just in case."

"Oh, I see. That makes sense, I guess." She picked up her purse. "But I wouldn't want a job where I could be called back from vacation at a moment's notice."

He shrugged again. "It's not so bad. I've only been re-called three times in fifteen years, and every time the company reimbursed me for the busted travel plans. But it's always a possibility."

"'Plan for the worst and hope for the best.' My mom always said that." Her smile was a little twisted and it touched something deep inside him, because he understood the loss she still felt keenly. "Is that how you process the fingerprints, too? With stuff you always carry with you?" Her tone conveyed merely casual interest, but he knew it wasn't.

"Yeah. I have a miniscanner attachment for my laptop."

"Ahhh, I should have guessed. Who's checking the fingerprints for you?"

A grenade this time, one he tried to deflect with humor. "What is this, Twenty Questions?"

"Nice try," she said softly. "Just answer, please."

If he hadn't known before, he would now—Savannah no longer trusted him. "Colleagues where I work," he said levelly. "And that's the last question I'll answer on this topic. You ready for lunch?"

The ship was passing through Wu Gorge during lunch, so Savannah was grateful she and Niall were early enough to get a table by the window. Lush, green and shrouded in mist, the Twelve Peaks that lined the gorge rose majestically and impressively on both sides of the boat.

"It's so beautiful," she murmured to the woman who'd taken the chair next to hers at the table. Her nametag read Debbie S. "So peaceful. Don't you think, Debbie?"

"Absolutely. This is the second time Bob and I have taken this cruise," she replied, indicating the smiling man on her other side. "I came down with a horrendous sinus infection the first time, even though I had a mask with me to wear in crowds," she explained. "I missed most of the side excursions. Poor Bob had to go by himself. But even though I felt terrible, I sat on the balcony outside our room because the scenery was just too beautiful to pass up."

Conversation at the table segued into discussions of other places people had been, especially other river cruises the tour company offered in the heart of Europe, the Baltic states and Scandinavia that these seasoned and well-heeled travelers had taken.

Niall, on Savannah's other side, was noticeably silent. And she wondered about that. He'd always been an excellent raconteur, holding his own in any table conversation and making the other guests laugh uproariously at times with his amusing banter.

Then it came to her. It made no sense whatsoever, but somehow she'd wounded him with her questions earlier, questions that clearly conveyed she didn't trust him anymore. She hadn't thought she could hurt him, but she had. And her tender heart gave her no peace.

But he lied to you, she reminded her heart. *He lied. Probably from the beginning.*

Out of the blue, she remembered two seemingly contradictory quotations her mother had often used: *Tell the truth and shame the devil*, a commonly used variant of a line from Shakespeare, and Robert Louis Stevenson's: *The lie of a good woman is the true index of her heart.*

And when Savannah had questioned her mother about it, she'd explained they weren't really contradictory at all. The first merely meant that honesty—as a general rule—was usually the best policy, though not always. Sometimes silence was best; to spare someone's feelings, for instance, rather than speak an unpalatable or hurtful truth. And sometimes a lie was warranted. A lie with the best intentions.

She glanced at Niall, who was turned away from her and gazing out the window at the gorge through which they were passing, and it suddenly occurred to her how like these mountains he was. Despite his seeming conviviality, he was really a solitary man. Stoic. Aloof. There was a quiet strength about him, too. A strength he'd never used against her, only to help her. Guarding her back as they climbed the Great Wall. Carrying her out of the crowd at the terracotta warrior museum. Chasing away the masked intruders outside her hotel room.

And making love to you as if it were the most important thing in the world, she remembered with a flush of warmth. *Proving you were wrong about yourself. Don't forget that.*

It all boiled down to a man she could trust, the lies notwithstanding. She reached under the table without thinking and clasped his hand, squeezing it reassuringly.

He turned around and their eyes met. She saw an apology in those dark brown depths for having deceived her. And at the same time, a steadfast determination to maintain that deception—whatever it was—for a reason only he could comprehend. Just as she'd known he'd lied to her, she knew this was the truth, too.

This didn't make everything miraculously all right between them. And though she hoped, she wasn't counting on anything after the end of this trip. But she *was* returning to her original resolution.

She was going to live her life one day at a time. She was going to accept the gift of this wonderful man for as long as she was allowed to have him. She was going to trust he'd never deliberately hurt her and make love with him secure in that trust for whatever time they had left. And she was going to love him unreservedly...for the rest of her life. Even if she never saw him again.

* * *

The man looked at the woman with dislike, masked by the role of loving husband he was forced to play. He leaned over to whisper in her ear, ostensibly a private word between husband and wife, but in reality a criticism he was burning to unleash.

"We could have been at their table if you'd noticed I'd left my jacket behind a little sooner."

She turned disbelieving eyes on him and whispered back, "*Your* jacket. Yours. *You* took it off on the sightseeing boat and left it there, not me. It's not my fault we had to go all the way back for it."

"Quiet! A fine partner you turned out to be. We would have been finished if you hadn't screwed up last night."

"Are you on that again? It was an *accident*. Just like you forgetting your jacket today was an accident."

He straightened and smiled for form's sake, then made a joke that had the whole table laughing. But when his gaze fell on his pseudo-wife, he made sure his eyes promised retribution.

Niall and Savannah detoured to her stateroom after lunch to don their jackets against the cool outside air, then took another stroll around the boat. Remembering his idea the first day on board, he led her to the prow of the ship.

"*Titanic* moment?" he murmured, drawing her out to the farthest point they were allowed to go. He set her in front of him while he stood at her back, his arms enfolding her like the couple in the movie, but careful not to take her by surprise.

She laughed, obviously delighted when the cool wind blew her hair out of its careful chignon. Then she dug a hand in her jacket pocket and pulled out her camera, holding it out at arm's length. "Smile."

A half dozen photos later, each one showing them both with crazy, wind-tossed hair, she gave up. "I don't care," she said, stowing her camera away. "I'm saving them, not deleting them."

He chuckled. "There goes your theory that I never take a bad picture."

"Hah! You still look gorgeous, even with wild hair."

He turned her in his arms. "You're the gorgeous one," he whispered as an ache built in his chest. Then he captured her lips for a kiss that couldn't even begin to convey what he felt because that couldn't be put into words, either. She was trembling when he finally let her go, and he pressed two fingers beneath her ear, just as he'd done last night. "Your pulse is racing again."

She nodded slowly, her gaze glued to his. "But this time I *am* turned on."

He kissed her eyelids closed. "I want you, Savannah," he breathed, realizing how pitifully inadequate that word was to describe how he felt. "God, how I want you. You're sweet and good and funny and sexy and so damn smart. But I..."

Her eyelids slid up slowly, as if she were surfacing from a drugged state. "You can't hurt me by wanting me, Niall. Not when I feel the same way. You can only hurt me by *not* making love to me." She smiled up at him and his heart ached again at the delicate beauty of her smile. "I seem to recall someone saying that love in the afternoon sounded pretty damn good." She tapped her lips with the tip of one finger as she pretended to be puzzled. "Hmm. Now who could that have been?"

Love in the afternoon wasn't better than make-up sex, Savannah acknowledged, but it was pretty darn close. At least with Niall.

"What happens when we run out of condoms?" she

asked as she pulled down the covers and plumped up the pillows.

He laughed softly and jerked the drapes closed, giving them privacy. "I bought the jumbo box. Forty-eight. I think we're safe for this cruise."

"I bought some, too," she volunteered, pulling the box out of the drawer where she'd stashed it and handing it to him. "The day we met."

His lips quirked. "Nice to know your intentions, but…" He put her box down and pulled his box out of his suitcase and handed it to her. "Yours are the wrong size."

"Oh." She glanced from one box to the other. "They don't…stretch?"

His hearty laugh made her laugh, too. "Yeah, they do, but not that much. And besides, you should know that if you stretch a condom past the tension limit, you run a greater risk of tearing." A semiserious, semihumorous expression crossed his face as he began stripping off his clothes. "If that happens, then why bother?"

"Good point." She thrust the box of condoms she'd bought back in the drawer, and when she turned around he was completely naked. Naked, and already impressively aroused.

Not quite comfortable just flinging her clothes off the way he had, she stalled and drew one of the packets out of the extra-large-size box. Suddenly curious, because he'd always donned a condom himself without her assistance, she ripped the packet open and stared at it in her palm for a moment, then glanced at him. Or rather, at a certain portion of his anatomy. And back at the condom. Then at him again. In all seriousness, she said, "I think this one might be too small, too."

His teeth flashed in a grin, and he drawled, "Why thank you, darlin'." He took the condom from her hand and efficiently rolled it on, proving her wrong. He then proceeded to undress her. Slowly. Torturing her with appropriate kisses in the most inappropriate places.

When she was finally as naked as he was and shaking from the force of her desire, he drew her onto the bed and pulled her on top of him. "What are you—" she began, but he cut her off.

"How about you do all the work this time?"

They dozed in the aftermath, and when they woke they just snuggled. This was almost as good as the sex for Savannah, lying in Niall's arms, listening to his heartbeat and watching his chest rise and fall. Sliding her fingers through the silky hair on his chest that was only a shade darker than his light brown mane. Running gentle fingers over the scar that could never be ugly to her because of what it stood for. Exploring the ripple of muscles that made her wonder how he stayed in such incredible shape.

Random thoughts swirled through her mind from their conversation earlier, and without thinking she started to ask, "Have you ever…" Then stopped when she realized it might be too personal.

"Ever what?"

Because she really wanted to know, she finished her question. "Not bothered?"

He got it right away; she didn't need to explain. "No," he said, his voice very deep. "Never. I've always protected the woman I've been with against pregnancy."

"Did you want to?" The follow-up question popped out before she could prevent it, and she sat up abruptly, tugging the covers over her breasts. "Sorry, you don't have to answer that if you don't want to."

He didn't respond one way or the other, so she peeked at him. "Once," he said finally, when their eyes met.

A shaft of pain struck without warning. She didn't understand why his answer hurt so much at first, until she remembered the woman he'd loved all those years ago, the one who'd told him the scar on his chest was offensive. The one who hadn't deserved his love. "Was it…the woman you loved?"

A faint smile touched his lips, but there was something in it that made her feel like crying. "Yeah. The woman I loved."

Niall had never given serious thought to fatherhood, other than to take precautions to prevent it every time. He adored his sister's little girl, Alyssa, and doted on her. And when he'd met his brand-new nephews, Drew and Caden— four months and one month, respectively—at Shane's wedding in July, he'd been taken with them, too, in a distant sort of way. But just as he'd never envisioned himself with a wife, he'd never figured kids would be compatible with the job he did and the life he led.

So Savannah's question had hit him like a tsunami. Because he'd realized in that instant just how badly he *hadn't* wanted to wear a condom…with her.

His younger brothers, Alec and Liam, were brand-new fathers. And the last time he'd seen them, they'd admitted they hadn't been anxious to be fathers, either. Until they'd met their wives, Angelina and Cate.

"I can't explain it," Alec had said. "Can you, Liam?"

Liam had pondered the question for a moment. "It's not some macho desire for a tiny human being in your image," he'd eventually said. "That's not it at all. And it's not even a desire to leave something of yourself for posterity— something that will live on after you." He'd paused for a second. "It's more like you want to create something with the woman who means the world to you, a tangible manifestation of the love the two of you share." He'd glanced at Alec. "Is that how it was for you?"

Alec had nodded. "You nailed it, bro."

All this flashed through Niall's mind in less than a minute. And as he pulled Savannah back down against his shoulder and cuddled her close, he acknowledged a bitter truth. Like his younger brothers, like his older brother, Shane, who'd confided to Niall that he and Carly were going to be trying for a baby starting with their honeymoon, *he* wanted to create a child with the woman he loved, too.

But that door was firmly closed against him. Forever.

Adam, standing on the outside looking back at the angels wielding a flaming sword to guard the gates of Eden, had nothing on the despair that filled Niall's soul in that instant.

Chapter 16

That evening, the riverboat passed through the five-stage locks of the Three Gorges Dam, which fueled the world's largest hydroelectric power station. As with everything else, Savannah wanted to experience it as it was happening, so she rushed through dinner in order to go out on deck for the night passage.

It was exciting at first. But then, as she confided to Niall, it became rather like watching paint dry. So they returned to her stateroom, where he immediately busied himself with his laptop, stretching his long legs out on the bed and using both pillows as a backrest. She sat cross-legged on the other bed and pulled her laptop out, too.

She downloaded the pictures she'd taken and put them in sequential, labeled folders, then updated the diary she was keeping about the trip—the places she'd seen, the people she'd met and how she'd felt everywhere she went. She made a face at the computer screen as she acknowledged she'd rather neglected this since they'd boarded the boat; Niall had monopolized her time.

"Not that I'm complaining," she whispered under her breath.

Niall looked up. "Did you say something?"

"Just talking to myself."

She put the photos of Niall in their own special folder with his name on it. And she started a separate diary just about him. Not about the sex, fantastic as it was. But every emotion he'd engendered in her, good and bad. From the way he'd overwhelmed her senses that very first day, to the moment she'd realized she loved him, to the fears of betrayal that had swamped her, to the acceptance that he wasn't perfect but she loved him anyway.

No one would ever read it but her, so she didn't worry she was betraying too much of her secret heart. She didn't worry about being politically correct, either. She was a strong, intelligent woman who'd carved a career for herself in a male-dominated field and had been wildly successful despite the obvious roadblocks. She firmly believed men and women should be judged by the same rules, should succeed on their merits and should receive equal pay for equal work. She knew she was as good as any man in her field, and in most cases better, far better.

But…

There was something particularly appealing about the protective shield Niall had erected around her.

And in her secret diary she didn't hesitate to lay bare her enjoyment of being looked after, taken care of, because she also knew that if Niall needed her, she would be there for him, too. But as she saw it, what he needed most from her was trust. Belief. And love.

Not the fairy-tale, happily-ever-after kind of love. Even her parents, who'd been her role models in so many ways, had had their ups and downs in their marriage. But through the good and the bad, their love had burned as an eternal flame. Steady. Unwavering. Happily-ever-after, but without the fairy tale aspect that couldn't be sustained over the long haul.

That's what she wanted with Niall. She knew he had it in him to give her. But what was even more important, she knew she had it in her to give him. Whether he wanted it, however, or was willing to accept it, she didn't know.

He cared. She knew that. He cared a lot. His words in the wee hours of this morning reverberated in her mind. *I don't give a damn about them. But I do give a damn about you. So for as long as you need me, I'm yours.*

Then there were those other words from this morning, too. *I don't want to hurt you.* And, *Don't fall in love with me, please. I'll only break your heart.*

That was the alpha male in him. Protecting her from every danger that threatened, as well as from himself.

He had secrets he couldn't or wouldn't share with her, which was a huge roadblock. And she didn't know what he'd lied to her about, or why—an even bigger obstacle. But if they could get past all that, they had a chance for the kind of happiness her parents had shared.

She and Niall were compatible in so many ways. Not just in bed, although they were incredibly attuned to one another that way—she didn't even have to touch him for him to be aroused, which was a very empowering feeling. But sex alone couldn't sustain a relationship for the long-term.

Relationship? a little voice in the back of her head whispered. *Let's be honest, shall we? It's marriage you're looking for. Marriage, with maybe a child or two. You're thirty-six. It's still possible. That's why you asked him if he'd ever considered not wearing a condom. Because in your heart of hearts you want his baby. Admit it.*

"Okay, okay," she muttered. "I admit it."

Niall raised his head again. "What did you say?"

"Sorry. Bad habit. Comes of living alone."

Obviously amused, he said, "I live alone, too."

"Well, then, you know what it's like."

He laughed. "Yeah, I'm afraid I do."

She tried to control her tongue, she really did. But the words came out willy-nilly. "Do you ever think about changing it? Living alone, I mean."

He stared at her for the longest time. Much longer than she'd thought he'd need to answer the question. There was something vulnerable in his face and his voice when he eventually said, "I've thought about it."

Her heart was suddenly pounding so hard it was all she could do to whisper, "Recently?"

You can't answer that! his conscience dictated. *She's in love with you—it's written all over her face. You answer that question honestly, she'll know you love her and she'll think the two of you have a future. Then when you get home and tell her the truth, the betrayal will devastate her.*

"Savannah…"

The hopeful light in her gray eyes died. "That's okay, Niall. I didn't mean to put you on the spot." She shut down her computer and scrambled off the bed, reaching for her purse. "I could use a cup of hot chocolate. How about you? There's a coffee station right by the grand staircase, on the starboard side, but you can get tea and hot chocolate, too. They even have little cookies. I could put some in a cup for you if you'd like, and bring—"

"Savannah." He moved swiftly to block her exit. "I can't let you go out alone. You're still a target, remember?"

She closed her eyes for a moment and bit her lip. Then she looked at him again, and what he saw in her face seared him. "It's just down the hallway, and I need to be alone for a bit. I'll be careful, honest."

"Savannah."

"Please," she begged.

Anger born of shame made him grasp her arms and demand roughly, "What the hell do you want from me? Blood?"

The silent tears suddenly welling in her eyes were the last straw, and he wrapped his arms around her. "Don't cry, Savannah. God, don't. You're killing me. Hit me, curse me. Slap my face and tell me to go to hell, but don't cry. I can't bear it."

She tore herself from his embrace and dashed the tears from her eyes. "I don't want to hit you, Niall. And I don't want to curse you, either. I just want a few minutes of privacy so I can get my emotions under control. Is that too much to ask?"

"I'll go for the hot chocolate you want," he decided suddenly. "You stay inside and bolt the door." He took a step back from her. "Fifteen minutes enough?"

Niall didn't wait for a response, just double-checked the lock on the balcony door and was gone before she could agree or disagree. She stood there and stared at the door for a minute, wondering what the hell had just happened here. Then she mechanically moved to the door and bolted it.

"Okay, yes, I started it," she admitted. *Stupid, stupid, stupid!* And she was supposed to be so smart. *What got into you asking that question?*

And crying? Oh please. *You resigned without giving the real reason because you were terrified of crying in front of the men at work, and then you go and cry all over Niall? Nice going.*

She went into the bathroom for a washcloth, ran it under the cold water and held it over her eyes to eradicate any signs she'd been crying. She glanced at herself in the mirror when she was done to make sure, then headed back to the other room and sat on the edge of the bed. She tried to figure out what she could possibly say to Niall to salvage the rest of this trip together, to put them back onto their friendly "just lovers" footing, but instead her brain kept focusing on the things he'd said. Not what he'd said so much as the way he'd said it.

And that's when the flame of hope was rekindled.

Because the note in his voice when he'd said, "I can't bear it," sounded awfully like a man who'd been pushed to the emotional breaking point...by the woman he loved.

Niall glanced at the coffee bar on his right, but kept on going. Hot chocolate would take five minutes, max, no matter how much he stretched it out, and he'd promised Savannah fifteen minutes at least.

He strode into the Lounge Bar and thought about ordering a glass of wine, but decided against it. One glass wouldn't affect him at all, he knew, but he didn't want to use alcohol as a panacea. He'd known a few heavy drinkers in his Marine Corps days, and he wasn't heading down that road.

He exited through one of the bar's side doors that would take him outside. It was cold and he'd come here without his jacket, but he figured he wouldn't freeze in the next ten minutes, so he pressed on toward the riverboat's bow.

He crossed his arms and tucked his hands under his armpits to keep them warm, then just stood there staring out across the water. Wondering what the hell had just happened with Savannah, how he'd lost control. How he'd almost told her *hell yeah!*—his thoughts on changing his single status were recent. Very recent. Then wondering how he was going retrieve his position as her lover after this.

Yeah, they could share her stateroom and sleep separately, that was always an option. Then he snorted in self-disgust. *Piss-poor option, Jones. You think you can sleep in the same room with her and not go crazy with longing?*

Going back to his own cabin wasn't an option either, because she still needed his protection 24/7. Which meant he had to think of something else…in the next few minutes.

No ideas occurred to him, however. *Nice going, Jones,* that derisive little voice whispered in his head. *You're always the man with the plan. So where's your plan?*

Plan. Plan. He had to come up with a plan. One that didn't involve lying to Savannah, because he'd lied to her enough. And she knew it, but she'd forgiven him. She'd taken his hand beneath the table at lunch, telling him plain as words could make it that she still trusted him even though he'd deceived her. That she had faith in him. That she knew there was a valid reason for his deception. *Why is that?*

The answer was staring him in the face, and had been, he realized, for days. Despite doing his damnedest to keep Savannah from falling in love with him…he'd failed.

Don't lie to yourself, the insidious internal voice said implacably. *You didn't do your damnedest to keep her from falling in love with you. Just the opposite. You did everything in your power to* make *her fall in love with you. You just didn't realize it.*

"You're right," he whispered. Then laughed softly when he remembered Savannah saying talking to oneself was a bad habit single people easily fell into.

He glanced at his watch and realized with a start he'd been gone far longer than fifteen minutes. He abruptly about-faced and headed back. Determined to do whatever it took to salvage their remaining time together.

The man and the woman sat in the front of the Observation Lounge, a little apart from the other passengers but still where they could watch Niall Johnson on the other side of the glass as he stood facing away from them.

"We're running out of time," the woman reminded him as she sipped at her wineglass.

"You think I don't know that?" he growled.

"What does Spencer say?"

His smile was unpleasant. "He says to do whatever it takes."

She gaped at him. "Murder? You're going to kill Johnson to get him out of the way?"

"No choice. He's in the way."

"But—"

"No buts. He's in the way, and he has to go."

"How?"

He smiled again, the smile of a stone-cold killer. "I'm working on it."

Savannah still hadn't figured out what she was going to say to Niall when she heard his forceful rap on her door. She looked through the peephole just to be on the safe side and confirmed that yes, her tall warrior was standing there, one arm propped against the doorway, his entire body radiating impatience.

She fumbled with the bolt and threw the door open, then stared in puzzlement at his empty hands. "Where's my hot chocolate?"

She couldn't have hit on a better opening line to break the ice if she'd tried, because he picked her up—just put his hands on her waist and lifted her right out of the doorway and into the room, letting the door swing shut behind them. He set her down, bolted the door, then turned back to her.

"Let's get one thing straight." His voice was all dominant male. "We have no future. None."

"Okay." He wasn't telling her anything she didn't already

know deep down, although it still gave her a pang to hear him put it into words.

"But that doesn't mean I don't love you."

"What?" She stared blankly, unable to wrap her head around it at first.

"You heard me. I love you. You love me. But this tour is all we have."

"What?" she repeated, because she still couldn't grasp what he was saying. He loved her? Not just cared, but loved? As in...*loved*?

The growl that emanated from his throat sent tingles down her spine—the good kind—and she opened her mouth to say something. What, she wasn't quite sure, but maybe... *God, yes, I do love you.*

Only he didn't give her a chance. His mouth closed over hers, swallowing her words as their tongues tangled. He lifted her up again almost effortlessly, and she wrapped her thighs around his hips. He was already aroused, and she whimpered with need that flared out of nowhere.

He released her lips momentarily, but only to give them both a chance to breathe, because his mouth descended again in short order. *Ravaged* was the only word to describe it—but in the very best way. And she did the same to him. She clung to his shoulders and rocked against his hardness, kissing him as if her life depended on it—*which it does*, she thought in that fraction of a moment when she could think at all.

They fell onto the bed, still locked in each other's embrace, and Savannah surfaced just long enough to realize the frantic hands tearing at his clothes belonged to her. Just as he was stripping off her jeans, her sweater, her panties and bra. He left her just long enough to retrieve a condom and roll it on, then tested her readiness with two fingers that drove her insane.

"Please," she panted, aware she would have said anything, done anything, if he would just—

She arched to take him deeper when he slid inside, moaning at the incredible sensation that never failed to surprise her, no matter how many times he—

Pleasure rocketed through her as her body tightened involuntarily. Again. And again. Throbbing around him as he continued his steady pace of *shallow, shallow, shallow, deep.*

He gave her no respite. "Yes," he whispered against her ear when the second orgasm whipped through her, something she couldn't possibly hide because she sobbed and clung to him, but he never stopped. She was mindless now, every nerve ending clamoring for more. More of everything. More of Niall. Knowing he loved her was the *more* she needed, an aphrodisiac she'd never imagined.

But finally even Niall's willpower cracked, and the intensity of his thrusts told her he was close. "Yes," she gasped as her third orgasm overtook her. "Yes."

He arched deep one last time, an inarticulate cry on his lips as he came with her.

Niall's arms were trembling and his lungs rasped for breath as he collapsed onto Savannah, totally drained of everything, including any strength whatsoever. Then he quickly shifted to the side, taking his weight off her so she could breathe, too.

Still embedded within her, he caught her chin and turned her face to his. "I didn't want to wear a condom this time either," he said, his voice husky with meaning. Pressing himself deep one more time for emphasis.

She blinked. "You didn't?"

He shook his head. "Not this time. Not any time with you." He saw the dawning wonder in her eyes, but quickly nipped it in the bud by adding, "Just because that's what I want, doesn't mean I can ever let it happen. I can't."

"Why can't you?" Her voice was small.

"I told you. We have no future."

"Oh. Right." He thought that was the end of it, but he should have known better. "Why is that again?"

Chapter 17

Niall groaned Savannah's name, his arms tightening around her as he ruthlessly quashed his hopeless dream. "Children just aren't possible for me." The shocked expression on her face told him she'd misunderstood, and he quickly amended, "They're *possible*, or I wouldn't need a condom. But raising a child is a huge commitment, not just in terms of time and money, but in emotional support, as well. The job I do…it's not compatible with a family."

He wondered what she was thinking when she gazed up at him with those sorrowful gray eyes, but all she said was, "I understand."

"Good." *Not good,* part of him insisted, but he ignored that little voice. He gently withdrew, then climbed out of bed to discard the condom.

He stepped into the shower for a minute, and once again found a towel waiting for him in Savannah's hand when he came out. They exchanged places, and though he told himself not to, he couldn't help it. He watched, the breath catching in his throat when her hand went between her legs with the bar of soap.

He cursed himself for a pervert and stomped into the

other room, savagely tugging his clothes on as fast as Savannah had taken them off. Then just stood there in the middle of the room, his imagination working overtime as the water in the shower continued to run.

Finally he couldn't take it anymore and headed for the door. "I'm going to get your hot chocolate," he called. "Bolt the door after me."

He ran into the Thompsons at the coffee bar. "Hi, Niall," Mary Beth said in that breathless way she spoke, as she filled a cup from the urn marked Decaf. "Isn't it nice we have this right here on our deck and don't have to go up or down for a late-night coffee run?"

"Your stateroom is on this deck?" he asked slowly. With all their comings and goings, he and Savannah hadn't run into the Thompsons in the corridor. And his boss hadn't yet sent him the passenger manifest with the stateroom assignments, so he hadn't known.

"Oh my yes." She handed the cup of coffee to her husband. "Rooms on this deck are more expensive, but Herb insisted, isn't that right, honey?" She didn't wait for a response. "Nothing but the best for us, just like you and Savannah."

She served herself a cup of coffee from the urn marked Regular. "And before you warn me, let me say I can drink caffeine any time of the day or night, and it never bothers me at all. Never interferes with my sleep. Not Herb, though. He can't drink anything with caffeine after three in the afternoon, or else he's awake all night, poor baby."

Niall glanced at the poor baby, whose expression conveyed embarrassment about having his personal limitations exposed to a relative stranger, but long-suffering. Niall smiled in commiseration. Mary Beth was still talking.

"I wish they'd planned some kind of entertainment for this evening," she complained. "Who wants to watch a four-hour lock transition? Fifteen minutes was enough for Herb and me, wasn't that right, honey? We noticed you and Savannah didn't stay long, either. Guess you had something better to do." She didn't waggle her eyebrows, but he knew exactly what she meant.

"Of course in the old days, people didn't go on cruises together unless they were married," she confided, as if she were eighty instead of fiftysomething. "But nowadays..." She sipped at her coffee. "I was just saying to Herb the other day, we have to hand it to you and Savannah, booking separate rooms at the hotels and on this cruise. Maintaining the conventions even though it's obvious to everyone the two of you are a couple."

Niall almost rolled his eyes, but then he focused on what she'd just said. Mary Beth and Herb knew he and Savannah had separate rooms. And their stateroom was on Deck Five. Which meant...

He surreptitiously gave Herb the once-over. *Could he have been the man on Savannah's balcony?* he wondered. Possible. Herb was in decent shape and looked strong enough. And the henpecked husband could be an act. Mary Beth and Herb were such stereotypes it was almost as if they wanted him to think they couldn't possibly be the bad guys.

"More money, of course," Mary Beth continued. "A lot more. But this way no one's sensibilities are ruffled." She sipped at her coffee again. "So..." she said archly. "Are we going to be celebrating some happy news on this cruise? I was just saying to Herb the other day that the way you look at Savannah reminds me of the way he looked at me when we got engaged." She giggled. "So incredibly romantic. Is there an engagement in the near future?"

A sudden urge to throttle Mary Beth before she could put that question to Savannah possessed him, and he quickly turned to empty a packet of hot chocolate mix in a cup, then fill it from the Hot Water urn. "We're discussing it," he said evenly. If the Thompsons were the attempted kidnappers, it wouldn't hurt for them to think he and Savannah were a couple headed for the altar, so they wouldn't suspect he was an agent who just might know more than they wanted him to know.

He stirred the powder mix until it was completely dissolved, then threw away the stirrer and popped a lid into place. "I'd better get back to Savannah," he told Mary Beth with a smile. "She's waiting for her hot chocolate."

"Isn't that sweet, Herb?" Mary Beth gushed to her husband. "So chivalrous, just like you. Bye for now," she said, looking at Niall again. "Are you and Savannah taking the tour of the Three Gorges Dam? The buses depart right after breakfast, you know. Maybe we'll be on the same bus—wouldn't that be fun?"

Fun like a dose of poison ivy, he thought, but merely smiled again and said, "Anything's possible. Good night."

"Remind me to tell you something," Niall said when she opened the door at his knock. "But drink your hot chocolate first."

"Thanks." She took the cup from him and dutifully drank it while he powered up his laptop and checked his email, unwilling to inform him that she only drank hot chocolate when she was upset, and she wasn't upset anymore. Okay, yes, he'd told her they didn't have a future. And he'd told her children weren't on his To Do list. But…

He'd admitted he loved her. How incredibly uplifting, even if nothing ever came of it. He'd also confessed he didn't want to wear a condom with her…and he'd never *not* worn one before. Which meant two things, both of them glorious. First, he didn't want there to be a barrier between them of *any* kind, physical or emotional. Second, if he could allow himself to have children, he wanted to have them with her.

So no, she wasn't upset any longer. She had an uphill battle ahead of her, knocking down those walls he'd constructed around himself, getting him to confide in her the secrets he thought put him beyond forgiveness.

But she'd fought uphill battles all her life—her career was a perfect example. Her enochlophobia was another. As Niall had reminded her, she'd made great strides in overcoming it. No one who'd never experienced unreasoning fear could truly understand how debilitating it was. But she'd fought her fear down numerous times. She hadn't conquered it, and maybe she never would. But she'd never stop trying. Just as she'd never stop trying with Niall, now that she knew she was loved.

"So you think it's the Thompsons?" Savannah asked Niall after he'd disclosed his encounter with them. They were sitting on the small sofa in the living area, the drapes open to the night sky and the lights on the shore, but the balcony doors closed against the cold night air. She held two fingers against her lips as she tried to reconcile the shadow she'd seen cast in dark relief against the drapes with her memory of Herb Thompson.

"Not saying it is, not saying it isn't," he replied. "Just that circumstantial evidence doesn't exclude them. Could Herb have been the man you saw?"

Skeptical for no reason she could name, she compromised. "Maybe. I only got a glimpse of him, so I can't swear one way or the other." But she didn't really think so. Herb was roughly the right height, give or take an inch, and he was roughly the right weight, give or take a few pounds. But it just didn't seem *right*. Like the equation the other day, the one with the backward sign. "Let me think about it for a bit."

"While you're thinking, I'll keep checking."

She thought of something else. "None of the fingerprints have helped?" She remembered sneaking the juice glasses out of the dining room and then back in. Sneaking them back in had been much more difficult.

He shook his head. "Not exactly. None of the prints are on file. And I wasn't able to lift a print from the stairwell or your balcony or the railing on the top deck. So I can't even cross-match to the fingerprints I do have."

"That tells us something anyway, that none of the fingerprints are on file."

"Yeah. It tells us that either none of the fingerprints we've obtained belong to the kidnappers, or—"

"Or they're not known to the police or any federal agency."

He smiled in admiration. "Exactly."

"Do you buy that the kidnappers are neophytes?" As soon as she'd used the word she thought better of it. "That means—"

"I know what it means. And no, I don't think they're newbies at this. Could they be good enough or lucky enough to never have been caught before, and therefore never been fingerprinted before? Maybe. But if they're not in one of the databases, that tells us a couple of other things, too."

It only took her a minute to figure one of them out. "They've never held a job where they had to be fingerprinted, either. Like me. I had to do that for my security clearance."

"Right. But a lot more people are being fingerprinted for their jobs these days, and not just those with security clearances. Teachers, for example. It's a sad commentary on the world we live in. And yet, you wouldn't want a convicted rapist or pedophile to be hired as a teacher, would you? Of course not.

"And one other thing," he continued. "Whoever they are, they're not legal US immigrants. All legal immigrants have to be fingerprinted." He was silent for a moment. "With more and more people being added to the databases, we're drawing closer to the day when everyone will have to be fingerprinted and have their DNA on file, not just those who're arrested for a crime. Good in one way, because—"

"Because if all these fingerprints you lifted were on file, we'd know if they really are who they say they are."

"Yeah, but on the other hand, it's a frightening loss of freedom for those who haven't done anything wrong." Niall sighed heavily, and Savannah squeezed his arm in empathy.

"So what's our next step?" she asked softly.

"Spencer Davies is under observation. I can't go into the details, but before you ask, yes, they obtained a court order."

She considered asking how he knew but decided against it. He'd probably lie to her again, and she didn't want that. He already had enough on his conscience. "Yes, but what are *we* supposed to do?"

"Keep doing what we're doing. Stay vigilant. Obtain a few more fingerprints. Sorry," he told her. "We're back to that for now. And we need to review the background reports I have, see if we can spot a discrepancy."

"We? You mean you're going to let me help?"

He smiled faintly. "It's your life on the line, and you're the smartest woman I know. Smarter even than my sister. So yeah, I'd be stupid if I didn't recruit your assistance with the investigation." He hesitated. "This has to stay confidential, though. You can't talk about anything you learn."

"Don't be insulting. The US government has entrusted

me with information maybe a thousand people in the world know. I've never leaked a word."

A rueful smile touched the corners of his mouth. "I stand corrected." Then his smile faded and he was dead serious. "That's why you're a target, Savannah. Why Spencer Davies thought he could get away with kidnapping you and throwing suspicion on the Chinese government. Because of what you know, not just because you're smart enough to help him salvage his obsolete missile."

Savannah woke the next morning with the feeling she'd forgotten something but had no idea what. That happened sometimes when she was working on one of the complex algorithms that were incorporated into the software of a missile. It had happened when she'd come up with the breakthrough design that was the basis for her latest patent application. She'd struggled for endless days trying to figure out why her idea didn't work and had pretty much given it up as a worthless cause. Then—*ta-da!*—the solution had appeared in her sleep.

So she knew there was no point in trying to force herself to remember. It would come to her, she was sure.

Niall was still sleeping, so she lay there quietly, hardly daring to breathe, as the early light of dawn crept around the edges of the drapes and into the room. He'd looked so exhausted when they'd gone to bed last night, and though he'd made preliminary moves indicating he intended to make love to her again, she'd called a halt.

"The spirit is willing—" she'd murmured in a teasing fashion, reminding him they'd been burning the candle at both ends for the last few days "—but I'd kill for an uninterrupted night's sleep."

He'd laughed, but he'd acquiesced. And she could have sworn there was a trace of relief in his laugh. So instead they'd just snuggled together under the covers until they'd fallen asleep. Or rather, until he'd fallen asleep as if a light switch had been turned off. She'd watched him for a few minutes, cherishing this private time with him when all his defenses were down.

Then she'd realized something momentous. Niall trusted her. Really trusted her. He would never have let himself fall asleep before her if he didn't, would never have left himself vulnerable that way. Which was a glorious revelation where a man like Niall was concerned, and meant she was one step closer to her goal of convincing him they had a future.

She'd smiled tenderly at that thought and had eventually drifted off, still smiling.

Now she was awake before him, which meant he really had been bone-tired last night; even Niall's iron constitution had limits. She held off getting up as long as she could, but finally the call of nature couldn't be ignored. She tried to slip out from under the weight of his arm without waking him, but the moment she moved, his eyes shot open and he was instantly alert.

"Shh," she whispered. "Everything's okay, I just have to use the bathroom."

"What time is it?"

"Early." She didn't know exactly without turning to look, but she could tell from the amount of light in the room that dawn was just breaking. "Go back to sleep."

He was standing right outside the bathroom door when she opened it. One arm was propped against the doorjamb and a yawn cracked his face. He was still naked, and—she peeked—semiaroused.

"I wanted you to go back to sleep," she protested.

When he finished yawning he slid his free arm around her waist, pulled her close for a good-morning kiss, then murmured in her ear as he nuzzled her, "When I'm awake, I'm awake."

She shivered from the nuzzling and his hands, not to mention he smelled heavenly. *Testosterone?* she thought distractedly. *Pheromones?* Whatever it was, it was working. Before she could become too aroused, however, he tugged down the oversize T-shirt she wore that had inexplicably—okay, *not* inexplicably—ridden upward when his hands had made a foray north.

"Hold that thought," he told her as he kissed her one last time, stepped into the bathroom and closed the door behind him.

"Oh, like you did that when *I* asked you to," she called through the bathroom door, and was rewarded by a masculine rumble of laughter. She dressed quickly and was brushing the nighttime tangles from her hair when he emerged.

"I thought we were going to take up where we left off," he said mildly.

But when she replied, "Payback's a bitch, isn't it?" he laughed and agreed.

She continued brushing her hair, watching him dress out of the corner of her eye. She sighed a little when he covered up all his gorgeous muscles with clothes. He still looked mighty tempting, and for just a moment she toyed with the idea of—*no!* she told herself firmly, brushing so hard her scalp complained. She was not going to turn into a sex maniac just because he was a sex god.

Don't try to make up for all the orgasms you missed out on for the past twenty years in one week, she chastised herself, then started chuckling at the thought.

"What's so funny?"

"You'd never get it."

"Try me."

So she told him. Before she'd met Niall, she would have

been aghast at herself, discussing something so intimate with a man, but it seemed natural to confide in him, even something like this.

He grinned the grin that took ten years off his face and drawled as he'd done before, "Why thank you, darlin', you just made my week."

She couldn't help it; she returned his grin. "You've accounted for what I missed in my teens," she admitted. "But you have your work cut out for you now."

He had her in his arms so fast he took her breath away. "I'm up to the challenge, Savannah," he murmured, rocking an impressive bulge against her most sensitive parts. "Try me."

"I've *been* trying you."

A wicked twinkle appeared in his eyes, and his voice dropped a notch. "Try me again."

Chapter 18

They breakfasted with three new couples, one of which was the Williamses, Tammy and her husband, Martin. Savannah had brought her carry-on bag, knowing Niall would purloin the juice glasses afterward.

"Are you and Martin going on the Three Gorges Dam excursion this morning?" she asked Tammy, taking a sweet roll from the basket in the center of the table and dividing it into two, then slipping half onto Niall's plate without conscious thought.

"I think so. Not much else to do. You?"

"Of course. It's a shame in one way so many people had to be displaced and so much beauty was destroyed when it was built—I would have loved seeing the Three Gorges before the dam was constructed. But when you think about what this means in terms of flood control on the lower Yangtze River—why, one flood alone killed more than three hundred thousand people and left roughly forty million homeless! Not to mention the amount of hydroelectric power the dam has generated ever since it became fully operational…" She stopped because Tammy was looking at her blankly, as if this was all news to her. "Well, anyway, the answer is yes, we're going."

She glanced at Niall on her right, sharing an intimate smile with him. Without prompting, he said, "If we have time either before or after, we'll probably stop off at the Yellow Ox Temple for a few minutes. Another photo op for Savannah."

Everyone at the table laughed because she was already famous within their little tour group for the number of pictures she took everywhere they went.

"This might be a once in a lifetime opportunity," she protested. "I'm keeping a photo-journal of my travels."

"Good for you," said a distinguished, silver-haired man on the other side of the table. They'd been introduced, but she didn't remember his name and his name badge was on his jacket, hooked over the back of his chair. "I wish Martha and I had done that. Our kids chipped in to give us this trip for our fiftieth anniversary—first class all the way, mind you, with a Deck Five stateroom. They gave us a digital camera, too, but we haven't taken many pictures."

A nod and a rueful smile from the man's wife made Savannah volunteer, "I could send you the pictures I've taken, if you'd like. I could put them on a thumb drive for you when I get home and mail it to you."

"Would you?" the man said. "That would be… Well, that would be so generous of you." He pulled out a pen and a business card, jotting down something on the back, then handing it across the table to her. "That's my company card, with our address and phone number on the back. I'm semi-retired, but you can reach me at either phone number if you need to." He patted his wife's hand. "Just think, Martha, we *can* show the kids how incredible this trip has been." He looked up at Savannah and said fervently, "Thank you so much."

* * *

Savannah tried not to let the juice glasses clink against each other as they went back to her stateroom after breakfast to lift the fingerprints. She watched Niall work in silence, and when he was done, she offered, "I can tell you right now it's not Martha and her husband. I don't remember his name, but—"

"Anders. Martha and Anders Mortenson."

"Right. It wasn't him on my balcony. He's too tall. And besides—"

"And besides, you can't see a seventy-something man rappelling down the side of the boat, even if it was just one deck?"

"Well…yes."

He grinned at her. "Men don't fall apart at forty, you know. Or fifty. Or sixty. Or even seventy. He looks in pretty good shape for his age. I'll bet Anders and Martha still have a fairly active sex life."

"Niall!" She could feel a flush crawling up her neck and into her cheeks.

"What? You don't agree?"

"I don't go around imagining other people's sex lives."

"No? You should. Imagine Mary Beth and Herb. You think she can stop talking long enough for him to whisper sweet nothings in her ear?"

She gasped, then laughed so hard she had to bury her face in one of the pillows from the unmade bed. Her eyes were streaming and she was still having trouble controlling her mirth when she raised her head. "Oh my God, Niall, you are so *bad*!"

"Yeah," he chuckled, "but you love me anyway."

That sobered her, and she realized she'd never said the words to him. He'd said them to her, but… "I do, Niall," she whispered. "I love you with all my heart."

He went very still. "I know," he said slowly. "I know you do. I didn't want you to, because I didn't want to hurt you. That's all loving me will give you—pain."

An ache began in the region of her heart at the desolate expression on his face, and she breathed, "How can you know that?"

"Trust me, I know."

"I won't accept that."

"You have no choice."

If Savannah had been a different kind of woman, she would have given up when Niall said, *You have no choice.* But people had been saying the same thing or something similar to her all her life, from her earliest teachers to her high school guidance counselor to her doctoral advisor. Even when she'd gotten out into the real world, even in a company that actively encouraged women in the STEM fields—Science, Technology, Engineering and Math— she'd still encountered far too many people who'd told her, *You can't do that.*

She'd proven them wrong, all the way down the line.

She hadn't risen to the top of her profession by being faint of heart. *If you can fight in one arena, you can fight in another*, she reminded herself fiercely as the bus she and Niall were riding on took the hill turn that led to the Three Gorges Dam's visitors' center.

A tiny voice of doubt raised its ugly head. *Yes, but in the past you always had your parents in your corner, believing in you. Your mom, leading by example. Proving that a woman could accomplish anything she wanted if she was willing to fight for it. And your dad, always letting you cry on his shoulder and then challenging you to prove the naysayers wrong. Encouraging you to push yourself further. To excel.*

Her parents were gone. They would never again tell her to stand tall, to put one foot in front of the other and keep going, even if it was only an inch at a time.

But they were still with her in spirit.

That realization silenced the voice of doubt. She didn't need the cheers from the sidelines; her cheerleaders were embedded in her heart, her soul. Her memories. She could do this. She and Niall had something worth fighting for, and she wasn't giving up. Ever.

Niall was propped against the wall in the visitors' center, waiting for Savannah to exit the ladies' room, keeping a watchful eye on the crowd milling around the diorama of the dam that took up much of the space.

He spotted Tammy and Martin, who'd been on the bus with Savannah and him, heading out the door, and mentally catalogued that fact as automatically as breathing. At the checkout stood Mary Beth and Herb, buying several of the overpriced souvenirs the visitors' center offered the gullible foreigners, and an expression his mother often quoted came to mind: *A fool and his money are soon parted.* He stifled a chuckle, thinking, *Truer words were never spoken.*

He was also thanking his lucky stars Mary Beth and Herb had *not* been on their bus here. Thinking of the Thompsons made him think of Savannah, however, which led right into the memory of her face this morning when he'd told her he knew she loved him...but she had to accept they had no future. She hadn't argued with him, but her very calmness told him she was angry. Angry and determined. He hadn't been exactly sure what that determination meant, but he'd had a pretty good idea.

She'd seemed normal on the bus here, though. Well, normal for a woman forced to process a truth she didn't want to accept. And her sudden animation as they approached the gates of the dam, the way she whipped her camera out to take pictures, made him hope she'd finally come to terms with the absolute finality of their relationship.

Problem was, *he* was the one having difficulty accepting it.

"Michael's Family, please assemble outside by my sign," came the voice of their tour guide through Niall's earpiece. "We are leaving in five minutes. Five minutes, Michael's Family. Finish your purchases, please, and assemble outside by my sign."

He glanced at his watch. "Come on, Savannah," he muttered. "Why do women take so long in the bathroom?"

He raised his eyes just in time to see the flash of a knife in the hands of a total stranger aimed straight at his abdomen. He reacted without thinking, parrying the thrust with such force he felt and heard a bone crack. He didn't need to hear the man's sudden howl of pain to know he'd broken something—wrist, forearm, he wasn't sure. All he knew was that the knife fell from the man's suddenly useless hand before he bolted through the crowd, though not before Niall memorized the stranger's face.

He gave chase. "Stop that man!" he yelled in English, then repeated it in Mandarin. But the crowd merely responded by gawking, then scattering as the man forced his way through them. With his good hand, the assailant shoved an elderly Chinese woman toward Niall, who was barely able to catch her before she hit the ground. The man burst through the door and was gone. By the time Niall set the woman on her feet and dashed after him, it was too late. The would-be assassin had disappeared.

Savannah heard the announcement through her earpiece and finished washing her hands. She'd just decided her hair didn't need brushing when the muffled sound of some kind of a commotion reached her. She hurried outside expecting to find Niall waiting for her, but he wasn't there. She craned her neck to look over the top of the unusually animated crowd, but she still couldn't spot him.

She'd just screwed up her courage to make her way alone through the chattering sea of humanity when the door opened and Niall walked in, heading right for her. "Oh thank God," she whispered fervently. Could she have done it on her own? Yes. But now she didn't have to.

Niall bent down just before he reached her, and used his hankie to pick something up off the ground. When he stood, she saw it was a wicked-looking knife with what appeared to be a six-inch blade.

"What...?"

His face was grim. "Someone definitely wants me out of the way. And this time they *did* have murder in mind."

The man moved away from the tour group to take the call he'd been eagerly awaiting, unable to keep the anticipation out of his voice. "Yes?"

"Unsuccessful."

Anger and disappointment made his voice harsh. "What the hell happened? No," he said quickly. "Not over the phone. Meet me at the..." He glanced around, looking for the largest concentration of visitors. "The fountain. We'll find somewhere private after that."

"I cannot. I am on the way to the hospital."

"What? Why? No," he repeated, "don't tell me over the phone. Too dangerous. Send me an encrypted text the way I showed you."

There was a hesitation at the other end. Then a reluctant, "That might be a problem. I cannot use my right hand."

He cursed under his breath and considered the risk of having their conversation electronically intercepted against his need to know what had gone wrong. "Then tell me," he barked.

"He saw me. I do not think I betrayed my intentions until the moment of attack, but somehow he was faster. He broke my arm. I barely managed to escape."

"Did he see your face?"

"I am sure he did. I will lay low for a while, and not just because of my broken arm."

There weren't enough curse words in the English language to encompass a monumental fubar like this, the man thought. But all he said was, "You do that."

He disconnected, then sought out his supposed wife, who was pretending to take pictures of one of the locks below. "Unsuccessful."

She looked at him, and for a fraction of a second he thought he saw relief in her eyes. "What happened?"

He told her in clipped tones. Then, because he was furious at the failed attempt and still angry over the other night, he said, "I'm beginning to think you're a jinx."

Niall made a police report, of course. *Not that it'll do much good,* he thought but didn't say as he recited the details of the assault to his third set of...well, not interrogators, exactly, but their questions certainly came across like an interrogation. He couldn't tell them his near-certainty of the real reason behind the attack. That was out unless he wanted to bring unwanted attention on both Savannah and himself. Unless he wanted them to be detained indefinitely.

So he didn't volunteer anything other than the facts as they'd occurred and a thorough description of the perpetrator, then agreed with the policemen when they theorized it was merely an attempted robbery of a wealthy American.

Not exactly wealthy, he thought with a flash of amusement he didn't allow to show on his face. He wasn't hurting.

He was the best there was at what he did, and his government recognized and rewarded it with a decent salary, which he rarely had time to spend. He could have made a hell of a lot more money in the private sector, he mused, but that wasn't who he was.

And he'd made a few good investments over the years. *Comfortable* was a better word to describe his financial position, he figured. He could afford his little luxuries without worrying about breaking the bank, but he wouldn't call himself wealthy.

The local police finally let Niall go, with profuse apologies for the inconvenience and an offer to take him back to the Three Gorges Dam. An offer he declined after a quick check of his watch. "I'm afraid there isn't time," he told the policemen. "Our riverboat is supposed to depart at noon."

"We could take you and your companion to the dock," one of the officers said in his precise English. "It is the least we can do by way of apology for this unfortunate incident. We hope this will not be a blight on your visit, and that you will not hold it against all of China for one man's greed."

"I'll take you up on the ride," he replied, "but don't worry. The same thing could have happened in any major city in the US. I don't blame China." *Especially since if I'm right, this has nothing to do with China at all*, he thought privately.

The three men walked out of the interrogation room and found Savannah waiting for Niall in the front hall. She'd insisted on accompanying him to the police station even before he could tell her she had to; he couldn't risk her being left unguarded in his absence. But he was touched her concern for him overrode her desire to visit the dam, one of the highlights of this tour.

He hadn't been worried about her being on her own, either, while he was being questioned. He couldn't imagine any place safer from kidnapping than under the watchful eye of the front desk sergeant in a Chinese police station.

"Are you okay?" she asked anxiously.

Conscious of the eyes all around them, he kissed her cheek, whispering in her ear at the same time, "Follow my lead." Then he stepped back and said, "Not a scratch, honey, I already told you. Sorry you had to miss out on seeing the dam. I'll make it up to you."

"No big deal," she assured him. "I'm just glad you're okay."

The trip back to the riverboat got them there ahead of the buses. With plenty of time before departure, they strolled through the bazaar between the boat dock and the bus lot, with its aggressive shopkeepers touting things they could have bought anywhere, but buying nothing. Although, Niall noted with an internal smile, Savannah was a sucker for the children tugging at her sleeve trying to sell her useless items. He had a sneaking suspicion she would have purchased something from each one if he hadn't been with her.

The riverboat was docked at the foot of the Yellow Ox Temple, so they stopped to peer inside and for Savannah to take pictures. "I'm sorry about the Three Gorges Dam," he told her again as he leaned against a stone pillar in the shape of a lion at her command.

"You really think I care about that?" she asked incredulously. She hugged him quickly, then let go and stepped back to take the picture. "You could have been killed."

If not killed, seriously wounded at least, which would leave you unprotected, he told her in his mind. The danger to himself he didn't care about. It was par for the course. The danger to Savannah? *Unacceptable,* he thought, his mouth grim.

"Smile, please."

He complied because it was the least he could do after depriving her of visiting the Three Gorges Dam that morning. And besides, he'd move heaven and earth to give her anything her heart desired.

He, Alec and Shane had always teased Liam unmercifully about being a knight in shining armor when they were younger. Not that he and his other brothers weren't honorable. They were. But they'd never considered themselves particularly chivalrous, unlike their baby brother.

You owe Liam an apology, he told himself now, gazing at the woman who'd become his world in just over a week. Because for the first time in his life he understood the true nature of chivalry. And where Savannah was concerned, it looked a lot like…him.

Chapter 19

They holed up in Savannah's stateroom after lunch to read the background reports on the people from their tour group. Niall put the files on a thumb drive to transfer to Savannah's computer so they could both read them at the same time.

They took their laptops out onto the balcony. The afternoon sun shone warmly and it was just too nice a day to stay indoors. One or the other of them would look up from time to time, drink in the beauty of Xiling Gorge, then dive right back into their work.

Finally Savannah straightened with a regretful sigh and closed her laptop.

"Nothing?" he asked, and she shook her head. "Same here."

"I keep getting the feeling I'm overlooking something." Then she confided her thoughts immediately upon waking this morning while he'd still been asleep. "It's frustrating, because I *know* it's there. I just can't put my finger on it."

"I know the feeling." He logged off his laptop and shut it down, then stood and held out a hand. "Want me to take that in for you?"

"Sure. Hang on a sec." She turned her computer off,

closed it and handed it to him. "Now what do we do?" she called after him.

"I know what I want to do." He reappeared in the doorway, raising and lowering his eyebrows suggestively, just in case she didn't get the message.

"What, again?" she teased.

"Gotta work off some of that backlog." And he winked.

She pealed with laughter, loving this playfulness between them. "Oh well, if you insist." She stood, feigning reluctance, then squealed when Niall pounced and hefted her over his shoulder caveman style. "What are you— You can't— Put me down!"

"Your wish is my command, fair maiden," he said, dropping her on the bed and coming right down on top of her, pinning her beneath him. She squirmed, but instead of dislodging him, only succeeded in fueling her own arousal... and his.

But as he stared down at her for long moments, the playfulness drained away. And in its place was the desolate expression from this morning. The one that meant he was already saying goodbye to her.

It hurt so much she could scarcely get the words out. "Why do you look at me that way?"

"No one will ever love you the way I do, Savannah. No one."

"I know." And she did. She just didn't understand why his loving her wasn't a good thing.

"Just remember that when—" He clenched his jaw, and she knew it was to hold back the words that would explain.

Her throat ached, and she cradled his face between her hands. "Will you ever tell me why?"

"If I had a choice, I would never tell you," he admitted in a voice so low she could barely hear him, his internal struggle reflected in his expression. "If I had a choice, I would keep you and marry you and give you all the babies your heart desires."

"Niall…"

He overrode her. "But I don't have a choice." His voice was hard. Implacable. "So yes, when this trip is over…when you're safely home… I'll tell you."

A sudden spurt of anger made her say evenly, "Do I get a choice in all of this?"

"What do you mean?"

"If my choice is between having you in my life and knowing your terrible secret, I choose you. I don't want to know. Ever. I mean it, Niall."

He bowed his head, and for a moment she thought she'd won. Then he raised his head and looked her full in the face, the regret in his eyes telling her she hadn't. "You're an angel for making me that offer, Savannah. But if I accepted, the secret would always be there between us. Even if you could live with not knowing, I couldn't live with not telling you. My conscience would tear me apart. And that would tear *us* apart. I know it."

So much pain. She couldn't bear seeing him in so much pain. "Why can't you tell me now? Oh. Right," she corrected herself before he could say it. "You have reasons. Valid-in-your-mind reasons why you can't tell me why you can't tell me now."

Her convoluted sentence made him smile reluctantly. "Yeah. I can't tell you why I can't tell you."

Okay then, she thought. But she still wasn't giving up. Niall was just like one of her algorithms. Complex. Layered. An equation within an equation. Sometimes they were straightforward, but not usually. Lots of times you had to take a step back and look at things from a different perspective. Approach the solution from a different angle.

She drew a calming breath, then did just that. "We have no future, that's what you said."

"Right."

"You also said you love me."

He didn't answer at first. Then, "I do."

"But you also said, and I quote, '…this tour is all we have.' Did you mean it?"

This time the wait for his response was longer, and she held her breath until his deep voice replied, "From the bottom of my heart."

"Then would you please make love to me?" She forced a teasing note into her voice. "There's all that backlog, remember?"

Niall made love to her as if it were the last time, though Savannah hoped and prayed it was not. He touched her everywhere with a gentleness that made her heart weep, but she kept her tears to herself and reveled in what this said about him. When he finally rolled on a condom and slipped inside, she was so ready for him she came almost immediately— not the earth-shattering explosion she'd come to expect, but rather like the undulations of waves that went on endlessly.

"Oh, Niall…"

She used every tool in her arsenal to show him how much she loved him. From sighs and moans to whispered words of love and longing. Telling him how he made her feel so cherished. Adored. How he felt deep inside her. Laying her heart bare.

He held on as long as he could, but then she touched him where they were joined and he lost control, driving into her with a desperation born of need. And when she arched and cried his name, clinging to him as release washed over her again, he let himself sink into her one last time as if he could claim her as his by holding tight and never letting go. Then he rolled them over and kissed away the tears that followed.

"No tears," he soothed. "Remember?"

"Can't help it. Oh, Niall, it was so beautiful I never wanted it to end."

Balm for his wounded soul. He'd wanted to make it perfect for her. And he had. But she'd made it perfect for him at the same time. Had any woman ever opened her heart to him this way? He couldn't remember.

"It was…" He cleared his throat. "Pretty special for me, too."

"What are you going to do?" the woman asked the man. "There's only the rest of today and a full day tomorrow. Then we dock at Wuhan the following morning. After that we fly to Shanghai."

"I know the schedule," he snapped. "You don't have to remind me."

"You don't have to bite my nose off. I was just wondering—"

"We're down to one local since the other one got his arm broken," he said, ruthlessly cutting her off. "Which means it won't be so easy to smuggle her out of the country. We might have to wait until we return stateside."

"But didn't Spencer say it had to be done in China? To throw suspicion on the government here?"

"I know what Spencer said. But he also told us she would be traveling alone, nothing about this Johnson character." He brooded for a moment. "I don't know who he is or what he does for a living, but he's good. Too damn good. Makes me wonder."

"About what?"

"He spotted that trip wire. And he broke Ming Li's arm in the knife attack, without receiving so much as a scratch," he said, putting the man's surname last as most English-speaking people did. "That tells me something."

"Tells you what?"

He ignored the question. "And he never lets her go anywhere alone. Almost as if he suspects something. Makes me think maybe he's a cop or a Fed."

"They're sleeping together," she protested. "Would he do that if he was a cop or a Fed?"

"They're sharing a stateroom. Doesn't mean they're sleeping together any more than we are. Double beds in that room, too." He pondered their options. "If Chao Li can find someone to replace his brother," he said eventually, "we still might be able to..." He thought some more, then reached a decision. "There's one more shore excursion before we reach Wuhan, the trip to the school in Jingzhou tomorrow. It's nothing special, so she might not be planning to go. You'll have to make sure she does."

"How am I supposed to do that?"

"You're a woman, aren't you? Don't most women go gaga over anything to do with brats? There's supposed to be some kind of show at that elementary school, with the kids singing and dancing. Play up that angle. Do whatever you have to do, but make sure she's on that bus!"

"There's an employee talent show in the lounge this evening," Savannah reminded Niall as they dressed for dinner. "Want to be my date?"

"Very funny," he replied. "You go, I go. You go nowhere without me, even with a bunch of witnesses around you. It's as simple as that."

"I'm not talking about that. I asked if you wanted to be my date for the evening."

He froze. "We're way past dating," he said finally.

She rolled her eyes at him. "Could you just answer yes or no?"

"What's different about being your date as opposed to the man keeping you safe?"

She tilted her head to observe him. "For one thing, if you were my date I could think of you as arm candy."

"Arm—don't you have that backward? Men have arm candy, not women."

"Ahhh, I knew you were a sexist pig."

"Sexist—" She let her eyes twinkle at him, and he laughed abruptly. "Okay, I'll admit I'm not as...enlightened...as I could be. Blame the way I was raised. But I'm not sexist. At least I don't think I am. I *have* learned a thing or two from the women in my life."

Her smile faltered. "The women in your life?"

He tucked his Henley into his jeans and zipped up. "My sister. My three sisters-in-law. And my mom, too, in some ways." Then he seemed to get what she'd thought he meant, and he said gently, "You're the only woman in my life the way you mean, Savannah." He walked toward her, his expression morphing from serious to teasing. "So if you want me to be your arm candy, just say the word."

Savannah and Niall arrived in the lounge early enough to get prime front row seats for the talent show. She waved at Anders and Martha Mortenson, sitting in the more comfortable lounge chairs on the side. "Should we move, you think?" she asked Niall doubtfully, resettling herself on the straight-backed chair she'd chosen and realizing why the Mortensons had picked the spot they had.

He shook his head. "It's a trade-off. Better view here, more comfortable there."

"Okay, as long as you're good with it."

She was kicking herself two minutes later, however,

when Mary Beth plumped herself down in the chair next to her. "Well, hi there," the other woman said brightly. "I thought I recognized the back of your head sitting all the way up here."

Savannah pinned a smile on her face. "Oh, hi, Mary Beth. Where's Herb?"

"He's getting us a drink at the bar." She set her purse down on the seat next to her to save it for her husband.

Niall started to rise, saying, "I should have asked you. Did you want something?"

But Savannah tugged on his sleeve, mouthing, "You traitor! Don't you dare desert me with Mary Beth!"

He chuckled, but he sat back down.

Mary Beth babbled on and on. Even when her husband joined her with their drinks, she barely paused to take a sip before she was off and running again on every topic under the sun. The Three Gorges Dam today. The talent show on her last cruise. The shore excursion to the elementary school tomorrow. "Some people at dinner said they're not going, but I wouldn't miss it. I hear in addition to the show the children will put on for us, you actually get to visit some of the classrooms and sit with the children and ask questions. Are you and Niall going?"

"I think so." She hadn't discussed it with Niall, but if she wanted to go he would go, too. He wouldn't even argue about it. He would just…go. That thought filled her with warmth, and she clasped his hand, smiling wordlessly when he looked her way.

The room was filling up quickly, but Savannah noticed no one had taken seats on the other side of the Thompsons. *Gee, I wonder why*, she thought facetiously. If she'd seen Mary Beth in this row, she would have avoided it, too.

Then suddenly a couple took those seats, and she recognized Tammy and Martin. Her gaze met Tammy's, and she read sympathy in the other woman's eyes that she was sitting next to Mary Beth.

When the houselights went down and the spotlights came on, Savannah discovered the one thing that would shut Mary Beth up—a glittering extravaganza. She leaned over to whisper in Niall's ear, "Oh thank God," and was rewarded with his strangled laughter.

Two hours had never passed so swiftly, especially since she was spared Mary Beth's running commentary, which would have spoiled the talent show for her. At the end when all the performers returned to take a bow to a standing ovation, the audience was invited to come forward for pictures with the performers. Savannah would have gone—she'd taken numerous photos during the show and would have liked a few close-ups—but Mary Beth surged forward, camera in hand, and Niall whispered, "Time to get while the getting's good."

She choked on a sudden laugh but dutifully edged through the crowd with Niall's arm around her shoulders. They found themselves outside the lounge finally, Tammy and Martin right behind them, and the cessation of noise was noticeable. "Cup of hot chocolate?" Niall asked, indicating the coffee bar just a few feet away.

Savannah shook her head. "I wouldn't mind a cup of hot tea, though. How about you? Coffee? Tea?"

"I'm good."

"Tammy? Martin?"

Tammy said, "I could go for a cup of herbal tea. They have the best tea here, don't you think?"

The two women chatted as they prepared their beverages, while the two men stood a little apart not saying much, waiting for the women.

"What are you doing tomorrow?" Tammy asked casually.

"There's that shore excursion to the elementary school," Savannah replied. "Mary Beth says it's actually better than what's in the itinerary. Are you and Martin going?"

"Oh yes. My sister's a teacher, didn't I tell you? She was particularly interested when I mentioned it to her. So I'll go and take some pictures for her. How about you?"

Savannah grimaced. "Only if I can be on a different bus than Mary Beth." When Tammy laughed softly in understanding, she added, "Oh, I know that sounds terrible, but she almost never stops talking! I get a headache just thinking about it."

"Me, too," Tammy commiserated. "We wouldn't have taken those seats tonight, but there really weren't any others except way in the back, so…" She chuckled. "If you really want to visit the school, don't let Mary Beth stop you. Tell you what. Go down early and we will, too. We can take seats right across from each other. How does that sound?"

"Sounds like a plan." She fit a lid into place over her tea. "Well, if we're going down early, we'd better call it a night. See you in the morning." She caught Niall's eye and the two of them headed down the hall toward her stateroom, Tammy and Martin a few paces behind.

It wasn't until they were in her stateroom with the door bolted behind them that Niall said, "That's interesting."

Savannah put her tea down on the nightstand and turned to look at him. "What's interesting?"

"The Williamses have a stateroom on this deck, too."

Chapter 20

The suddenly stricken expression that came over Savannah's face made Niall sorry he'd mentioned it in one way, but in another... *She's really too trusting*, he thought. *The Thompsons. The Mortensons. The Williamses. And me.*

"You really think it's them?"

He shook his head. "No more than anyone else on this deck. But they just moved to the high probability list, along with the Thompsons and the Mortensons."

"They seem so...nice. So...so ordinary."

So do I, he could have said, but didn't. Someday he'd make a clean breast of it to Savannah, but not today. "That's how the confidence game works," he told her, a harsh edge to his voice. "Very often it's the people you'd least suspect. Take you, for instance."

"Me?"

"You look sweet and innocent, good and kind. All the things you are. But someone who was trained to suspect that when something looks too good to be true it probably is, someone who didn't know you, could be misled into thinking you were something other than what you are." *The way I was misled...before I met you.*

She didn't answer, and he wondered what she was thinking. He didn't have long to wait to find out. "You're talking about you," she said softly. "You thought I was too good to be true."

Well, hell. "The thought had crossed my mind. But not for long."

Her voice softened even more, and an expression he couldn't read entered her eyes. "So you've been trained to be suspicious...of everyone."

There was no point denying it. "Pretty much."

"That has to make for a very difficult life. Not being able to trust anyone."

"I trust a few people. My family for sure. Those I work with, for the most part." He shrugged. "Other than that... yeah, it's rough, but that's the job I chose. The life I lead. I have no regrets." *No regrets about the trust thing*, his conscience corrected. *But hell yes, you have regrets. About Savannah. About accepting the assignment in the first place. About making her your target.*

It only took him a couple of seconds to realize his conscience was wrong. If he'd never taken the assignment to begin with, if he'd never come to China, never made Savannah the target of his investigation, where would she be now? Kidnapped? Held prisoner by Spencer Davies somewhere, until she came up with the solution to his obsolete missile?

And ultimately...murdered. That was the bottom line. Without his intervention, Savannah probably would never have known what Spencer Davies had planned for her until it was too late. So in a way, accepting the original assignment had turned out to be a good thing after all.

Don't get carried away feeling all noble, Jones, his conscience reminded him. *You think Savannah would buy that logic? Yeah, serendipity is wonderful, but it only goes so far.*

All of a sudden he realized he'd allowed the internal argument between himself and his conscience to block out what Savannah was saying, and he was forced to ask, "Can you repeat that?"

"I said I'm glad I don't have your job. Yes, my job entails— entailed," she corrected swiftly, "a certain level of secrecy. But I only had to worry if someone tried to find out exactly what I did, about the missiles I worked on. Stuff like that. I never had to be suspicious of everyone over *everything*." She leaned into him suddenly, placing her hands against his chest so she could reach up and kiss his cheek. "I'm so sorry," she whispered. "Sorry you have to live this way."

"Don't feel sorry for me. I chose this life, remember?"

"Yes, but did you know it would be like this going in?"

The question made him smile. "Not exactly." He slid his arms around her waist and pulled her closer to deflect any more questions on this subject. Once he had her body exactly where he wanted—plastered against his—he deliberately injected humor into his voice. "We're a fine pair."

"What do you mean?"

His lips quirked. "I'm too suspicious, and you're too trusting."

That enigmatic expression returned to her face. "Maybe I am," she admitted. "I wouldn't exactly call myself a Pollyanna, but I do tend to look for the good in people." She took a quick breath, then blew him away when she added, "Like you, Niall...but I don't have to look hard. The goodness in you shines like a beacon."

"I'm not—" he started to protest, but she cut him off by the simple expedient of placing a finger over his lips.

"Oh, I know you're not perfect. And you probably wouldn't be an easy man to live with—a woman would have to make all kinds of concessions. But I also know you're a good man at heart."

Which left him with nothing to say. But apparently she

considered that conversation closed and wasn't expecting him to say anything at all, because she began running her hands over his chest and down, tugging his Henley from his jeans as if she had only one thing on her mind...and it wasn't talking anymore.

He laughed softly when she reached for his belt buckle as if she had every right in the world. *Which she does*, he acknowledged. He'd given her that right...until the end of this trip. He just hadn't expected this level of self-confidence from her in this arena so quickly, but he loved it.

She unzipped his jeans and slid her hand inside to free him before asking, "What's so funny?"

"You. Me. Us. *This*," he groaned when her hand stroked over him with assurance. "You would never have done this a week ago. But now..."

Her slow, knowing smile killed him. "You said I'd be good at it," she murmured. "I'm just proving you right."

The sun was shining but the air was decidedly cold when Savannah opened the door onto the balcony the next morning, shortly after the riverboat docked. "Brrr," she said, shivering, and quickly closed the door.

She turned just in time to watch Niall dress with an economy of motion that always amazed her, tugging on jeans and another Henley, this one in navy. He seemed to have an inexhaustible supply—*thank goodness!*—a notion that made her smile to herself. There was something so basically masculine about a Henley. Especially the way Niall filled one out.

"You have anything warmer than that light jacket?" he asked, sitting on the bed to put on his socks and shoes.

She shook her head. "Not really. I tried not to pack too much, because seasoned travelers recommend packing light. You should know. But I can do layers. A sweater, then the padded vest I bought in Beijing the very first day and my jacket over top." As she said this, she pulled a sweater out of the drawer and the vest and jacket from the closet.

"Gloves?"

"Of course." She patted her jacket pockets. "What about you?"

"I'll do the layer thing, too."

"Then we're all set."

"Well…after we have breakfast," he reminded her with a smile. "And one other thing."

"What's that?"

"This." *This* was a kiss that curled her toes. "Good morning," he whispered when he finally raised his head to gaze down at her. "If I didn't say thank you last night, let me rectify my omission." He kissed her again. "Thank you."

Because her parents had raised her to be polite, there was only one way to answer this. "You're very welcome." Then she couldn't help it. She smiled. "But I enjoyed it, too, so it was a win-win all the way around." When he raised a quizzical brow, she said, "It's true, Niall. I'll be honest, though, I never thought I would. But I did. So you don't have to thank me any more than I have to thank you for—" She cleared her throat, suddenly self-conscious in a way she hadn't been self-conscious a minute ago. "Well, you know."

"Well, you know?" His eyes twinkled at her. "No, I'm afraid I don't know what you're talking about," he teased. "Explain it to me, please."

She narrowed her eyes at him playfully. "You know exactly what I mean, so don't pretend."

He waggled his eyebrows in an exaggerated fashion the way she loved, then leaned to whisper a few extremely explicit words in her ear. Words that caused anticipatory tin-

gles everywhere and made the color rush to her cheeks…
but didn't offend her at all.

"Yes, please."

"Tonight," he promised. "Or this afternoon. We sail
at noon, right?" He nodded, answering his own question.
"Definitely this afternoon."

Savannah climbed aboard the bus with Niall right be-
hind her, only to find Tammy already on board…with Mary
Beth in the window seat beside her instead of her husband.
"Where's Martin?" she blurted out, then quickly added,
"And Herb? Aren't they coming?"

Tammy grimaced. "Martin bailed. Said it didn't sound
like a fun way to spend the morning, so he was just going
to walk around on shore and see what there was to see. He
promised he'd be back on the boat in plenty of time before we sail."

"Herb said he wasn't feeling well after breakfast and was
going back to bed," Mary Beth volunteered. "But I think
that was just an excuse," she added, in a way that didn't
bode well for the missing Herb.

"Oh. Well." Savannah couldn't think of anything to say,
so she took the window seat on the other side of the aisle,
hoping Mary Beth wouldn't chatter the entire way. "Sorry,"
she mouthed at Niall, apologizing for making him take the
aisle seat *and* having to accompany her on an outing that
probably wouldn't appeal to him.

He grinned wickedly and replied in an undertone, "I'll
let you make it up to me later." *The same way you did last
night*, his eyes told her. Which not only made her feel less
guilty, but also reminded her of what Niall had promised
her was on the agenda for this afternoon, and she shivered
in a delightful way.

The bus filled up quickly after that, and Savannah noticed most of the women were accompanied by their spouses, including Martha's husband, Anders Mortenson. Sotto voce, she said, "Guess it won't be so boring for you after all."

The twinkle returned to his eyes, and he winked. "I'll still let you make it up to me."

The man waited until the buses had departed, then casually walked off the boat and mounted the wide stone staircase leading to the road. He strolled in leisurely fashion until he was out of sight of the riverboat, then walked purposefully toward the intersection where he would be met, as arranged.

Chao Li turned around to greet him when he got into the back seat of the small, nondescript rental car. "This is my cousin, Li Feng," Chao said, using the Chinese custom of stating the surname first as he indicated the man behind the wheel. "He flew in late last night, as you requested. He speaks only a little English—not like my brother and me—but he was in the army until last year. And he can be trusted."

"Good." The man got right down to business. "You have everything I asked for? Does your cousin know the plan?"

"Yes and yes."

"Good," the man said again. "I trust nothing will go wrong this time around." He tried but failed to keep the condemnatory tone out of his voice. "I warned you this man Johnson is dangerous. Your brother was lucky only his arm was broken, and not his neck. I'm paying you for results, not for another failure."

Chao's face was impassive. "Understood."

The outdoor pageant was well underway on a makeshift stage next to the soccer field. A dozen fifth and sixth grade schoolgirls were performing a welcome dance dressed as butterflies—albeit butterflies with warm tights and jackets beneath their costumes—for the two hundred or so tourists who'd come from the boat for this purpose. This school was funded by the cruise company, and though Savannah knew the motive wasn't entirely altruistic, since the shore excursion to visit the school was a big draw for some of the passengers, she was still glad to see it. Anything that contributed to education for girls was a good thing in her mind.

Savannah was standing in the front, close to the stage so she could take pictures with her camera. Niall was right behind her, his arms wrapped protectively around her waist as he kept the rest of the people at bay. The crowd wasn't so dense it had engendered in her the fear that was never far away, but she wasn't complaining. She exulted in being held this way by the man she loved. Niall's protectiveness made her feel cherished in a heart-deep, I'm-here-for-you-always kind of way.

Maybe he was right when he said this trip was all they had, although she wasn't conceding that—not by a long shot! But if so, at least she'd take this memory with her… like all the other wonderful memories she'd stored up.

A dozen boys dressed as ancient warriors with swords and shields took the stage when the girls were done, and Savannah couldn't help the rueful smile that tugged at the corners of her mouth. *Gender stereotypes are alive and well*, she thought. Boys as warriors. Girls as butterflies. *Oh well. At least Niall knows I'm no butterfly. He's a warrior, no question. But so am I in my own way. I've known that about myself since the day I went to work in missile guidance. I never served in the military, the way Niall did, but I serve the military. They need me just as much as I need them to protect our country and me.*

She almost turned around and told Niall what she was

thinking, but decided this wasn't the time and place. *Soon, though*, she promised herself. She wanted him to understand the patriotic side of her, if he didn't already. Maybe it wouldn't make a difference, but it might. And she would use every weapon in her arsenal to convince him he was wrong—they *could* have a future, if they were willing to fight for it.

I'm willing, she confessed to him in her mind. *You said it yourself, Niall, I'm a fighter. I'm not giving up. Ever.*

She stayed in the shelter of Niall's arms until the show was over and the principal invited the crowd to pick a classroom in the school to visit for the next half hour. "The children are eager to talk with you," the principal said in her excellent English. "We hope you are just as eager to talk with them."

Savannah waited until most of the people around them had turned and started toward the school building—being a fighter notwithstanding, no way was she going to tempt fate by trying to force her way through the crowd—and she loved that Niall didn't try to encourage her to leave before she was ready. He understood without her saying a word.

Eventually, though, he turned her slightly in his arms so he could look down into her face and asked in a deep rumble, "You ready?"

"Mmm-hmm."

"Then lead the way."

A few stragglers were still around, taking pictures of the children, who'd quietly and obediently lined up next to the stage and were waiting for the adults to leave. Savannah couldn't resist snapping a few shots herself. The children were so adorable, their cheeks reddened by the cold but excitement on their faces. And it was apparent the principal hadn't been exaggerating—the children really were excited about their upcoming interaction with the school's visitors and could scarcely contain themselves.

Savannah and Niall made their way across the soccer field, walking hand in hand beside the two lines of children, their teachers and the last of the visitors. They were almost to the school when all of a sudden Niall said, "Son of a bitch!" in a furious undertone, then, "Down! Everybody down! Sniper!" followed by a jumble of words that made no sense to her, just as shots rang out.

Savannah found herself flat on the ground with Niall covering her as panicked screams from the children resounded all around them. Followed shortly by whimpers of pain.

Despite having the breath knocked out of her, she said frantically, "Niall, the children."

"I know." He rolled off her, then dragged her to the shelter of an open door into one of the downstairs classrooms. "Stay here." Then he was gone.

"Oh, hell no," she whispered to the man who could no longer hear her, and raced after him toward the first of the downed children, a little girl no more than five or six.

"I told you to stay where it was safe," Niall barked at her as he quickly checked the little girl's wounds with gentle hands. "Here," he said roughly, scooping the child up and bundling her into Savannah's arms. She didn't bother answering, just ran toward the school. She relinquished her precious burden into the beckoning arms of one of the teachers, then turned and raced back to Niall's side.

"Flesh wounds, thank God," he told her, placing another child in her arms. This one was heavier, and she was breathing hard by the time she arrived at the open doorway. She turned once more, only to stop short when she almost bumped into Niall, who was carrying a boy in each arm. "That's it," he told her as he handed the boys over to their teachers, and when she looked out into the schoolyard, she saw he was right. Everyone except the four wounded children had managed to scramble to safety.

Now Savannah could hear sirens in the distance and realized she'd been hearing them in a corner of her brain for some time. Then and only then did it hit her—Niall could have died. She didn't know for sure who the sniper had been aiming at, although she couldn't imagine anyone except Niall being the intended target, but when bullets were flying no one was safe.

She shuddered and her knees shook, but she managed to stay on her feet. "Are you okay?" There was blood on his jacket, and she ran her hands over him to reassure herself he hadn't been struck by a bullet, that the blood wasn't his.

"I'm fine. You?" He was doing the same thing to her, which was when she realized her jacket was stained with blood, too. Contact blood from the two children she'd cradled in her arms.

"I'm okay. It's not my blood."

Niall wrapped his arms around her and kissed her fiercely. Again and again. Then he set her away from him and demanded just as fiercely, "Why the *hell* didn't you stay where I told you to stay?"

"Excuse me?"

"You had no way of knowing that sniper was finished." His voice was harsh. Strained. "You could have been killed. Next time—"

She cut him off firmly. "Next time, assuming there is a next time, I'll probably do the same thing I did today. Yes, I risked my life. But so did you. And you did it first." He opened his mouth to argue, then closed it, words unsaid.

"Well, look at that," she said softly, smiling up at him. Letting her love and admiration show on her face. "I guess *I'm* one of the women in your life, too." And when his eyebrows pulled together in a question, she prompted his memory. "You know. Your sister? Your sisters-in-law? The ones you said have taught you a lesson or two?"

At first Niall just stared at her. Then his lips tilted up at the corners, and an expression she could have sworn was respect crept into his eyes. Followed closely by approval. Then love. And her heart swelled.

Chapter 21

Once again Niall and Savannah were transported to a police station in the back of a cruiser; only this time they were both asked to give statements. "I didn't see anything," she explained over and over in the little interrogation room she was shown into. "I just heard the shots. And when Niall— Mr. Johnson—went back to help the wounded children, I went with him."

She knew Niall had seen something. His curse that only she'd heard was a dead giveaway, but she wasn't going to say anything about it to the police. If Niall wanted to volunteer that info he was free to do so, but that was his call to make. In the meantime, all she could do was repeat… endlessly…the little she knew.

Niall had debated with himself about exactly what he would say in his statement to the police as he and Savannah had been driven to the station. If he told them he'd seen the sniper, he stood a good chance of being politely "detained" as a material witness. Which would mean the riverboat would depart without him. Nothing the tour company could do about that; he couldn't expect them to inconvenience the other five hundred passengers because of one man.

And he had no way of knowing for sure what Savannah would choose to do if he was forced to stay behind. Continue on the cruise and the rest of the tour in Wuhan and Shanghai without his protection? He didn't think so, but the alternative was no better. Stay with him here in a city where she knew no one, didn't speak the language and would be completely defenseless while he was being interrogated? Neither choice was acceptable. Not for him. Which meant he would tell the police the truth. Just not the whole truth.

"What went wrong?" the woman asked the man in the privacy of their stateroom once they were both back on board.

"You were there," he snapped. "What the hell do you think went wrong? Chao and I were all set to snatch her the minute Chao's cousin took him out, but he didn't die, damn it. He didn't even get hit! He should be dead, but he's not, because he spotted Chao's cousin with the sniper rifle. Don't ask me *how*, but he did. He's good, I told you. Too damn good to be anything other than a professional. I'm calling a halt to this right now, before we're caught red-handed."

"What will Spencer say?"

"I don't give a damn."

"But our bonus depends on—"

"No amount of money is worth it if I'm in jail. Or dead."

"But—"

"I said no!" He made a slashing motion with his hand. "We're done here. End of discussion. If Spencer still wants her, he'll have to wait until she's back stateside. For now, we just enjoy what's left of the cruise and the tour. We fly home afterward, and so will she. Then, when *he's* out of the picture..." He smiled, but it didn't reach his eyes.

It lacked only five minutes of the noon hour when Niall and Savannah were dropped off at the top of the wide, stone stairway leading down to the dock. She held his hand tightly as their feet skimmed down the steps, then they practically ran the rest of the way, boarding the riverboat just before the ramp was pulled up in preparation for departure.

The engines were already fired up, and she could feel as well as hear them on this lowest deck, where the crew lived. As soon as she and Niall turned in their shore excursion cards, one of the crew members spoke into a walkie-talkie, and the boat moved smoothly away from the dock.

They stepped into the elevator and Niall pressed the button for Deck Five. Lunch was already being served in the dining room on Deck Two, but they both knew they couldn't carry their bloodstained jackets into the dining room with them.

Savannah let out a huge sigh of relief. "We made it," she told Niall. "I wasn't sure we would."

He shook his head. "The boat wasn't going to leave without us. The police called ahead to let the captain know we were on our way."

Her curiosity piqued, Savannah asked, "How do you know that?" When Niall didn't respond, she said slowly, "You overhead them. That's how you know. You speak Mandarin, and you overheard them."

"Let's have this discussion in your stateroom," was all he said.

"Okay." But her mind was already two steps ahead, and she nodded to herself. *That's what he was shouting right before the shots were fired, when you couldn't understand what he was saying. He was warning the children about the sniper...in Mandarin.*

She took a moment to thank God no one had been seriously injured in the attack. The police had received a status report from the hospital on all four children, and when she'd asked they'd been happy to share the good news with her—all the children were going to be fine.

Could it be that Niall's warnings in English and Mandarin had made a difference? Would more children have been injured if he hadn't sounded the alarm in their native tongue? There was no way to know for sure, but it couldn't have hurt and might have helped. Only...why hadn't he mentioned it before?

"So why didn't you tell me you speak Mandarin?" Savannah asked as soon as the door of her stateroom closed behind them.

"I don't recall the subject ever coming up," he temporized.

She gave him one of those long-suffering looks women had down pat. "Nice try," she said dryly. "Try again."

He considered what he should say. "It often pays to keep certain information to yourself in my line of work. I got into the habit of not revealing things about myself so long ago it's become second nature."

"Keep going."

He frowned and shrugged. He had nothing to fear from Savannah, so admitting this to her wouldn't be a risk. "I have...let's just say I have an affinity for languages." *Which has certainly come in handy in my job*, he thought but didn't volunteer. "Some I speak fluently, such as Russian, Arabic and Mandarin. Some I can get by with—most of the languages spoken in the Eurozone fall into this category. And some..." He grinned, attempting to deflect her curiosity with humor. "Some I can order food in a restaurant without embarrassing myself, but that's it."

She smiled, but he knew it was perfunctory at best. Then her smile faded. "I understand about not revealing secrets, Niall. I really do. So if you thought you needed to keep this information from everyone, including me, I'm good with that. And I meant it when I said if it's a choice between having you in my life and knowing your deepest, darkest secrets, I choose you. It's just…"

An expression of frustration flitted over her face. "It's just that I want to know you," she confessed. "So little things I learn about you from time to time might bother me, but don't worry. I'll get over it, I promise." She took a deep breath, then slid a verbal dagger between his ribs before he realized it was coming. "Just don't ever lie to me, please. I trust you. If you can't tell me something, just say you can't, and that will be the end of it."

She picked up her jacket from where she'd laid it over the back of the chair and held her hand out for his. "If I soak these in cold water while we're at lunch," she said when he silently complied, "maybe the bloodstains will come out. I have a little bottle of stain remover with me, too, for anything that's too stubborn."

When she disappeared into the bathroom with the jackets, he stood there for a moment, staring at the empty place she'd occupied. Remembering all the lies he'd told her. Wishing with all his heart he could take them back…but knowing it was far too late for that.

Savannah stopped cold just before they entered the dining room, and turned to Niall. "I was going to ask you about today, but I forgot."

He pulled her a little to one side so another couple could pass them. "What about today?"

"You saw him, didn't you." It wasn't really a question. "The sniper. That's why you cursed. That's why you ordered everyone down." He neither confirmed nor denied the accusation, and she understood. This was one of the questions he couldn't answer for some reason.

"I didn't tell the police," she said. "I only told them I heard the bullets."

He smiled faintly. "I figured you hadn't. Otherwise, they'd have questioned me about it, and they didn't."

"So you saw him, but you didn't recognize him. I know you, Niall," she said when he just stared impassively. "You'd tell me if you'd recognized him. So it wasn't Martin or Herb shooting at you. It could have been one of them since they weren't on the bus, but it wasn't."

"What makes you think—"

"He was shooting at you?" She snorted delicately. "Give me a break, Niall. Any idiot could have figured it out." Then an idea occurred to her. "There's one good thing in all of this."

"What's that?"

"It couldn't have been Anders Mortenson, or any of the men who were there with their wives. So that reduces our suspect list."

His answering smile was gentle. "Yes, but just because they were there doesn't mean they didn't instigate the attack. The same goes for Herb and Martin. They could still be responsible even if it wasn't one of them behind the rifle."

"Oh. Right," she said blankly. "So much for that theory."

He kissed her as if to take away the sting, then took her arm. "Come on, I'm famished. Let's eat first, then we can reassess where we are on the case."

* * *

They took a quick walk on the upper deck after lunch, but Savannah was too cold with only her padded vest, so they went inside. She would have walked right past the display of pearls the way she always did, but Niall stopped her. "You haven't used up your shipboard credit yet," he reminded her. He gestured toward the display cases. "Use it or lose it."

"I don't really need anything," she began.

"Come on, Savannah," he urged. "Today's the last day. We dock at Wuhan tomorrow morning, and it'll be too late then." He pointed to a pair of dangling pearl earrings in a shimmering blue-black hue prominently displayed in the case. "Those would look beautiful on you."

He could see she was tempted, so he told the salesclerk, "We'd like to look at that pair, please."

He angled the standing mirror so Savannah could see her reflection better as she held a pearl earring up to each ear. "I really shouldn't." But what he heard in her voice was, *Convince me*, so he set out to do just that.

"A souvenir of your trip," he coaxed.

"I bought this vest in Beijing."

"A vest? Get real." The saleswoman moved away a little, as if she realized Niall was doing a better sales job than she could do.

"I've taken thousands of pictures," Savannah protested half-heartedly.

His voice dropped a notch. "The only picture I'm thinking of right now is you wearing these pearls…and nothing else."

Warm color tinted her cheeks. "Okay," she conceded. "I'll take them."

Before the saleswoman could bring over her sales book, however, Niall told her, "We'd like the matching necklace, too, please."

"Niall!" Savannah whispered. "The earrings alone are more than my shipboard credit."

"Ah, but I haven't used mine yet," he whispered back. Then he said to the saleswoman, pointing, "No, not that one. The other one."

The other one was three blue-black pearls suspended in tandem from a slender white gold chain, on which seed pearls in the same hue were interspersed with crystals. The effect was delicate. Ethereal. And when he held it in his hand, he knew it was perfect for Savannah. More than anything, he wanted to think of her wearing it years from now, touching the pearls and reminiscing about the man who'd given her the necklace...along with his heart.

"We'll take it."

"Niall!" Savannah tugged at his sleeve in protest, but he ignored it and gave the saleswoman their respective cabin numbers. When she moved off to write up the sales, he smiled down at the woman who'd so quickly captivated the heart he hadn't known he had to lose.

"I want you to have it," he insisted quietly. "I want you to have something to remember me by."

Her eyes crinkled at the corners and she blinked rapidly, and for just a moment he thought she was going to cry right there. But then she said in a small voice, "I don't need things to remember you by, Niall." She placed her hand over her heart. "You're in here, and you always will be." She drew a trembling breath. "But if you want me to have the necklace...if you want to think of me wearing it... fine. I won't argue with you."

While Savannah downloaded the photos she'd taken that morning, Niall checked his email via his VPN-secure laptop. He'd sent off an encrypted message to his boss before lunch regarding the events at the school today and the conclusions he'd drawn, as well as his interrogation by the police, but he wasn't expecting a reply yet. Since China didn't observe daylight saving time, and since all of the country was in one time zone, noon here was midnight in DC at this time of year.

But he'd noted earlier he had several emails that might be replies to queries he'd previously submitted, including fingerprint analysis and requests for more detailed information on the Thompsons, the Williamses and the Mortensons. But Savannah had been waiting for him to go to lunch so he'd logged off, promising himself he'd deal with his inbox when he got back.

He quickly clicked through everything, tapping an impatient fingertip against the side of his laptop as email after email yielded nothing. He cursed mentally, then cursed himself for his impatience. *Since when do you expect miracles overnight, Jones?* his inner voice jeered. *You know damn well these things take time.*

Yeah, he knew that. But it had never been personal before.

He was just about to log off when another email appeared in his inbox, this one from his sister. "Burning the midnight oil, Keira?" he muttered, opening it. Then sat up straight as he scanned the first few sentences.

Sorry I'm sending you this so late, his sister wrote. But Alyssa has a bad cold so I was working from home today. She's finally asleep and I wanted to let you know ASAP I've hit pay dirt with Spencer Davies.

Pay dirt?

You know the NSA is listening to Davies's cell phone conversations, he read. And the FBI tapped his home and work phones.

"How the hell do you know that?" he asked under his breath. *He* knew it, but he hadn't told his sister. Then he shook his head in amusement. *Shouldn't be surprised*, he reminded himself. This wasn't the first time the agency seemed to know everything.

You've probably received negative reports from the NSA and the FBI, Keira continued. That's because Davies hasn't said anything incriminating so far. But...

His sister wrote the way she talked, and he could almost hear her breathless excitement. Davies's latest earnings call with Wall Street analysts hinted at something big coming, possibly in the fourth quarter, but no later than the first quarter next year. When you add that to what I already learned about DMFC and their obsolete missile—that news would make the stock tank, by the way—it makes you think he's found a way to redeem himself with the DoD, and therefore retrieve his position with Wall Street.

Something big. That could only refer to Savannah, and Davies's plot to acquire her brilliance by hook or by crook.

His fingers flew over the keyboard. Thank you very much! Then he clicked Send and logged off.

He glanced over at Savannah on the other double bed, completely focused on what she was doing. And he remembered the terror that had gripped him this morning when he'd spotted the sniper. Not for himself. For her. And his first reaction had been to get her out of the line of fire. Then, as if a filmstrip played in his mind, he saw her racing from cover to help him rescue the children who'd been shot. No one else had risked rifle fire...except her.

Savannah. So fearless for her own safety. So brave when the chips were down. So utterly and unbelievably lovable. Then he thought about Spencer Davies and his plans for Savannah—use her and kill her—and his blood turned to ice. "No," he whispered to himself. "Not happening."

She looked up at the sound and smiled at him. "Did you say something?"

In that instant he knew he couldn't do it. He couldn't walk away when this trip was over. Somehow he'd find a way to make it work for them. Just as he'd find a way to keep her safe, he'd find a way to keep her. Period.

Chapter 22

Savannah tried to hang on tightly to the remaining days with Niall, but they slipped through her fingers like water through a sieve. First there were five days and four nights… then three…then two… And suddenly it was the night before their flight home.

No more attempts had been made to kidnap her or to dispose of Niall, but she wasn't naïve enough to think they were safe. They'd never be safe until whoever was after them was caught. Until Spencer Davies—assuming this *was* all his doing—was arrested, tried and convicted, and his cohorts with him.

Niall had received confirmation before they'd left the riverboat that only the three couples they already knew had staterooms on Deck Five were also members of Michael's Family, which was welcome news. Not that Davies's cohorts *had* to be one of those three couples, but they were now the odds on favorites.

The tour company had reserved the last night of the tour for a special event in Shanghai, a performance by a troupe of incredibly talented acrobats. She didn't know how many pictures she'd taken, nor how much video she'd shot. And she'd gasped and applauded along with the rest of the audience at the acrobats' feats. But the entire evening had been bittersweet, despite the amazing show. All she could think of was, this was the last night with Niall…unless she could convince him they had a future.

Back in their Shanghai hotel room, Savannah cracked open a fresh bottle of water to brush her teeth, allowing herself to be distracted for a moment. She chuckled a little at the thought that she'd finally adapted to the necessity, so it would seem strange now to use tap water once she got home.

Niall appeared in the bathroom doorway. "Care to share the joke?"

"It's not really funny." She held up her toothbrush in one hand, the bottle of water in the other. "I'll never take clean tap water for granted again."

"Yeah. It takes not having something to really appreciate it." Then his smile faded. A muscle in his jaw jumped involuntarily. And all at once Savannah knew they weren't talking about tap water anymore.

Hope, never far from the surface, bubbled up like a clear mountain spring, and she carefully laid her toothbrush on the counter and set down the bottle of water. She couldn't bring herself to look at Niall directly, so she gazed at him in the mirror, her heart in her eyes. She hadn't realized she was going to say anything until the words escaped. "I thought I could do it, but I can't."

"Can't what?"

"Say goodbye." Her heart was pounding so hard the blood was thrumming in her ears, and she saw rather than heard his next words.

She swung around to face him, the fervent desire to believe she hadn't misunderstood making her voice shaky. "Say that again."

"I can't say goodbye, either."

She didn't know if she'd thrown herself into his arms or if he'd dragged her into his embrace, but somehow they were both holding on for dear life, peppering each other with frantic kisses and heartfelt whispers. Then he lifted her right off her feet, and she wrapped her thighs around his hips as he carried her toward the bed.

They lay together afterward in the jumble of bedding and clothes they'd practically torn from each other's bodies and strewn carelessly aside. Savannah being Savannah, she had to ask, "When did you know?"

"The last night on the boat."

She propped herself up on his chest and stared down at him in disbelief. "And you didn't tell me?"

He smiled faintly. "You didn't tell me, either."

She scrunched her face, then admitted, "You're right. I didn't."

"So when did you know?"

"The night you broke down and threw a declaration of love at me at practically the same moment you said we had no future."

He seemed stunned. "Then?"

"Well, let's just say I was determined to do my best to change your mind from that point on. I knew you thought you had valid reasons—reasons you couldn't share—but I've bucked the odds all my life, and I wasn't giving up. I wasn't ever giving up."

"But?"

"But I wasn't going to tell you. I was just going to keep trying no matter what. Then I realized that was such a...a... *woman's* response. Letting you have the final say when it's my life, too."

That made him laugh deep in his throat. "So you decided, 'The hell with what he wants, I'm going for it.'"

"Well...yes."

He rolled her over and settled between her thighs. "I like
this new, assertive you. A woman after my own heart, who
sees what she wants and doesn't take no for an answer."

"I was always that way where my profession was concerned," she confided, squirming a little to fit him at just
the right spot. "Only when a woman is assertive in business exactly the same way a man is, they call it aggressive. If I hadn't been so valuable to them—I won't say I
was indispensable because no one is indispensable—but
if I hadn't been so valuable, I'm sure they'd have—" She
faltered at the expression that fleetingly passed over Niall's
face. "What is it?"

"Nothing."

"Don't lie to me." The fierceness of her tone surprised
them both. "It's something. If you can't tell me, okay. Just
be honest and say that. But don't lie and pretend everything's fine when it's not."

"You're right. It *is* something." Frustration was evident
in his face and voice when he added, "But I can't discuss
it. Not without auth—"

"Authorization," she completed for him, her eyes wid-
ening with comprehension. And just like that she got her
first inkling of Niall's terrible secret, the one he'd been so
sure would tear them apart. *But then you knew he hadn't
been completely truthful with you all along*, she reminded
herself, remembering their conversation about the Defense
Security Service. Niall had denied working for them, but
there were other federal agencies. Lots of them.

"You work for the government," she said softly, nodding
to herself as everything started falling into place. "You

were sent to…guard me? Because they were afraid something might happen to me here in China?"

The blank mask was back in place on Niall's face, but Savannah was as sure as sure could be that she was close to the truth. "So…we didn't 'accidentally' meet. You planned it." She closed her eyes for a second, ravaged by devastating pain she didn't want him to see, as other things started making a horrible kind of sense, including how he'd known she was a PhD. "That's why it seemed as if you knew me," she whispered. "Because you did. Because you'd learned everything there was to learn about me. Because I was your assignment."

"Falling in love with you was never my assignment," he rasped.

The statement helped, but not enough. Not nearly enough. Anger made her icily polite as suddenly their positions in bed became intolerable. "Get off me, please."

"Savannah…"

"Please."

He cursed beneath his breath but complied, standing to pull his clothes back on with more deliberateness than she'd used when tearing them off. She thought about doing the same, but knew she couldn't stand naked before him. Not now. So she pulled the covers almost all the way to her chin, humiliation making her writhe internally. But she wasn't going to give him the satisfaction of knowing how badly he'd wounded her.

"I would appreciate it if you'd go back to your own hotel room now," she said in that same polite voice.

"No." The face he turned to her was implacable.

"I don't want—"

"I don't give a damn what you want. I'm not leaving you unprotected."

She wanted to say she didn't give a damn about what

he wanted, either, but the reminder of the danger made her pause. And that's when other memories came flooding back. Niall, so protective of her. *His job?* she couldn't help but ask herself, pressing mercilessly on the wound she'd just received.

Maybe, her heart responded once the pain receded a little. *But that wasn't his job talking when he yelled at you for risking your life when the sniper opened fired at the school. That was pure, unadulterated terror...because he loves you and was afraid you'd be hurt or killed. The same way you were terrified for him.*

She sat up abruptly, grabbed her blouse from the foot of the bed, and dragged it on without her bra, which she couldn't see anywhere. Niall stooped and retrieved her jeans from the floor, then handed them to her. She managed to wriggle them on beneath the covers without worrying about her panties. But at least she had the armor of clothing in which to face Niall, standing so she could finish zipping up.

Savannah considered, then discarded, a half dozen different things she wanted to say, but none seemed right somehow. She finally settled on the bald truth. "I still love you." She drew a shaky breath, pressing her hand against her heart. "And I know you love me. I *know* it, Niall. I won't say I understand, because I don't. And I won't say I forgive you, because I don't know if I can. But what you did doesn't erase what we feel."

All Niall really heard was Savannah telling him she didn't know if she could forgive him. *No more than you expected*, he reminded himself. *And she doesn't even know the worst yet.* His tone flat and emotionless, he said, "I told you we had no future. You just didn't want to believe it."

She raised her chin. "You said earlier you'd changed your mind about that. Was it a lie?"

Anger flashed to life and he wanted to roar a denial at her, but he held on to his temper and answered curtly, "No."

"Then you don't get to decide if we have a future or not," she insisted with intensity. "I do."

A rare moment of despair overcame him because the truth was far worse than Savannah imagined. If she wasn't sure she could forgive him now, how the hell could she forgive him when she learned his initial assignment hadn't been to protect her?

Then his jaw tightened as a phrase from his Marine Corps days came back to him—*never surrender.* Wasn't that what he'd be doing if he gave in to despair? Giving up? Surrendering?

Hell no! Not now. Not ever.

For a moment he thought he'd spoken those words aloud, until he realized from Savannah's expression he hadn't. But he couldn't leave things at that. "No," he said, as calmly as he could. "You don't get to make that decision on your own."

She nodded decisively after a minute. "Okay. But you don't, either."

"Agreed."

She crossed her arms in a way that reminded him of… him. Stubborn. Determined. "So where does that leave us now?" she asked. "I take it you're not going to tell me anything more tonight, not without *authorization.*"

"You take it correctly."

"Then…?"

"We have a long flight home tomorrow, and you need your sleep. I'm not going back to my hotel room—that's out. But I can sleep on the couch. At least I'm here if someone tries something."

"That's silly. I'm a lot smaller than you. You take the bed, I'll take the sofa."

"No." He wasn't going to argue, but he wasn't giving in on this point, either.

Her eyes narrowed stubbornly, and at first he thought she was going to insist on having her way. But then she offered, "We can share the bed. It's king-size, not like the doubles on board the riverboat. Plenty of room. We don't have to—" She stopped abruptly, as if she didn't want to remember all those nights they'd slept entwined. "You can stay on your side, I can stay on mine. It's only one night."

Share a bed with Savannah and not hold her? *Not* kiss her and caress her and make love with her? He was going to adamantly refuse when she effectively stymied him by saying in a deliberately insulting way, "Unless you don't trust yourself to be adult about this."

In his mind he heard the accusation his sister-in-law Carly had thrown at him before she'd married Shane. *Yes, and you're forty years old. Not a kid. Don't guys* ever *grow up?*

So he gritted his teeth. "I can be as adult as you."

A thought that ironically flitted through his mind in the wee hours of the morning when he woke to find a soft, warm, sleeping woman snuggled up against his back, spoon fashion...on his side of the bed.

All passengers on inbound international flights had to deplane at their first stop in the US, claim their luggage and go through Customs, then recheck their luggage and pass through airport security before proceeding to their ultimate US destinations. Niall and Savannah were no exception. She was surprised, however, when Niall didn't say good-bye at the check point, but instead followed her to the gate for her flight from Los Angeles to Tucson.

"What are you—?"

She never got to finish her sentence, because a man in

the uniform of a US Marshal approached them, flashing an official badge and addressing her. "Dr. Whitman?"

"Yes?"

"I've been assigned to accompany you to Tucson, ma'am."

She didn't answer, just turned to Niall, who said, "I have to report in." He glanced at his watch. "My flight to DC leaves in thirty minutes, but I wanted to make sure you get home safely, so I had my boss arrange security for you."

She ignored the Marshal and asked Niall in a low voice, "When are we going to have that conversation?"

He shook his head. "I don't know. I'll be back as soon as I can, as soon as—"

"As soon as you receive authorization to talk about… whatever it is you need to tell me?"

He didn't smile. "Yeah."

"And in the meantime, what?"

"You'll have US Marshals protecting you."

"You really think that's necessary? Here in the US?"

"Yes."

She sighed heavily. "Okay. But what happens if I don't hear from you in, say, a week? I have a couple of short trips planned for mid-November."

"More bucket list places?"

She smiled, willing him to smile back. "Yes."

Still unsmiling, he repeated, "You'll have marshals protecting you around the clock. Wherever you go." For a moment, he looked as if he would touch her, but he didn't. "You'll be as safe as I can make you, Savannah."

She blinked back sudden, unexpected tears, longing to say, *Not as safe as I've been with you.* Knowing in that instant she'd already forgiven him for the deception that had brought him into her life. Knowing that for a man like Niall, to whom words like *honor* and *duty* and *loyalty to one's country* were everything, he couldn't have turned down the assignment, no matter what he'd been called on to do.

But she couldn't tell him these things. Not now. Not in front of a witness. So she merely said, "Thank you. For everything." Hoping Niall would understand. His faint answering smile reassured her.

Then, without another word, he resettled his backpack on one shoulder, hefted his carry-on suitcase in one hand, turned and walked away.

Thank you. For everything.

Savannah's words echoed in Niall's head the entire flight back to DC. He dozed off and on, dreaming of her. On the Great Wall. In the Forbidden City. On the tiny boat in the middle of the Goddess Stream. Standing with her arms outstretched on the prow of the riverboat, unselfconsciously reenacting the *Titanic* moment.

And, of course, in bed with him. Numerous times.

He hadn't known until he met her what was missing in his life. But now he knew. And now he would do whatever it took to keep her, even if it meant giving up his job.

More than that, however, he would also do whatever it took to keep her safe. No one was going to be allowed to hurt Savannah, not while a drop of blood remained in his body. Even if it meant taking the law into his own hands.

Chapter 23

If there was one thing Niall hated above all else, it was traitors. But bureaucracy ran a close second. He was kept kicking his heels in DC for almost a week while the powers that be debated endlessly over what could and should be revealed to Savannah. Over what could and should be done about Spencer Davies and his plan to kidnap and then murder her.

This last was the most difficult, because there was very little proof. It was nothing but speculation on Niall's part unless the people Davies had hired to kidnap Savannah could be caught in the act and were willing to testify against him in exchange for a plea deal. And providing round-the-clock surveillance on Davies and the three couples high on their suspect list—not to mention the 24/7 protection on Savannah—was expensive.

Niall argued until he was blue in the face about not withdrawing Savannah's protection, even threatening to resign and protect her himself. Only one thing made this unnecessary—unexpected allies within the Department of Defense. Now that Dr. Whitman's loyalty to her country had been reestablished, her brilliance made her too valuable to the US government, even if she wasn't currently working for a defense contractor. As Savannah had stated, no one was indispensable where his or her work was concerned. But she came close.

It was a totally different story when it came to his personal life. Savannah *was* indispensable…to him. Which was why at first he positively, absolutely refused to have anything to do with the plan to catch Davies in the act using Savannah as bait, hatched by the same people who'd originally dispatched Niall to neutralize her.

The idea was presented in a high-level staff meeting attended by senior presidential advisors, the heads of the FBI, the Defense Security Service and the agency, as well as Niall and his boss, neither of whom knew why they'd been invited…until the discussion was well underway.

Niall stared at the president's National Security Advisor and, though it wasn't his place to speak, demanded abruptly, "Are you insane?"

Niall's boss cleared his throat, a warning that the question probably wasn't the most politic response. But Niall wasn't backing down. "You want to risk Dr. Whitman's life to set a trap to catch the man who intends to kill her?" He didn't say the words again, but his tone definitely questioned the sanity of the man who'd suggested this plan. "Doesn't that defeat the purpose? Sir?" he tacked on at the end for form's sake.

Before the man could respond, however, Nick D'Arcy, head of the agency and one of the most highly respected men in the capital, spoke for the first time. "Dr. Whitman doesn't think the risk outweighs the benefits. She has already agreed."

"What?" Niall stared blankly. "You've approached her?"

D'Arcy's smile was full of understanding, and though no one else in the room knew, not even his boss, that smile told Niall that D'Arcy was all too aware just how personally involved Niall was. *Someone told him*, he thought. *Did Keira somehow pick up on it? Is that how he knows?*

Then he remembered D'Arcy's nickname, which he'd heard his sister and her husband use more than once. *Baker Street. That's right. That's what they call him, because he's so omniscient, like Sherlock Holmes.* So maybe his sister hadn't betrayed him after all.

"The plan wouldn't work without her," D'Arcy explained. "There was no point escalating it to top priority unless she was on board. So, yes, I spoke with her myself. She was quick to understand this is really the only way. She had only one request, Mr. Jones."

"Which is?"

"She wants you in charge."

Well, that explains why you were invited to this top-secret meeting, Niall realized. He considered flat-out refusing to have anything to do with a plan that put Savannah at risk in any way…for the space of ten seconds. But after a quick perusal of the faces at the conference table, he concluded they were going ahead with this idea with or without him. And there was no way he would let Savannah do this without him.

He turned back to D'Arcy. "Break it down for me, sir. I need every detail, including what assets you're deploying and how you intend to keep Dr. Whitman safe through all of this."

Savannah had cancelled the road trip she'd planned to Hoover Dam and Las Vegas at the behest of Mr. D'Arcy. *Not cancelled*, she corrected herself as she sat in her office poring over all the photos from her China trip. *Postponed. I'm still going there. Eventually.*

But Mr. D'Arcy had pointed out how important it was to have a controlled environment until Davies and his henchmen were caught, and she'd seen the wisdom of his argument. So she was a semiprisoner in her Vail, Arizona, home for the time being.

It wasn't as if she was twiddling her thumbs, however. The postponement of her next trip was a good thing in one way, since it gave her time to catalog the remainder of her China photos and update her travel diary while everything was fresh in her mind.

But doing that also meant she couldn't relegate Niall to a corner of her mind, so the pain of missing him was a constant ache. So many pictures either featured him or brought back memories of having him with her when they were taken. Like the ones on the Great Wall. She would never have made it to the top without Niall, which made those pictures poignant reminders of him.

When she found herself mooning over the selfie she'd snapped of the two of them reenacting the scene from *Titanic* together, she resolutely took herself to task. "Concentrate!" she muttered. She clicked on the next photo, determined to get through this entire batch today. And that's when she saw it.

She almost missed it. She actually had her finger poised over the Delete button, because somehow the camera hadn't focused on Niall and her in the foreground—they were slightly blurry, and she had several other much better pictures of the two of them in that moment—but then she saw the couple in the background. The faces the camera *had* focused on, and the malevolent expression captured on the man's face. And all at once she knew.

"Oh, my God. It's them. Niall was right."

Which meant the emailed invitation to visit them in White Sands, New Mexico, the email she'd just received that morning and hadn't answered yet, was a lure.

The doorbell rang and Savannah automatically jumped

up to answer the door, but her US Marshal bodyguard stopped her before she reached it. "Please, Dr. Whitman," he reminded her patiently. "I'll get that."

"Sorry. I keep forgetting." She retreated to the hallway as her bodyguard drew his gun before moving to the door and checking through the peephole, but the moment he opened the door and she saw Niall framed in the doorway, nothing could stop her.

She threw herself into his arms, babbling, "It's them, Niall. I know it. I saw their picture and I suddenly knew it was them. And White Sands. I remember telling her White Sands is on my bucket list. That's why she invited me to visit them there."

His arms closed around her in comforting fashion, but all he said was, "Whoa. Back up. Take a deep breath and start from the beginning."

She buried her face against his shoulder and did as he asked, breathing deeply. *I'd know him anywhere*, she thought distractedly, *just by his unique scent.* Then she forced herself to start over. "I was going through my China pictures just now. Cataloguing them. And there's this one picture—no. I shouldn't tell you when I can show you."

She dragged him by the hand into her office, the Marshal trailing after them. She unlocked the screen saver, then pointed to the photo in the center of the screen. "See? I can make it larger if you—"

"No need." Niall's face was grim. "It's not proof that would stand up in court, but you're right. It's them. Now what's this about White Sands?"

"I've always wanted to see it—the sand dunes, I mean. And when she and I were talking one day about all the places I want to visit at least once in my lifetime, we specifically discussed White Sands National Monument."

Savannah paused for breath. "She's been sending me

emails ever since we returned from China. And I…" She faltered, then admitted, "I've been writing back to her. She seemed so nice! I didn't want it to be her…them…and I… I guess subconsciously I told myself it *wasn't* them. So when she wrote to me—just a chatty email about how tough it was getting back into the normal swing of things after the leisurely pace of our China trip—I replied. I was careful, honest," she reassured him. "I know better. But we've kept up a casual correspondence. And I mentioned I'd postponed the trip I'd planned to take this week because something had come up.

"Then this morning…" Savannah gulped. "This morning she emailed me an invitation to go stay with them. She said they live not too far from White Sands National Monument, so I could kill two birds with one stone. Visit them and cross the sand dunes off my list." Her voice dropped to a whisper. "If I'd been stupid enough to accept…"

Savannah stopped when Niall's eyes lit up, and she recognized that expression. It was one she was sure she'd worn when she solved some tricky problem.

"That's just what you're going to do," he told her. "You're going to accept her invitation." He then proceeded to lay out the plan he'd devised, which was as detailed as if he'd had hours to come up with it instead of mere seconds. And once again Savannah was in awe at just how quickly Niall's mind worked. Another in a long list of reasons why she loved him.

The convoy stopped at the agency's safe house on the outskirts of White Sands Missile Range, or WSMR, to set Savannah up with the audio transmitter and GPS tracking device she would wear for her meeting. And—hopefully—her kidnapping. Since White Sands was less than five hours by car away from her home in Vail, Niall had decided Savannah would drive rather than fly under normal circumstances.

The convoy was composed of Savannah and Niall in her car, her US Marshals bodyguards in another car and a pair of special agents from the FBI's office in Phoenix in a third vehicle. But the "assets" assigned to this case also included special agents from the Defense Security Service and the agency, who were meeting them at the safe house.

"Just talk and act normally," Niall told Savannah for the third time. "Try to forget you're wearing a transmitter."

"You said that already," she reminded him.

He glanced at the other agents surrounding them, then framed her face with his hands. "We'll be listening the entire time," he promised her. "And we'll stick as close as we can without tipping them off."

"I'll be okay," she reassured him. "Spencer Davies needs me alive, remember? He won't kill me until afterward."

"Yes, but..." An expression of frustration crossed his face. "That's Davies. If something goes wrong during the kidnapping or handover, they could kill you in a heartbeat rather than leave a witness who could testify against them. We already know they won't stick at murder. And they don't care who gets caught in the cross fire, either."

"I'll be okay."

His voice was rough when he said, "If there were any other way, I—"

"I know." She smiled at him. "But there isn't." Her smile faded. "I love you," she whispered. "If something goes wrong—not that it will, but just in case—I wanted you to know I understand why you did what you did. And there's nothing to forgive."

His hands tightened on her arms, and pain slashed across his face. His tone betrayed him when he whispered her name in return. "You don't know the worst," he began, but she shushed him.

"Not now. I need all my wits about me right now. Don't tell me something that might distract me."

He nodded his understanding. "But when this is over…"

"Agreed. I'll listen to anything you have to say when this is over." She wanted to kiss him, but not in front of all these agents, so she patted his cheek instead. "Just know that no matter what, it won't make a bit of difference to how I feel."

"Don't screw up this time," the man told the woman as he checked his Ruger nine-millimeter handgun, "or you'll be sorry."

"I'm already sorry. Sorry I hooked up with you in the first place." When his scowl turned ferocious, she added, "I'm the one who got her to come here, remember. If it wasn't for me—"

"If it wasn't for you, we would have had her in China," he reminded her viciously. "I'm still docking your share of the payoff for that colossal blunder."

She muttered something he didn't catch. "What did you say?"

"I said you'd better not try it," she flared at him. "Who came up with the idea to get her here? Me! Not you, me! You try cheating me out of my rightful share and you're the one who'll be sorry."

You just signed your death warrant, he thought. *When this is over…* But he allowed nothing of what he was thinking to be reflected in his face, and instead snapped, "Fine." *You'll get what's coming to you*, he added in his mind. *Oh, yes, you'll get exactly what you deserve.*

Savannah drove up to the address she'd been given, pulled into the driveway and parked. "There's a For Sale or Rent sign in the front yard," she said for the benefit of the men who were listening via her electronic transmitter. "Makes sense. I doubt they really live here." She took a deep breath and let it out slowly. "Here goes."

She rang the doorbell and pinned a smile on her face. *Just talk and act normally*, she heard Niall in her mind. So when the door swung open she said brightly, "Hi, Tammy. Thanks so much for inviting me. This was such a great idea!"

"Well hey, Savannah, come on in. You found us without a problem?"

If she'd been as clueless as Tammy obviously took her for, Savannah would have missed the furtive glance the other woman cast out into the street before closing the door, as if she needed to reassure herself Savannah was alone.

"GPS is a wonderful thing," she replied as if she had nothing but this visit on her mind. "So what's with the sign in the yard?" she asked artlessly. "Are you and Martin moving?"

"Oh." Tammy's tiny hesitation was a dead giveaway, but Savannah pretended to accept the other woman's explanation, nodding when Tammy said, "The real estate market seems to be recovering finally, and Martin thought we should test the waters." She quickly changed the subject. "You made good time."

Savannah followed her lead. "I did. I was so excited about seeing you and the sand dunes, I could hardly wait to get on the road this morning." Her face ached from smiling so much, but she kept going. "I know we said we'd just take it easy this afternoon and visit the sand dunes tomorrow morning, but I'm not tired at all. Where's—"

She stopped abruptly when Martin Williams—*or whatever his real name is*—walked into the room, a gun in his hand. "Martin?" She didn't have to fake the fear in her voice, but she forced herself to speak so Niall and the others would know exactly what was going on. "What are you doing with that gun?"

Niall sat in a nondescript white van parked a block away, listening intently to every word. And he didn't miss the quaver in Savannah's voice as she said, "What are you doing with that gun?"

She'd known something like this would happen. He'd rehearsed a half dozen possible scenarios with her and what she should do in each case. Most important? *Don't resist*, he'd hammered home. *Let them kidnap you. Let them take you to Spencer Davies. Whatever you do, don't make them panic.*

But there was knowing, and there was *knowing*. Savannah wasn't a trained agent. Yet everything rested on her ability to pretend surprise and shock at what was going down. If at any point the Williamses felt threatened, there was no way he could get to her fast enough to prevent them from killing her.

"Come on, Savannah," he whispered, even though she couldn't hear him. "You can do it. I know you can."

"Tammy?" he heard her say, with the perfect amount of stunned disbelief. "What's going on?"

"I'm sorry, Savannah, but we have a job to do."

"I don't understand." Bewilderment was evident in her voice.

Niall nodded to himself, but spoke to Savannah. "Good touch. I'd believe you were clueless, too, if I didn't know better."

"Cut the chatter." Martin's voice, but all pretense was gone. The seemingly nice guy had been replaced by the ruthless killer Niall knew him to be. "Scream and you die. It's that simple. Now turn around." Apparently she didn't turn fast enough, because the next thing Niall heard was, "I said turn around!" Followed by a cry of pain.

"What are you— Why are you tying my hands? No, please don't put that over my head. I swear I won't scream, but if you want to gag me, okay, just don't… Tammy, you know I have enochlophobia. I can't stand people coming up behind me when I'm not expecting it, and I—"

The rest of her words were garbled, as if she'd been gagged. Then muffled, as if a hood had been placed over her head. And Niall took a knife to the gut when he heard the tiny whimper Savannah couldn't suppress.

Chapter 24

Savannah lay prone on the floor in the back of the vehicle she'd been forced into. *Van?* she wondered. *SUV?* Trying desperately to distract herself from the unreasoning fear that had begun when Martin had pushed her blinded self in front of him toward the garage, then bundled her into the back of...whatever she was in the back of.

She had no way of knowing anything about the make, model or color of the vehicle, and she had no way to communicate with the agents listening anyway. She just hoped the tracking device she'd been fitted with was working, because she wanted to be rescued. Soon.

Niall will find you, she comforted herself. *He will.*

He'd been sure she wouldn't be taken to Davies's headquarters—no way to keep her presence there a secret. Which meant someplace else. Someplace she could be safely confined, yet still be allowed to do the work Davies needed her to do. For now.

Niall had theorized two different possibilities for where Martin and Tammy would transport her after the kidnapping, and only one wouldn't require she be tracked there. Spencer Davies's sprawling estate near Alamogordo was already under surveillance. If they were taking her there, the agents would see it. Or at least, they'd see the Williamses' vehicle arrive. But if Davies had fitted up another location, the only way Niall would find her was by her tracking device.

My money's on another location, he'd told her on the drive to White Sands. *Even though Davies has done his best to throw suspicion on the PRC, he won't risk having you imprisoned in his own mansion. No way to keep it secret there, either. But if I were him, I'd make sure wherever you are, it's not too far away. Since he needs you alive, at least for now, he'll need to check on you constantly, make sure you're okay.*

So their destination was somewhere in or around Alamogordo, which was less than an hour away from White Sands. Which meant wherever Martin and Tammy were taking her, she'd find out pretty soon.

The van Niall was riding in was fitted out with the very latest technology, courtesy of the agency, including state-of-the-art recording equipment and a sophisticated tracking system that would have been the envy of many of the other alphabet-soup agencies...if they'd known about it.

The high-tech nature of the setup in the van distracted him for a minute with the realization there'd been no opportunity to remove the worm from Savannah's laptop. *Can't forget to do that*, he reminded himself.

Then Niall shoved the thought aside as immaterial right now. He focused his attention on the map on the computer screen in front of him, and the little blue electronic dot that indicated Savannah's position.

They'd tracked her electronic beacon easily for the past forty-five minutes, staying far enough behind the Williamses' SUV so they weren't tagged as a tail, but close enough they were never in danger of losing the signal. They were on US 70, heading for Alamogordo, just as Niall had theorized. They'd passed White Sands National Monument a while back, and Holloman Air Force Base, too, when he noticed a shift in direction of the blue dot. "Turn right," he told the special agent driving the van, who obediently took the fork that led away from the city, toward the mountains to the east.

The electronic signal came to a complete halt ten minutes later and stayed that way. "Pull over." When the van halted, Niall watched the signal, but it didn't move. He clicked to throw an overlay on the screen, a satellite image of the earth in that location so crisp and clear it, too, was top secret, because the US didn't want its enemies to know just how good their satellite cameras were.

But… "There's nothing there," Niall said blankly, staring in disbelief. No buildings. Nothing but mountain foothills, sparse trees and scrubland.

Then something happened he hadn't been prepared for. Something that scared the living daylights out of him. The blue dot simply…vanished.

"Equipment malfunction?" one of the FBI special agents asked when Niall and the rest had assembled for a hastily called confab.

The driver of the van shook his head. "Not possible. That equipment has never failed before. *Never.*"

"There's a first time for everything, and…"

All at once an idea occurred to Niall, and he tuned out the pissing match between the agents from the FBI and the agency. He fished his cell phone out of his pocket and moved away, then hit speed dial for Keira. When she picked up, he said without preamble, "I need to know if Spencer Davies obtained a building permit in the last year. For anything. And if so, I need to know exactly what and exactly where."

"Is that all? Piece of cake. Give me five minutes, ten max. I'll call you right back."

But his phone buzzed for an incoming email before five minutes had passed. He swiped a finger over the touch screen, and sure enough it was from Keira. When he clicked on it, he saw a series of numbers in a format he instantly recognized. Then his phone rang.

"Did you get my email?" she asked. "Those are—"

"GPS coordinates," he finished for her.

"You got it. Davies applied for and received a permit at the end of August for construction of a bomb shelter on a remote area of his estate in the foothills east of Alamogordo. Three guesses how he got that approval in record time," she added dryly, but not waiting for a response. "Work was completed mid-October—apparently he paid the construction company a huge bonus to get it finished early."

"Thank you *very* much!" And though his brain was already assimilating this knowledge into the situation and what they could do about it, he took a moment to say, "Anyone ever tell you you're a lifesaver?"

Keira laughed and said in an understatement, "Oh, once or twice."

The FBI and the agency guys were still verbally duking it out, with assistance on both sides of the argument from the Defense Security Service men, so Niall ignored them and climbed into the van. He keyed in the coordinates from his sister's email, and confirmed that, yes, they were an exact match for Savannah's last known location before her beacon disappeared.

He jumped out and got everyone's attention by putting two fingers in his mouth and letting out an ear-piercing whistle. "I know why the signal was lost," he announced. "And it has nothing to do with equipment failure."

"Keep walking," Martin said, one hand on his gun, the other shoving Savannah forward. He'd removed the hood and the gag—*thank God for small favors!* she thought—but he'd left her hands tied. They moved deeper and deeper into the side of the mountain, and Savannah knew a moment of despair.

Niall had been right, this definitely wasn't Spencer Davies's mansion outside Alamogordo. But there was no way a signal would penetrate the inches-thick concrete walls, no matter how good the electronic equipment was.

The despair was banished when she reminded herself she wasn't going to die until she solved the problem with Davies's obsolete missile. *He has to know it won't happen overnight, regardless of how brilliant he thinks you are. And Niall will move heaven and earth to find you.*

Maybe the agents working this case wouldn't catch Martin and Tammy. If the Williamses escaped today, even if they were caught at some point in the future, it would only be her word against theirs that they'd brought her here at gunpoint. A good defense attorney could easily cast reasonable doubt on the voice recording's authenticity. And their fingerprints weren't on file, either, which meant they both had clean records. They could fool a jury the same way they'd fooled her.

There was little chance of putting pressure on them to testify against Spencer Davies if they weren't caught in the act of kidnapping. Which meant his house of cards would stand…for now.

Even if she somehow escaped or Niall managed to eventually rescue her, again it would only be her word against Davies's that he'd had her kidnapped. Would a jury believe her? Would it even go to trial, or would the prosecutors decide there just wasn't enough evidence?

No way to know the answers to those questions, she admitted. *But you'll still be alive no matter what.*

Unless she did something stupid, like make Martin and Tammy suspicious the Feds were on the case. Like refuse to work on Davies's obsolete missile. Like let it slip she knew Davies intended to kill her, eventually.

"Savannah's not in imminent danger," Niall said, reminding himself at the same time as the other men, "unless the Williamses think they're trapped. If that happens…" He didn't finish the sentence because he refused to let himself dwell on that possibility. Failure was not an option. "So whatever we do, we can't let them know we're out here.

"If they're waiting for Davies—and I think they are because they want to be paid—then they won't leave until he arrives. That means we have to know where Davies is at every moment." He bent his gaze on the FBI special agents, whose agency was tasked with the round-the-clock surveillance on Davies. "Where is he now?"

"Eyes in the sky from Holloman say his Range Rover just left the house, heading east toward these mountains," the senior FBI special agent replied. "He's on a private road, so there's no way to put a tail on him. But aerial surveillance is better anyway, out here in the middle of nowhere."

"Agreed. But I want continuous updates. And I want to know the minute he arrives at the entrance to the bomb shelter."

He glanced at the US Marshals who'd been guarding Savannah right up until she drove to meet the Williamses. "You've got broad latitude where Dr. Whitman is concerned. You do whatever you need to do to keep her safe. Understood?"

A trio of *yes, sirs* answered him, and he turned back to the men from the FBI, the agency and the Defense Security Service. "Nobody makes a move until I give the word, you got that?" It was highly unusual for a representative of Niall's agency to be put in charge of a joint federal task force like this, especially when both the FBI and the agency were involved, but he *had* been placed in command. He wasn't going to risk something going wrong because someone hadn't got the message.

He nodded in response to the chorus of acknowledgements. "Okay then. Everyone knows the plan. Let's do it."

Savannah's hands were going numb. She'd accurately assessed Martin as the leader, so she addressed her request to be untied to him. He considered her docile plea, then said, "Alive, you're money in the bank to me. Dead, you're worthless." He raised his gun and added, "But I'll kill you if I have to."

Savannah nodded her head and said, "I understand. I won't try anything, I swear. But I can't feel my hands."

Martin glanced at Tammy and ordered, "Do it." And Tammy complied in untying her.

So at least she was free. Not that she intended to do anything with her dubious freedom. But Spencer Davies would arrive eventually. He'd pay the Williamses and they'd be gone. Then she'd reassess. For now, though, she intended to be the model prisoner.

Dramatic rescues made for good press, but they also put the victims in grave peril, and Niall had no intention of risking Savannah's life. So while part of him was chomping at the bit to storm the bomb shelter and shoot it out with the Williamses like some kind of modern-day Wyatt

Earp at the gunfight at the O.K. Corral, the rational side of him knew better.

She's not in imminent danger, he told himself when Davies arrived at the entrance to the bomb shelter, parked and got out of his Range Rover carrying a brown leather briefcase, which Niall figured was the payoff.

She's not in imminent danger, he repeated when Davies went around to the back of the Range Rover and extracted a smaller case from where it was tucked inside one of the wheel wells. Opened it. Then took out a pistol and a clip, inserting the latter into the former.

Niall's gun finger twitched on the Beretta's trigger, and he so wanted to take Davies down, hard. Not because of the attempts on his own life, but because the scumbag thought he could get away with kidnapping Savannah by casting doubts on her loyalty, using her for his own nefarious purposes and then, when she'd accomplished what he wanted her to accomplish, killing her to get rid of the evidence.

But... *She's not in imminent danger*, Niall reminded himself for the third time.

Once Davies entered the bomb shelter, Niall silently signaled his men to move in and take positions close to the entrance. There couldn't be any gunshots that might be heard inside, so they had to take the Williamses down quietly when they exited and arrest them without gunplay.

Still, when the couple walked out into the sunlight with the briefcase Davies had carried inside, it gave Niall great pleasure to spring from his hiding place and press the barrel of his Beretta against the base of Martin Williams's skull. "Move and you're dead."

The man froze. Niall had no intention of shooting, but Williams didn't know that.

"Drop the briefcase." Again, Williams obeyed.

"Now hand over the gun, nice and easy," and Williams did exactly that.

Then one of the FBI special agents was there, clapping cuffs on Williams and intoning, "You're under arrest for kidnapping and attempted murder. You have the right to remain silent…"

The other FBI agent was doing the same to Tammy Williams, and Niall heaved a sigh of relief that so far everything had gone according to plan. Now all they had to do was wait for Davies to exit, arrest him and free Savannah from her concrete tomb.

But the minutes crept by with no sign of Davies, and doubt crept into Niall's mind. Had something gone wrong? Had Davies heard the arrests, quiet as they'd been? Had he barricaded himself inside with Savannah as his hostage? Was there another exit from the bomb shelter, one they knew nothing about? Yes, the Range Rover was here, but if Davies knew the Feds were here also, he could be trying to escape any way he could.

Then he heard a single gunshot.

Chapter 25

"You shouldn't have done that," Savannah told Spencer Davies, as the echoes of the gunshot still reverberated around the room. She'd been determined to remain cool and collected at all costs, but her heartbeat had rocketed when the gun went off. Then she reminded herself Davies was only trying to intimidate her by firing over her head, and she drew a calming breath. "I merely said—"

He backhanded her across the cheek. "Don't tell me what I should or shouldn't do, you bitch," he spat. "You'll do as you're told, or the next time…"

She pitched her tone to be reasonable, despite the pain that made her want to lash out at him. "I merely said I'll do my best, but I can't give you a time frame."

"You have one month. One month, you hear me? Our stock price is plummeting, and Wall Street won't wait." He clenched his teeth. "This is all your fault to begin with. If you'd accepted my job offer a year ago, I wouldn't have been forced to these extremes. Do you know how much you've cost me? Do you?"

He waved wildly at the room around them. "This alone set me back millions. Not to mention what I had to pay for your kidnapping. But all that's a drop in the bucket to what I'll lose if DMFC has to declare bankruptcy."

Savannah saw movement behind Davies out of the corner of her eye, but by sheer will forced herself not to look directly. "Okay," she said, placating the furious man in front of her. "One month." She stood slowly, keeping a watchful on Davies's gun hand, and moved toward the classified computer setup, deliberately diverting his attention. "I think I have everything I nee—"

A guided missile in the form of her warrior lover hit Davies from behind. The gun flew across the room, and Davies was knocked sprawling, a hundred eighty pounds of solid muscle and bone atop him.

Savannah raced for the gun, then turned toward the two men wrestling on the ground. It was an uneven match. Niall had Davies pinned in seconds, one arm twisted behind his back. Niall wasn't even breathing hard when he said, "I'll break it if I have to," in a voice that begged Davies to give him a reason.

Davies's cries of excruciating pain were music to Savannah's ears for a few seconds, payback for the blow he'd given her—her cheek was already swelling up and she knew there'd be a heck of a bruise. But then she came to her senses. "Don't, Niall. He's not worth it."

He tightened his hold and looked up, running his worried gaze over her. "You're okay? I heard a gunshot, and I—"

"I'm fine. He was just trying to intimidate me." A soft smile spread over her face. "Niall to the rescue again. I knew I could count on you."

Everything seemed to move swiftly after that. Davies was arrested and taken away in handcuffs. All three suspects were isolated from each other in the back seats of separate vehicles, per standard procedure, and the FBI special agents draped crime scene tape over the entrance, pending a search warrant. "Might not be necessary under the circumstances," one of them said, "but no point taking a chance any evidence we collect will be tossed on a technicality."

"Speaking of evidence," Savannah said with a rueful grimace, "it's too bad you weren't able to record the conversations in the bomb shelter. Not only did Davies admit to everything, but Martin pretty much confessed, too." She thought back. "He said something to the effect that alive I'm worth money to him, but he'd kill me if he had to."

"Yeah," Niall agreed. "That would have been explosive evidence, if we had it."

One of the special agents from the agency spoke then. "Actually, we do."

Savannah blinked. "What do you mean?"

"Belt and suspenders," the special agent said obscurely. "That's the agency's unofficial motto, didn't you know?" He reached for the electronic device Savannah was wearing, which was disguised as a necklace. "May I?" When she nodded, he unhooked the chain, then cradled the locket in his hand. "State-of-the-art," he reminded them. "This serves three purposes. Electronic beacon. Audio transmitter. And audio recorder."

"What?" Niall and Savannah both said almost simultaneously.

The agent climbed into the van and fit the locket into a piece of equipment, then hit a button that converted the electronic recording to a computer audio file. He opened the file, fast-forwarded to nearly the end, then hit Play.

"Belt and suspenders," said the recorded voice. *"That's the agency's unofficial motto, didn't you know?"* A pause was followed by, *"May I?"*

Every word clear as a bell.

"I'll be damned," Niall said. Then his brow darkened. "Why the hell didn't you tell us this up front?"

A sheepish expression crossed the agent's face. "Need to know. You know?"

Savannah couldn't help it—she started laughing. Niall's face was a thundercloud, the FBI agents were obviously miffed and the Defense Security Service agents looked intrigued.

"'Need to know,'" she chortled. She caught Niall's eye, willing him to see the humor in this. "Oh yes, if there's one thing I understand, it's the concept of 'need to know.'"

Two days later, Niall still hadn't had a single moment alone with Savannah. Endless rounds of questioning by FBI and Defense Security Service agents who hadn't been part of the task force, as well as federal prosecutors eager to hear everything that had transpired, had effectively kept him away from Savannah.

Then Niall was urgently recalled to Washington and dispatched on another assignment, to Russia this time, with no opportunity to get a message to Savannah. He'd considered turning the assignment down—how could he possibly be effective when his every thought was focused on Savannah and the case against Davies and the Williamses?

But the US needed someone who spoke fluent Russian who also had the skills to safely extract a long-time deeply embedded spy and his family, a spy whose cover the government feared was about to be blown due to leaked documents that were making their way piecemeal onto the internet. Time was of the essence, and lives were on the line. So Niall went.

It was very late when Niall walked into his minifortress apartment in DC eight days later, mission accomplished.

He turned off the alarm automatically—keying in the code, submitting his thumbprint for identification and announcing his name for the computer.

Not his real one, of course. He'd deliberately used his brother Alec's middle name when setting up the security alarm. So if someone tried to force him at gunpoint to disable the security system all he had to do was use his real middle name, Aspen, and the silent alarm would be triggered.

Aspen wasn't too bad as middle names went, he'd always thought, especially compared to his brothers. Their mother had tried to make up for the ordinariness of Jones by giving all her children unusual first names. But she'd taken things a step further, giving them middle names of the places where she'd thought they'd been conceived. Which was why his brothers were named Shane Breckenridge, Alec Loveland and Liam Thermopolis Jones. Even his sister, Keira, wasn't exempt from this convention, although she'd gotten lucky. Sedona was a pretty middle name for a girl, and a lovely place to be named after.

He dropped his carry-on suitcase by the door and was headed for the kitchen when he heard a sound he wasn't expecting. He reached for his Beretta M9 in his ankle holster, then made his way on cat feet to the open bedroom door. The shower was running in the master bathroom, and the light was on. Niall crept to the doorway, ready to take out whoever had breached his ultra-sophisticated security system, then froze.

Savannah whirled around, but her scream never made it past her lips. She turned the water off and reached for the towel hanging from a hook over the shower stall. She wrapped the towel around herself and tucked the edge firmly in place before saying in as calm a voice as she could manage given the way her heart was still jumping, "Hello, Niall." Then realized although he wasn't planning to shoot her, he was one pissed off male.

"How the hell did you—how did you know where—who let you in?"

Correctly interpreting the series of unfinished and finished questions, she answered, "I tracked down your sister, Keira, through Nick D'Arcy. He didn't want to tell me how to reach her, but I played my trump card—I said he owed me for having let myself be used as bait." Her smile conveyed she was more than a little pleased she'd thought to use that as leverage. "Keira told me a few things about you, then she directed me to your brother, Shane. Shane told me the rest and he's the one who let me in."

"Where the hell is the US Marshal who's supposed to be guarding you?"

"Umm…yes, well. About that…"

"Don't tell me you gave him the slip."

"Okay, I won't tell you."

"Savannah…" *Very* pissed off, his mouth a tight line even when he spoke her name.

"I'm just teasing," she said quickly. "I don't need protection now that Spencer Davies and the Williamses have been arrested. Oh, and by the way," she added, "they're not really the Williamses. In fact, they're not even married. Tammy took a plea and spilled her guts. After which Davies scrambled to take a plea, too. He confessed everything. And I mean everything, including the false statements he made to the DoD about me, making it appear I was a traitor. Only Martin, or whatever his real name is, is insisting on a trial."

When Niall just stared at her, she said, "Could you point that thing somewhere other than at me? Just in case, you know, it accidentally discharges?"

He cursed under his breath—he seemed to do that a lot lately, she'd noticed—then bent down and tucked the gun in what she could see was an ankle holster. He radiated cold anger, but all he said when he stood up again was, "You have five minutes to get decent, then you have a hell of a lot of explaining to do. I'll be in the living room."

He was going to kill Shane. No question about it, his brother had a lot of nerve. Niall had given Shane use of his apartment a few months back, when someone had been trying to assassinate Shane and he needed a safe place to stay. Niall had never bothered to remove Shane's access from the security system, but that didn't mean his brother had the right to—

Niall whipped out his cell phone and hit speed dial, but the phone rang and rang before going to voice mail. He didn't waste time leaving a message, but he did send a text. He didn't bother with the niceties, just typed:

What the hell were you thinking?

Then he fumed, needing a target for his anger but unable to vent. His phone dinged for an incoming text two minutes later.

Calm down before you blow a gasket. You'll thank me later.

Like hell he would. He was just about to dash off a scathing response when Savannah entered the room. He didn't hear her. He didn't see her. But he sensed she was there, and when he turned around, he was right. How had he known? He was so dumbfounded by the realization he *had* known, that he was speechless, and Savannah spoke first.

"Before we say things we might regret, would you just answer one question honestly?"

"Question being?"

"Are you glad to see me?"

That stopped him in his tracks. Glad? Of course he was. *Then tell her, dipstick.* He tamped down his anger, born of exhaustion, guilt and frustration that he'd had to leave the country before he'd been able to confess everything to her, and quietly admitted the truth. "Yes."

She was in his arms before he knew it, and the minute he touched her, he lost it. Then he was carrying her into the bedroom, stripping her out of the clothes she'd just put on and tearing off his own. He managed two instances of sanity. "I need a shower." A statement Savannah dismissed with the contempt it deserved. And, "Condom."

To which she replied, "No, you don't. I'm on the patch now."

Niall had never not used a condom. But he'd had himself tested twice a year anyway, just to be on the safe side, because he would never put a woman at risk. So he didn't hesitate when Savannah made him that offer. And when he was deep inside her with her legs locked tightly around his, he whispered, "I've never—"

"I know. You told me before." She undulated against him in a way designed to drive him insane, snapping every last leash on his restraint. Then he proceeded to make love to her until she joined him in madness.

They lay locked in each other's embrace afterward. And though Niall had never imagined making his confession in bed, he couldn't bear to let her go. "So if you spoke with Keira and Shane, you know my name isn't Johnson," he said slowly.

"I know."

"There's more."

She stroked his cheek in soothing fashion. "I know that, too."

His heartbeat accelerated. "I've killed people."

He thought she'd be shocked, but all she said was, "So have I."

He raised his head to stare at her, his eyes wide with disbelief, and she explained, "Not directly, no. But indirectly, yes, through the missiles I've helped design. I'm realistic enough to accept that as the lesser of two evils. I trust our country and our military to only use the weapons I helped create when it's absolutely necessary." She was silent for a moment. "I know you, Niall. You killed for one reason and one reason only—because they were bad people and you had no other choice."

He digested what she'd said, amazed she understood. But he still hadn't admitted… "I could have killed *you*."

Then came the bombshell. "I know."

His arms tightened around her as disbelief warred with hope, and he couldn't think of a single thing to say.

She drew a deep breath. "I figured it out after Davies confessed. I can't say I understand my feelings on the subject, because I seem to be somewhat conflicted about it. Of course I'm glad you *didn't* kill me—I don't have a death wish. But knowing how much the government trusted me with information only a very few people have access to, I can see why some people might have thought it necessary to kill me to prevent me from betraying our country after the lies Davies spread about me."

He shook his head. "Killing you was always a last resort. Only if there was no other way. But still…"

"Yes. But still."

"I very quickly realized those who dispatched me to stop you were way off base," he rushed to add. "But still…"

Savannah smiled, a brief movement of her lips, and repeated, "But still." She hesitated for a few seconds before saying, "It wasn't easy getting past that—don't ever think it was. I was devastated at first. But then I remembered telling you that if my choice was between having you in my life and knowing your terrible secret, I would choose you."

Tears slowly filled her eyes, but she blinked several times in an obvious attempt to hold them back. "I gave you the perfect out, Niall, *but you refused to take it!* That told me the kind of man you are at heart."

He couldn't have spoken right then to save his life, but Savannah wasn't finished.

"Don't you see, Niall? I fell in love with a man who puts honor and duty above everything, even himself. Even me."

The tears spilled over, and though he desperately wanted to kiss them away, part of him still felt he no longer had the right despite her words.

But then she smiled through the tears and added, "I fell in love with a man who could make that difficult choice and then tell the truth about it. Even though you thought you were cutting your own throat by being honest with me."

She kissed him, her face wet with tears, and he kissed her back, putting his entire soul into it. Then he raised his head, his own eyes suspiciously damp. "So…what you're saying is…you forgive me?" His stern conscience needed the words.

"I love you, Niall Aspen Jones," she whispered, peppering him with kisses. "I told you before and I meant it— there's nothing to forgive."

Epilogue

There were still hurdles to overcome, of course, and no one knew that better than Niall. So after he dried Savannah's tears, after he responded to her fervent avowal of love the only way a red-blooded man could do, he led her back into the living room for a serious discussion.

He'd already realized that if any woman could understand and accept the secrecy surrounding his work, it was Savannah. But still…

"Assuming I don't resign, I can never tell you anything about my job," he began, gazing down at her left hand in his, thinking that the only thing he would change about it was the addition of a slender gold band on the fourth finger.

"Resign?" He could hear the bewilderment in her voice. "Why would you resign?"

"You live in Vail and you work in Tucson. I live and work here in DC. It might be possible I could relocate and still keep my job—I spend a lot of time on the road, as you've probably already figured out—but it would be inconvenient. DC is my home base, the place I go for assignment briefings and refresher training to stay the best at what I do. Commuting would put a strain on both my job performance and us. I don't want to risk, either."

She laughed softly and shook her head. "I *don't* work in Tucson, remember? I resigned. And I put my house on the market the day I returned from White Sands."

"What?"

"My job is flexible. Yours isn't. There are plenty of defense contractors in and around Washington, DC, I can work for," she assured him. "There's even a division of my former employer located across the river in Virginia."

"Yes, but…"

"Don't take this the wrong way, but I can pretty much write my own ticket where my work is concerned, you know." She tried to look modest, but failed miserably. "If that's the only thing you're worried about, you're worrying for nothing."

Sudden relief made him laugh softly. "Yeah, those three patents—"

"Soon to be four," she reminded him in all seriousness.

"Right, soon to be four. The woman I'm marrying is brilliant, and everyone in her field knows it."

"The woman you're—" She caught her breath. "Is that a proposal, Mr. Jones?"

"Not exactly."

"Oh." Excitement gave way to disappointment, followed by what could only be described as acute embarrassment, and Niall realized she'd misunderstood.

"It's not a proposal, Dr. Whitman. It's a statement of fact." And he winked at her.

Her slow smile warmed him. "Oh, really? A statement of fact?"

"Hell yeah. You can't expect to continue taking advantage of me the way you did from Beijing to Shanghai without there being some price to pay." He nodded judiciously.

"I think marriage is warranted—there's nothing like making the punishment fit the crime."

She gasped in fake disbelief, easily falling into the play-acting routine they'd established in China. "Me? It was *you.* You're the sex maniac. I'm just your innocent victim."

She squealed with laughter when he said, "Hah!" and threw her over his shoulder. "Let's see who the real sex maniac is," he teased, carrying her into the bedroom. But all desire to tease her left him when he had her pinned to the bed. And the only thing he could think of in that instant was that if he'd never been sent to China, he would never have met Savannah.

"You have to marry me," he breathed, staring down at the woman who held his life in her hands. "You have to."

Her gray eyes went all misty. "Just try to stop me."

He closed his eyes and bowed his head for a moment, trying to take it all in. When he looked at her again, he vowed, "You'll never regret it, I swear."

"I know I won't." She blinked until the mist cleared from her eyes, then her lips quirked into a teasing smile and her expression turned mischievous. "Especially if you work off that backlog."

* * * * *

"Just what is it that you want me to do?"

Serena threw her hands up, angry and exasperated. "I
don't know," she cried, walking back around to the front
of the building. *"Something!"*

"I am doing something," Carson shot back. "I'm trying
to find the person who killed my brother," he reminded
Serena.

From what she could see, all he was doing was spinning
his wheels, poking around on her ranch. "Well, you're
not going to find that person here—and you're not going
to find Demi here, either," she told him for what felt like
the umpteenth time, knowing that no matter what he said,
her cousin was still the person he was looking for.

HRSEXP1217

"If you don't mind, I'd like to check that out for myself," Carson said, dismissing her protest.

"Yes, I do mind," she retorted angrily. "I mind this constant invasion of our privacy that you've taken upon yourself to commit by repeatedly coming here and—"

As she was railing at him, out of the corner of his eye he saw Justice suddenly becoming alert. Rather than the canine fixing his attention on Serena and the loud dressing down she was giving Carson, the German shepherd seemed to be looking toward another one of the barns that contained more of the hands' living quarters.

At this time of day, the quarters should be empty. Even so, he intended to search them on the outside chance that this was where Demi was hiding.

Something had gotten the highly trained canine's attention. Was it Demi? Had she come here in her desperation only to have one of the hands see her and subsequently put in a call to the station? Was she hiding here somewhere?

"What is it, Justice? What do you—?"

He got no further with his question.

The bone-chilling crack of a gun—a rifle by the sound of it—being discharged suddenly shattered the atmosphere. Almost simultaneously, a bullet whizzed by them, so close that he could almost feel it disturb the air.

Find out who's shooting at Carson and Serena in
COLTON BABY RESCUE by Marie Ferrarella,
available January 2018 wherever
Harlequin® Romantic Suspense books and ebooks are sold.

www.Harlequin.com

Get 2 Free Books,
Plus <u>2</u> Free Gifts—
just for trying the Reader Service!

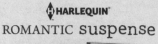

LOVE
Harlequin
romance?

Join our Harlequin community to share your thoughts and connect with other romance readers!

Be the first to find out about promotions, news, and exclusive content!

Sign up for the Harlequin e-newsletter and download a free book from any series at

www.TryHarlequin.com